PRAISE FOR
The Gift of Hope

"McKanagh's story sparkles with humor and hope."
—Charlotte Hubbard, author of *Morning Star*

"Kristen McKanagh's *The Gift of Hope* is pure joy to read, with endearing Amish characters and heartfelt relationships!" —Rebecca Kertz, author of *Finding Her Amish Love*

"Upbeat and sweet. . . . I can't wait to read Kristen's next book. Truly a gift that will stay in my heart."
—Emma Miller, author of *A Summer Amish Courtship*

"As with anything written by this author, readers are treated to an amazing offering. . . . If you want something different and need an escape from the worries of life, get your hands on *The Gift of Hope* and enjoy." —Fresh Fiction

"The story is magical, well described, with a wholesome romance and believable characters you want to root for. I loved this book!"
—Romance Junkies

The Unexpected Gifts Series

THE GIFT OF HOPE
THE GIFT OF JOY

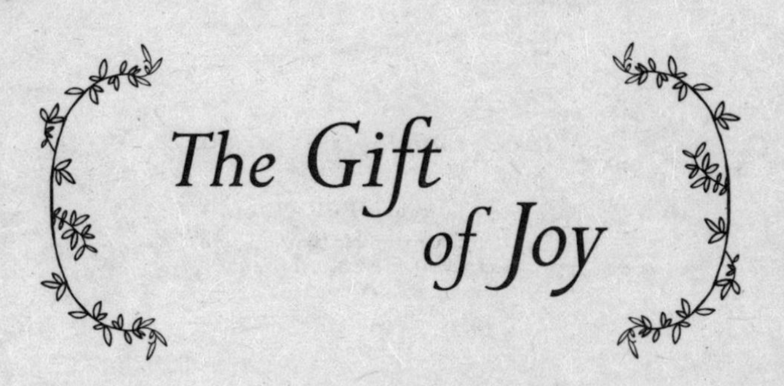

UNEXPECTED GIFTS

Kristen McKanagh

JOVE
New York

A JOVE BOOK
Published by Berkley
An imprint of Penguin Random House LLC
penguinrandomhouse.com

ISBN: 9780593199886

First Edition: April 2022

Printed in the United States of America
1 3 5 7 9 10 8 6 4 2

Book design by Gaelyn Galbreath

To Anna.
For being an inspiration and a friend.

Chapter One

JOY TRIED NOT to limp or rub at her sore backside as she paused at the edge of the tree line to observe the area around her family's home.

The large barn where her dat housed the horses he trained—for Amish as well as Englischers—partially blocked her view. Beyond that lay their old family farmhouse with its well-cared-for clapboard siding; flourishing garden, thanks to her mamm's careful attention; and sheets drying on the line. At this hour of the day, Dat would no doubt be either in the barn or the paddock, also hidden from her view, and Mamm in the house, expecting Joy home soon to help with dinner.

If she could make it inside without anyone seeing her in this state, Joy could change her dress, and no one would be the wiser. Mamm wouldn't know that she'd tried to repair the fence in the back pasture on her own. Anna Yoder didn't like her only dochder doing what she called "man's work." Not when she was trying so hard to get that same dochder married off.

Joy brushed at the large streak of dirt across the skirt of her blue dress, to no avail. At least this wasn't her favorite yellow dress. Even if she could clean herself up more, the additional insult of a large rip wasn't something she could hide from her parents' eyes, which were sharp enough to see even a small one.

Guilt tweaked at her heart, because she had been going against their wishes, even if she had only been trying to help. Unfortunately, the fence might be in worse shape now.

That was the least of her worries, though.

Cautiously she made her way through the tall, green summer grasses of the open field between the trees and the barn, accompanied by the hum of the bees working away at the wildflowers. Luck was with her, and she reached the red-sided barn unseen. Sticking close to the building, she scooted her way down the long side. A quick poke of her head around the corner showed no one in sight. With careful steps, she inched along. She was almost to the wide, open barn doorway when the low rumble of Father's voice had her stumbling to a stop, her heart leaping like a hop toad in the creek that ran through the woods.

"It saddens me to hear that, Joshua," Dat was saying.

Joshua Kanagy, no doubt. One of their closest neighbors, he was here often, helping with the horses.

Joy paused and, to her shame, moved closer to the doorway to listen better.

Her girlhood fellow adventurer no longer paid her much attention, unless she made him. Not since he'd grown "too old for shenanigans." His words, not hers. A hurt that had worked its way under her skin like a splinter, but she'd been determined not to let it fester. Forgiveness had always come easily for Joy. All Amish practiced it, but she had never had to try.

"You know I have appreciated working with you," Joshua's voice sounded now.

Appreciated? As in the past, but not anymore?

Dat's heavy sigh was easily distinguishable. "I must admit I had hoped you might apprentice under me."

Joy had to put a hand over her mouth to hold in her gasp.

Joshua *was* quitting. Except . . . he couldn't. He was *born* to do this work. Dat said his hands were blessed by Gotte, that Joshua was a born horse trainer. He was here every chance he had. Why would he give up such a gift?

"Amos and Samuel might take over someday," Dat continued. "But training horses is a wonderful gute business, enough to go around, and they won't be old enough for years yet. Are you certain?"

She wasn't sure what Joshua's reaction to that was, because only silence greeted her ears before Dat spoke again. "I appreciate that you must honor your parents' wishes and continue your family's work."

Understanding settled over her like her mamm's knitted winter shawl. The shop. Joshua was quitting to help run his family's gift shop in town.

Joy clenched her hands in fists at her side to keep from running into the barn to argue. Cry out that anyone with half an eye could see that Joshua didn't want to work the shop the same way he did with horses. Gotte didn't pass out blessings of ability and passion to everyone, but He had to Joshua. How could he not honor that? How could his parents not see?

But she'd been trying lately to be less impetuous and had already landed herself in trouble once today. A cooler head prevailed, and she stayed put.

Except Sugar Cookie, the poorly named massive orange-and-white barn cat who didn't like anyone, decided at that moment to slink by, hissing at Joy as if she'd moved into his territory.

"Shoo," she mouthed at the thing, waving her hands. He stopped right in the open barn door and batted a paw at her, his pinched and graying face curled in a snarl.

"Go away," she mouthed next.

Sugar Cookie glared then finally turned up his nose, tail in the air, and slunk away. Joy held her breath, hoping neither man heard or saw anything amiss.

They didn't. "This is *my* choice," Joshua was saying. "Please do not say anything to Mamm or Dat."

Her own dat remained silent, and no surprise there, because Joseph and Ruth Kanagy were part of their close-knit Amish community but, as their nearest neighbors, were also close and dear family friends.

"Very well," Dat said, the words heavy.

That was all? "Very well" and let Joshua walk away? He couldn't be pleased about this.

This is none of your concern, Joy Yoder. Her mother's voice sounded in her head. Always Mamm's voice when common sense tried to override her natural spontaneity.

Silence inside again. What were they doing?

The sound of footfalls nearing where she stood had her jumping to scramble back around the side of the barn. She pulled up as she rounded the corner, plastering her back against the wood as Dat stomped away, off toward the house.

She peeped after him, waiting until he disappeared inside before hurrying into the cooler darkness of the barn with its familiar smells of sweet hay, leather, and horseflesh. It took a few blinks for her eyes to adjust after the bright sunlight outside, but then she spotted him. Joshua stood at the other end, putting away equipment.

Dark hair that all three Kanagy brothers had inherited from their dat was sticking up in all sorts of ways. Which meant he'd been running his hands through it, a sure sign she recognized from childhood. Joshua was bothered. He had the sleeves of his shirt rolled up, and her steps slowed as his arms flexed, hefting a freshly oiled saddle onto a rack on the wall. Joy wasn't sure when she'd noticed that Joshua had grown into a man, but every so often she found it . . . distracting.

And improper, she reminded herself in that mental Mamm voice again. She should be interested in who that person was, his character, not his physical appearance. Usually, Joy didn't find that a problem. Probably because Joshua had a kind heart, too. All the girls in the district talked about him.

"You can't go," she called out as she got closer.

Joshua straightened abruptly and whirled around to face her. "Joy?"

His gaze skated over her disheveled appearance, and he gave her *that* look. The one he'd started giving her when he'd reached the age to start Rumspringa. Without her, because she was a little over two years younger. About the same time that he told her he was too old to play anymore.

Joshua's face, arranged in a deep frown, clearly said, *What did you do this time, Joy?*

What he said out loud was, "Ach du lieva. What did you do, Joy?"

At least he'd left off the "this time" bit.

"You're a mess," he continued. "There's a rip in your dress, and where's your kapp?"

Her hand flew to her head, and she grimaced to find it

uncovered, her dark hair no doubt a tousled knot. She'd tried to heft a fence post and ended up tumbling into the dirt to get pinned under its weight. Now she'd have to go back to the field to fetch the head covering.

"Ach vell, I fell, but I'm unharmed," she said with a dismissive wave of her hand. Then stepped closer, tipping her head to gaze up at his face. "You *can't* quit horses, Joshua. You love them. You love them so much, you fall asleep in the stalls sometimes. And Dat says you have the best hands in all of Indiana. You know you do."

She stopped to take a breath.

He cocked his head, arms crossed, though she caught a flash of sadness in his dark eyes. She wasn't wrong about this. "Eavesdropping again?" was all he asked, though.

She wrinkled her nose. "As if I do that often." She might get herself into unusual situations, but listening to others without permission was not typical. "You didn't answer me."

Joshua twitched a shoulder, tension settling across his broad back like a burden. He was hating this as much as she guessed he would be.

Without thinking, she took one of his hands in both of hers, like he had once when she'd been a little girl and skinned her knee jumping out of his family's buggy. "Why are you doing this?" she asked softly.

She shouldn't be holding his hand. They were both in their twenties now, no longer kinder to excuse such a gesture. Certainly not sweethearts. But Joshua had always been one of her favorite people, and he was hurting. She could no more keep herself from offering comfort than her younger brothers could keep out of mischief.

"I grew up a while ago," Joshua said. "Now I should accept my responsibilities. All of them."

Always with the growing up. For a person who liked to tease as much as he did, the man was a contradiction.

"But Aaron doesn't work in the shop anymore," Joy pointed out.

Joshua's brother now worked for the Troyers making custom furniture. Obviously the Kanagys would understand if—

"Hope works in the shop now, taking his place," Joshua pointed out. "I don't have someone to take mine."

Aaron's brand-new wife, Hope, was a sweetheart and perfect for Aaron and for the gift shop. It was so tempting to offer to help Joshua by taking his place. Joy had other dreams—like turning her quilting hobby into a shop that not only sold materials and quilts, but held classes and quilting get-togethers for Amish and Englisch alike. When she let herself daydream, she could easily picture doing that from Joshua's family's adorable store.

Except her mamm's own rules about working stood in her way.

Her mamm had watched several girls a bit older than Joy get jobs in nearby towns to help support their families. Englischer jobs, with the permission of the bishop and their Amish community, of course, thanks to the shrinking options in their region of northern Indiana. Several of those girls had eventually jumped the fence, or they remained unmarried . . . and Mamm had made her rules.

Joy sighed, because no matter how she thought through it, she couldn't see a different answer for her old friend. "I'm sorry, Joshua."

He smiled his thanks, though it didn't quite reach his eyes, then he glanced down. His hand tensed in hers a heartbeat before he pulled away.

Heat flamed into Joy's cheeks as he also stepped back,

apparently not able to put distance between himself and her forward ways fast enough. Her impetuous nature would get her into serious trouble one day, and not just embarrassing situations with men.

Not that this was that kind of thing. This was Joshua.

"A man is never old until his regrets outnumber his dreams," she said. Her grossdawdi used to say that before he'd died.

Joshua chuckled and her heart warmed at a shared joke, because he'd heard that phrase often enough from everyone in her family. Used to, it would make him wink at her. Not this time.

Instead, he sobered and pointed at her dress. "You'd better get changed before your mamm sees you like that."

Joy grimaced. He wasn't wrong. Mamm's wrath wasn't worth risking, so she nodded. "I'll see you tomorrow at Gmay."

Before he could say anything, she scurried toward the smaller door leading outside located at this end of the barn. She checked that no one was about.

"Joy," Joshua called, much louder.

"Shhhh—" She swatted a hand in his direction even as she turned to find out what he wanted. "What?" she whispered.

Joshua suddenly grinned, his handsome face turning into something else entirely. Into the boy who had once been her hero, dark eyes twinkling with the delight of a shared adventure. "Don't get caught," he whispered back.

JOSHUA HAD TO bite back laughter at the sight of Joy Yoder bent over at the waist, peeking out the barn door. Somehow, even on the worst days—and this counted as that—she always managed to make him laugh.

Granted, usually Joy's plans, promises, and schemes didn't end up with her in such a shambles. Most involved helping other people, which no doubt she'd been trying to do when she ripped her dress. He didn't buy that oh-so-casual "I fell" story for a second.

A disheveled wreck with the dirt and the tear and the missing kapp, her mamm was like to take a switch to her if she caught her. He would be sneaking about, too, if Anna Yoder was his mamm. Not that Anna wasn't kind and wunderbaar. She simply had certain ideas when it came to her only dochder.

He was tempted to offer to go distract Anna so Joy could slip in the house unseen, but where would the fun be in that? Watching from back here was a lot more entertaining.

Joshua crossed his arms and waited for her to make her move.

For once her face, the side of it at least, was cast in a serious frown, dark brows drawn down over her eyes, and no dimple in sight.

This isn't grown-up behavior. He could practically hear his own mamm. A lament she'd shared with him almost daily as a child, thanks to his own behavior. Not as much anymore, because he took things more seriously these days. The step he'd taken today to devote himself to the family gift shop was part, parcel, and proof of that.

Telling Mervin Yoder that he was going to quit helping out with the horses had left an ache right in the center of Joshua's chest. He rubbed at the spot and hoped Gotte would take it away soon.

But he'd seen his own fater's face when Aaron had asked to leave the store to move into his own carpentry and furniture-building business. Dat had been disappointed. After all, their shop, A Thankful Heart, had been in Dat's family for generations yet. He'd made no secret of his dream that his sons would one day run it together. Even if Joshua's own wishes tugged him in a different direction . . . that was selfishness speaking. Gotte had already provided him a solid life and future—running the store with his family.

That's what he'd do.

Even if every hour spent in there crawled like the box turtle he found crossing their dirt driveway once. Maybe he'd settle into the job better now that he'd removed the temptation of working with horses.

After all, in order to mold his people, Gotte often had to melt them. That had to be what this was, and Joshua was trying to be faithful about it.

Though sometimes knowing the Lord's will and wanting to follow it were two very different things.

Joy telling him he couldn't quit—her big dark eyes all concerned like a doe-eyed mama bear, such a Joy-like combination—didn't help. After all, he was trying to follow Gotte's calling for his life. How was he supposed to do that if he was being yanked in opposite directions? He couldn't keep going the way he was, dividing his loyalties between himself and his family, or he'd eventually fray, then rip right down the middle, like a worn-out lead line.

Joy jerked, as if she was going to start for the house, then pulled up short and settled back in her hiding spot.

"What are you waiting for?" he asked her, not lowering his voice. Because she still hadn't moved.

"I can see Mamm in the kitchen window." Joy continued to whisper, and he grinned.

This reminded him of the time she fell into old Mr. Fischer's pond—well, he'd pushed the boat they'd "borrowed" out into the water with her in it, and the boat sank.

She'd had to sneak into the house under her parents' noses then, too. Of course, she'd been only five at the time.

Things had changed since then.

Like that odd moment when he'd glanced down at his hand in Joy's. Despite the dirt under her fingernails from whatever she'd been getting up to, he'd suddenly realized she had lovely hands. Long, slim fingers, pale against his darker, rougher skin, and soft despite the hard work of cleaning and mending and gardening that he knew she did every day.

He hadn't been able to let go of her fast enough, and even then, he'd stepped back.

From Joy of all people. His playmate since childhood, and until he'd gotten too old for such things, maybe his closest friend other than his bruders. He wasn't supposed to be noticing things like how she smelled of sunshine and sugar cookies.

Or how much she'd grown up, despite currently being bent in half as she watched her house like the worst thief ever.

He'd never finish these last chores he'd promised Mervin he'd get done before leaving if she didn't get herself safely inside. Shaking his head, Joshua moved closer.

He'd meant to tug her out of the way so he could check for himself what was happening in the house. Only the second he put a hand on her arm, Joy swung around with a gasp. He was close enough that she bounced off his chest like a rubber ball and would've gone down had he not instinctively reached out to catch her.

The action pulled her near and they both stilled and sort of stared at each other a long beat. He blinked, because for the first time, he noticed Joy's dark eyes had a lighter inner ring around the pupil. Golden almost. Lovely.

Joshua frowned. What was wrong with him, noticing such things? This was Joy.

He was about to let go when a small voice piped up from directly behind her. "What are you and Joshua doing, Joy? Playing tag?"

Chapter Two

JOY PRACTICALLY JUMPED out of her shoes at the question and whirled to find her two bruders—Amos and Samuel—standing by the door. No one had been anywhere near the barn two seconds ago. Sneaky buwes.

Of course they would come by when she and Joshua had gotten caught up in the strangest moment. He'd stared at her face as though he had never seen her before. An unfamiliar and annoying warmth had started to rise in her cheeks when he didn't stop.

Perhaps she should be grateful for the interruption.

"And where did you come from?' she demanded, hands on her hips, ignoring the man at her back.

Amos and Samuel were her cousins in truth, but they'd lived here with her family almost all their lives—after their parents were killed when a car hit their buggy—and Joy considered them her bruders. Everyone did. Twin expressions that were a humorous combination of guilt and sly intent slid across their freckled faces. Angelic ones that got them out of more trouble than Joy had ever managed to get into.

"Nothing," they said in unison.

Knowing she'd get nowhere asking, she squatted and said instead, "Can you help sneak me inside? I don't want Mamm to see me like this."

"Corrupting your younger bruders yet? What will Leroy Miller say?" Joshua demanded from right behind her. Followed by a *tsk* of his tongue.

She shot him a quelling frown over her shoulder. How did he know Mamm had set her heart on Joy and the bishop's son?

Joshua held up both hands as though warding off her ill humor, even if his lips were twitching.

Turning back to the wide-eyed scamps in front of her, she raised her eyebrows in question. Amos glanced at Samuel, who grinned then ran off.

"Where's he going?" she asked as he sprinted across the grass, past the garden, and into the house as fast as his six-year-old legs could go.

"He's our scout," Amos said proudly, as though this was a longtime setup and they were letting her in on the secret.

Together—Joy terribly aware of Joshua watching all this from close behind her and doing her best to ignore his presence—they watched the house. Sure enough, after a few minutes Samuel stuck his dark head out the back door and waved frantically.

"Let's go," Amos said.

He took her hand in his and they ran, and she was certain a deep chuckle followed her out the barn door—Joshua, of course.

As soon as they were inside, Samuel, waiting for them

in the mudroom, stooped over and, sneaking around on his toes in a wildly secretive manner, glanced carefully over his shoulder. "Go up the back stairs," he whispered.

Though his whisper was more like a harsh yell. Amos jumped at his bruder, clamping his hand over his mouth.

"Oh, sis yucht, Samuel," he muttered. Older by a year, Amos was the self-appointed wise leader of the two. Samuel, sweeter, younger, and she suspected the brains behind their operation, nodded.

"Hurry," Amos said to Joy.

"Denki," she whispered, and received two gap-toothed grins in return.

Sometimes she loved those boys more than she'd ever realized could be possible. Mamm might tear her hair out over them, but she loved them with all her heart, too.

Safely in her room, Joy blew out a breath of relief. She could admit that trying to fix that fence on her own had been a foolish idea. Deerich. Except with Joshua around less lately, Dat had more work than he could handle. Not that he ever said anything, but she'd wanted to help.

Now that Joshua wasn't ever coming back . . .

Joy paused with a change of clothes in her hands, staring at the floor, vacantly trying to figure out why that left an odd ache, akin to a pebble in her shoe, sitting in the center of her chest. She rolled her shoulders, trying to make it go away. It had to be worry for Dat. Amos and Samuel were helpful around the barn, but too young to be able to do much with training horses, or mending fences for that matter. And she wasn't allowed.

Mamm's edict.

No unmarried dochder of the Yoders was going to be seen doing man's work. She was to help Mamm with the house and garden and find herself a decent Amish man to marry and have a family of her own. Joy had her doubts about that last part. Not that she didn't wish to marry. She did.

The problem was . . . she had dreams about what that would be. While her grossmammi and grossdawdi, Mamm's parents, had been gone a few years yet, they were still in her heart. They had married for love, and that's what Joy wanted. The way Dawdi had looked at her mammi as though she were the sun and moon and stars.

Only lately, she wondered if that dream was childish. Her parents were a gute example. Theirs had been an arranged marriage and they suited each other well. Loved each other even, though differently, softer. Until recently, marriage had always been a distant future in her mind. When she was "old enough." An age that had somehow crept up on her.

But who would take on a somewhat progressive Amish woman who tore her dresses, or dreamed of owning a quilting shop one day, or tended to laugh too loud and smile in church?

She straightened suddenly. Maybe her parents would make an exception about her working if it meant keeping Joshua around to help Dat. After all, if she took his place in the gift shop, then he could stay. It had worked for Hope and Aaron.

In a flurry of activity, Joy threw a clean dress on, stopped in the bathroom to check her appearance and fix her hair under a fresh kapp—she'd go back to get the other one later—then ran downstairs to help her mater with dinner.

"Weren't you wearing your blue dress earlier?" Mamm asked as Joy's foot hit the bottom step of the back stairs. She didn't even turn from the sink where she was peeling potatoes to look. Eyes in the back of her head, her mater.

"Not recently," Joy hedged. Lying was a sin.

Mamm hummed, which could mean anything—agreement, disbelief, not really caring. At least she didn't say any more, and they got down to the business of preparing supper.

Finally, the family gathered around the table, and after their time of silent prayer, Joy broached the topic. "Dat, I happened to be walking near the barn when you were talking to Joshua Kanagy today," she said.

"Ach jah," he murmured as he passed the bowl of boiled potatoes to Mamm, exchanging a glance with his wife Joy couldn't quite interpret. "Unfortunate, but I respect his decision."

"What's this?" Mamm asked slowly.

Joy could hardly contain herself as Dat elaborated on how Joshua intended to devote himself fully to his family's business.

"That is too bad for us." Mamm frowned at her plate. "You *do* need the help, Mervin. Do you have anyone else in mind?"

"Actually," Joy jumped in. "I had an idea."

"You are *not* training horses," Dat said, his beard twitching as his mouth turned down and he glanced pointedly at Mamm.

"No, no." Joy headed off an argument about that. She loved the horses, but she didn't have Joshua's passion for them. "But what if I worked in the shop in his place?"

Mamm dropped her cutlery with a clatter. "Joy Yoder, we have discussed this."

"But I wouldn't be working for money. It would be an even trade." Aaron's wife, Hope, had done something similar before they married.

"No," Mamm stated categorically.

Joy turned pleading eyes in Dat's direction. "I *could* use the help, Anna," he murmured.

Her mother huffed. "And who would help me around the house and with the buwes?"

"We can take care of ourselves," Amos protested, and Samuel nodded fiercely.

"Nae." Mamm picked up her fork and knife, her mouth pinched.

Here it came.

Sure enough . . . "No dochder of mine needs to work like those girls going to Englischer jobs. She needs to focus on her own chores and responsibilities and finding a fine Amish man to marry and start a family of her own."

Joy straightened in her chair. "Think of the nice Amish men I could meet working in the shop." People, Amish and Englischers alike, came from miles around to the quaint downtown of Charity Creek, and the Kanagys' gift shop was one of the most popular businesses.

Anna Yoder was not above using Joy's tender heart to get her own way. "Meet men from other districts so you would move away from me when you marry? Leave your family behind?"

Joy groaned in her head. She didn't dare out loud. "You know I wouldn't want that, Mamm."

She knew her mother only wanted the best for her. Not that Leroy Miller was that. She hadn't the heart to dash Mamm's hopes, but Leroy, a nice boy certainly, was too quiet. Not in the Amish way, but more . . . unable to speak up for himself. An unkind thought that she'd never share with anyone else. She felt bad enough thinking it in her head.

Besides, one of these days, when Leroy finally got up the nerve to ask her, Mary Hershberger was who had caught his eye. If he wasn't careful, Mary would give up waiting soon. That or sweet, shy Mary was going to have to develop a new personality and break with convention to ask Leroy to drive her home in his buggy after the Sunday singeon herself.

Joy really didn't see that happening.

But Mamm would figure that all out on her own. Eventually. The same way Joy hoped her mamm would also realize that she would marry when she was ready. Or not at all. She'd become an old maedel, happier alone than with the wrong man.

Her mater's expression softened, and she reached across the table to pat Joy's hand. "Your heart is in the right place, but we must find a different way. Gotte will show us."

Joy nodded, deflating inside like her favorite riding horse that finally stopped holding her breath when she was cinched up.

She should have known Mamm wouldn't go for that idea.

The rest of the meal and evening went on as they usually did. Cleaning up, getting her bruders to bathe and settle, and finally settling in bed herself, her mind still turning over the problem of Joshua, the horses, the shop, and her quilts.

Part of her was tempted to simply ask the Kanagys if they realized that their expectations were holding their son back. Except that would be judgmental and disrespectful, not to mention hurtful. Ruth and Joseph were not only two people she genuinely liked, but Joshua had told Dat he didn't want his parents to be troubled by his decision.

Even she wouldn't dare go against his wishes that way.

Why this was so important to her, she didn't dwell on. Joy put it down to not liking change. She never had. Mamm said that was what held her back from marrying. Plus, she wanted the people around her to find happiness.

She stared at the wood beams across her ceiling and pursed her lips in contemplation. Something had to be done.

The next morning, she had to drag herself out of bed after a restless night. Sunday morning went the way it usually did—breakfast, chores, dressing for Gmay and loading up in their buggy to travel to the church gathering, hosted at the Bontragers' house this week.

She lost herself in the flurry of activity when they arrived, bringing in the food they'd brought for the communal meal after service, greeting the other women, and finally lining up in their proper order to enter the barn, where service would be held. Joy sat with the other unmarried women her age, next to her friends Sarah and Rachel Price.

And through all of that, her mind had been focused on running through and discarding ideas. Solutions. Any solution.

They started the first song, known by rote since she was a young child, and Joy sang without thinking, though her heart was focused heavenward. Mamm was right. Gotte must have a plan here. If only she could see His path.

She raised her gaze from her lap, only to find Joshua seated directly across from her with the men on the hard benches. He was tucked behind Eli Bontrager, who was as wide as he was tall, but Joshua was taller, so she had no difficulty seeing his full face.

He *did* have a handsome face—strong featured and square jawed with deeply dark eyes that often crinkled with laughter. Despite turning a bit too serious and stuffy lately, Joshua was a fine and decent man, baptized in their shared faith when he was old enough to make that decision, as she had been. He was a hard worker, and kind, if a tad judgmental.

Joy's voice faltered, shock stealing the sound right out of her throat.

Because she knew. Right then and there, she knew exactly what she should do. As though he'd heard her thoughts, Joshua happened to raise his own gaze and caught her staring. Joy straightened and sent him a sunny smile. Gotte *did* have an answer, and He had supplied it to her.

Joshua shot her a warning frown, no doubt because smiling wasn't done in church. Nor, for that matter, was staring.

Dutifully she lowered her gaze and took back up the song, which suddenly soared in her soul. She couldn't entirely squelch the smile, though. Tonight at singeon was probably the best place to approach him, even though her excitement made her want to jump up and ask right now, or even after the service was over.

Still, church was no place to be proposing marriage to Joshua Kanagy.

JOSHUA DROVE HIS buggy to the Bontragers' for singeon alone, the sun directly in his eyes as he turned the horse's head west down the lane that would take him there. He was late because Aaron and Hope had come over. Joshua saw Hope all the time at the store, but Aaron, now that he lived in his own house and worked elsewhere, he hardly laid eyes on except Sundays. So he'd stayed to chat a bit.

Daniel hadn't felt like joining the Sunday get-together with the rest of die Youngie. Yet another example of how their lives were changing. They were no longer boys, running around in bare feet and playing pranks on each other. Despite being late, Joshua still found himself in no particular hurry. Maybe he was outgrowing singeon, too.

They were men now, meant to step into lives of their own. Why did that sound . . . endless?

He snapped the reins, hurrying the buggy down the road. Unfortunately, being on his own also meant he was alone with his troubles.

He'd hardly made it one day—a church day no less, when all Amish paused in their work—without wanting to go over to the Yoders'. The bay mare who'd been a fine producer for Mervin was set to drop her late-season foal any day now.

But that wasn't Joshua's responsibility, nae, not even his hobby, anymore. He should be thinking of the next vendor Dat had set his heart on bringing into the shop. Or figuring out a way to sell the quaint clocks that Mamm had been so sure would be snapped up quickly, but they hadn't sold one yet.

He shouldn't be thinking of the foal, or the yearling that was about ready to start groundwork to break him in as a buggy horse, or Joy Yoder's big eyes as she informed him that his talent with horses was Gotte-given.

Gotte had given him the store. If Gotte meant him to work with horses, he would've been born into the Yoders' household.

Joshua frowned over the memory of the bright smile Joy had shot him during service this morning. He knew that look. That look usually got him into a mess. But she hadn't approached him during the meal afterward. Not that she'd had much opportunity, with them surrounded by the entire community, but still, Joy wasn't exactly patient. Maybe she'd forgotten whatever bee had gotten in her bonnet. Either way, he should remind her that she shouldn't be smiling at men in church that way.

He turned off the road onto the dirt lane that led to the Bontragers' house, then pulled the horse to a stop, suddenly reluctant to proceed.

Perhaps he shouldn't go to singeon today. Not in the mood he was in.

The sound of chatter and laughter coming from the back yard filtered to him on the evening breeze, and he snapped the reins again. He was here. Maybe being around others would make him forget his problems. Other than getting to go to the Yoders' to work with the horses, going to singeon had always been one of his favorite things to do. Treats, friends, volleyball, and other activities, as well as singing hymns and favorite songs, all for die Youngie—the Amish youth in their teens and early twenties. What could be better?

Last to arrive, as he neared the large brick-sided house, Joshua spied a lone figure sitting on the two narrow steps leading to the Bontragers' front door. A girl, he could see, based on the yellow dress she wore and the white kapp covering her dark head, with her arms wrapped around her knees.

Joshua swallowed a groan.

Joy practically had an instinct for when he was in a bad mood. She'd pop into his life, usually making it better, her laughter infectious, like catching fireflies in a mason jar just to see them glow.

However, he suspected this had to do with why she'd smiled at him that way during Gmay.

Joy got to her feet, dusting off her skirt as he neared. Which meant he was right, and she'd been waiting for him. Probably to argue with him about giving up the horses. Sitting straighter, he arranged all his arguments in his head, like lining up the furrows in a field with a plow. The same arguments he'd offered to her father earlier today.

Sure enough, as soon as he pulled his horse to a stop beside the others, she ran across the yard before he'd hardly had a chance to get out.

"I need you to drive me home from singeon today," she burst out.

Joshua stilled in the process of unhitching his horse, Frank, from the buggy. This was new.

"Didn't you come in your own buggy?" he asked, before resuming his task.

"I had Dat drop me off."

"Why?"

"So I could ask you to take me."

He paused again and gave her a closer inspection over Frank's back. Even the horse turned his head to stare at her as though she'd spoken in tongues.

If this had been any girl other than Joy, Joshua would probably be fighting with himself about pride by now. Though, the honest truth was, he didn't mind being considered one of the better prospects in the district.

But this was Joy. She'd never acted that way around him.

Still, he couldn't help teasing her. "I think it's my job to ask you," he pointed out.

Rosy color tinted her cheeks, and not from the warmer-than-average August evening. That alone gave him pause. Making Joy blush was hard to do. He'd tried to tease her often enough as kids to know. So what was this about?

She bit her lip, then burst into speech. "I have something I want to discuss with you. The ride home is the best time. But I wanted to make sure you didn't ask another girl first. Because that would ruin everything. It won't be a problem. Because we're neighbors. You see?"

She paused, brows furrowing, looking like a tiny garden trowel had dug two perfect rows between her eyes. "You didn't already promise another girl, did you?"

Joshua followed that rushed and convoluted speech with the ease of long practice. "Nae," he said slowly. "I didn't."

"And Daniel didn't come with you." This she pointed out with ill-concealed satisfaction.

"That's right."

"So . . ." She tucked her hands behind her like a little girl and smiled beguilingly.

Joshua could only shake his head. "So . . . I guess I'll be happy to take you home," he said.

She bounced lightly on her toes, face lighting up. His own personal glow bug. "That's wonderful gute. You won't be sorry, Joshua."

Then she paused, mouth open like she wanted to say more before she gave her head a tiny shake and turned to walk away.

"Oy," he called after her. She turned and paused under the shade of a large maple tree, the sun dappling her dark hair and cheerful dress.

When had she changed from the child he knew into a lovely young woman? Still a whirl of positivity and plans, because she was Joy, but still . . . all grown up.

He frowned. "Are you sure you don't want someone else to drive you?"

She tossed a quick glance heavenward, as though appealing to Gotte for patience. "If there was, I would've asked him."

Uh-huh. "Not even Le—"

"Don't you say it." She cast a quick glance in the direction of where their gathered group of friends could be heard around the corner of the house.

Joshua chuckled though he held up his hands in surrender. So he was right about Leroy Miller and her mamm's aspirations toward that young man. Not who Joshua would choose for Joy, but maybe Anna Yoder knew better.

"Will you give me at least a hint?" he asked. "What are you so all fired up to talk to me about anyway?"

Joy tipped her head, clearly considering what to tell him. Then her dimple flashed—the danger dimple he called it, because it appeared only when she was really excited about a new scheme or promise.

"Marriage," she called back.

Then hurried away, under the clothesline and heading toward the back, while he stood there gaping after her, stunned speechless.

For once leaving the horse to his own devices, Joshua stumbled after Joy. No way could she toss a clangor at him like that and expect him not to immediately need an explanation. Knowing Joy, it could be anything. Was she thinking of getting married? Maybe Leroy had given in to Anna Yoder's blatant attempts to throw her daughter at him? Or was this about someone else?

She better not be trying to marry me off.

Marriage, when he finally entered into it, would be given the appropriate amount of consideration. His choice. Not someone else's. He wanted a nice, quiet, serious Amish girl. A biddable, decent in the kitchen, and easy to have around woman who would trust him to know what was best.

He caught up with Joy at the edge of a copse of trees that lined the backyard, dividing it from the Bontragers' farmable land.

Catching her by the elbow, he gently swung her around to face him, glowering at her. "What are you up to, Joy Yoder?"

She blinked at him with a guileless gaze, but he knew better than to trust that innocent face.

"We can talk about it on the ride home," she said, tossing a glance over her shoulder.

"Nae," he insisted. "We talk about it now."

Joy pursed her lips. "You have gotten so bossy, Joshua Kanagy. I hope you fix that before you marry, for sure and certain."

Oh, sis yucht. This marriage idea *was* about him.

"Whoever you have in mind for me, stop right there," he said.

Her chin went up in the air. "Even if she solves all your problems and lets you work with horses instead of at your family's shop?"

Joshua was already slashing a hand through the air with his next argument, only her words stopped him mid-slash, the words cutting off in his throat. "How could a wife do that?"

"Isn't it obvious?" she asked, all self-satisfied now.

He stared at her, not making heads nor tails of what she could be on about. Marriage was going to do all that?

He glanced over her shoulder to find several friends setting up the volleyball net within sight.

Nope. No way was he about to go through the rest of singeon worrying over what she had in mind and assessing every girl at the event as problem-solving material. Lovila Miller, Leroy's sister, perhaps. Probably Katie Jones.

See. He was already obsessing over it.

"Kumme," he said. Using the grip he still had on Joy's elbow, he tugged her back toward the buggy. Forget singeon. They were going to get this sorted out now.

Chapter Three

"WAIT. WHERE ARE we going?"

As Joshua practically dragged Joy back to the buggy, she lightly tugged against his hold, probably glancing over her shoulder. Hopefully no one was close enough to the corner of the house to see them. He didn't need to be answering curious questions for the next week or more.

"I'm driving you home now."

"But I promised Sarah—"

Joshua shook his head. "Go visit her tomorrow."

Joy gave a small growl of frustration, but she stopped trying to pull out of his hands, at least. Thankfully, she stayed quiet while he sat her in the buggy and fixed what he'd already done to unhitch Frank, who had stayed in place like a lamb. Then Joshua got them turned around and headed back down the lane and in the direction of Joy's house.

"Okay," he finally said, half reluctant and half hopeful. The way Joy always made him feel. She should sell pretzels the way she twisted things up. "Tell me all about this grand idea."

She remained quiet, though.

Long enough that he glanced over to find her clutching her hands in her lap. Nervous? Was Joy actually nervous about this now? That was unusual.

He reached over and put a hand over hers, stopping the restless action. "Tell me, Joy," he said in the same soft, low voice he used with a spooked horse.

She took a deep breath. "Joshua . . ." In a small voice. Another breath. Then even smaller, "Will you marry me?"

Lucky Frank knew the way home, because Joshua would have driven them right off the road and crashed the buggy. Even so, the horse tossed his head, and Joshua had to let up on the reins.

"Ach du lieva." Only that was all he could think of to say.

Shock had stolen the rest of the words from his head and tossed them into the summer breeze. How long had Joy been thinking this way about him? He'd had no idea.

"Joshua?" She said his name with such hesitance, it hardly penetrated the hard freeze going on inside him.

"Joshua." Firmer now, as though she was getting irritated with him. Then a huff. "Joshua Kanagy, bread doesn't take this long to rise. Say *something*."

His mind finally managed to latch on to words. "I think—"

"No," she cut him off. "Wait. Let me explain first."

She wanted to explain her feelings? This would only lead to embarrassment, for both of them. "I am flattered, Joy," he rushed to say. "But I really don't—"

"See. I knew you'd mistake the entire matter."

Joshua clamped his teeth shut. Mistake what exactly? That his childhood friend was in love with him? She'd just proposed marriage? Indignation welled up inside him. What a Joy thing to do, to jump right in and take away that special moment for her man.

"I'm sure there's nothing—"

"Oh, sis yucht. Pull over," she demanded, pointing a finger at a drive off to the right.

Joshua guided Frank to the graveled shoulder of the road then stopped the buggy. Trying to hold on to his patience, he turned to face her. Hard to do as he tried not to panic about hurting his sweet friend's feelings. But also . . . he needed to make sure she understood not to do this to the next man she thought she fell in love with.

Joshua shifted his weight, suddenly uncomfortable over that thought, the image of her proposing to another Amish boy in a buggy like this, the idea not sitting quite right inside his head.

"We are friends and know each other well," she started. "Too well maybe, but that can be useful if we use it right. I mean we wouldn't have to tiptoe around each other. You see?"

She shot him a bright smile.

Joshua didn't see anything. This was the strangest proposal he'd ever heard. Not that he'd been a part of any before this, but he was fairly certain this wasn't how they went.

"This isn't about love," she said next, and suddenly Joshua found himself unsure of what was up and what was down anymore.

"What's it about, then?" he asked slowly.

"Partnership."

The word settled between them for half a heartbeat before she was off again. "We would make wonderful gute partners. I mean we both have our faults. You can be bossy and a know-it-all. You laugh too loud at your own jokes and are a terrible tease. Oh, and you're too tall."

Too tall? He scowled. "I do *not* laugh too loud."

She flapped a hand like he shouldn't be bothered by the idea. "But those are all things I can live with."

Incredulity kept his mouth shut. Did she expect him to be grateful?

"I mean," she continued, oblivious to his reaction. "The buwes Mamm has picked out would be worse. Elam Yutzy's habit of never letting anyone else speak wouldn't work at all."

Not with talkative Joy it wouldn't. Anna Yoder wanted Joy to marry Elam? What was she thinking? He was a terrible choice.

She made a face. "And Leroy Miller—"

"Ha!" Joshua couldn't help himself. "I *knew* it."

Joy rolled her eyes. "But he's too quiet and doesn't have an opinion on anything."

"And you don't love him," Joshua pointed out. "Or Elam."

Marrying without love wasn't unusual. The Amish were a practical people. Though more and more matches were made for love these days, just as many were made for duty or because it made sense. However, Joy was more full of love than anyone he knew. "You've always, always said you want what your grandparents had. Even when you were little. I remember that much."

She sighed, giving him a look from those dark eyes that made him want to squirm. "I've grown up, Joshua."

He was beginning to see that, despite the torn dress and sneaking around the barn yesterday.

She plucked at an invisible string on her dress. "My grandparents had something special, but it doesn't always work that way. Romantic love, the way a lot of the girls around here talk about it or act . . . it's more often fast and fleeting and burns out, leaving a mess behind."

Joshua didn't like that the world had stolen that sweet dream from his friend, an ache for that lost innocence settling in his gut.

However, she shrugged then lifted her gaze to his, seeming unconcerned. Steady. Sure. "A relationship based on friendship and mutual respect, that is like building your house on rock instead of sand. I want a man to grow old with. Someone who I can build a life with."

The thought did appeal. Though . . . look at his bruder, Aaron, and how he'd found love with Hope. True love, not something rushed or forced. Was Joy right that what Aaron had, and what her grandparents had had, was a rarer gift?

"Why me, though?" Not that Joshua couldn't be solid, constant, or dependable. He could.

She bit her lip, a sure sign she was holding back. "Ach vell . . . What could be better if it allows you to work for my fater all the time? Then I can take over in the shop and my mater can't say anything about it."

Finally words that made sense . . . and the heart of the offer, he suspected. If one waited long enough, Joy usually got around to it. "I don't need to marry you, or any other girl, for that. I could get someone to take over in the shop. Except it would break my fater's heart, so I can't."

"Exactly." She clapped as though he'd made her point for her. "And if your *wife* is in the shop, *she* will be a Kanagy. Eventually your children, your dat's grandchildren, would take over. All Kanagys."

She straightened, her expression both optimistic and determined. "See what I mean?"

Unfortunately, he did. His stomach twisted into that Joy-caused pretzel knot inside him as he realized she was right.

He should have seen it sooner. Most of his friends were marrying. Aaron, too. Joshua had already been thinking of finding a quiet, traditional Amish girl to settle down with. Had even taken steps toward finding the right one.

Except Joy's idea meant the two of them . . . and Joy was anything but traditional.

No. He shouldn't even be considering this. "Well . . . you are too short for me." Where did that come from?

Rather than getting upset, she pulled a face. "I know," she lamented. "I hardly come up to your shoulder, but you can live with it."

True. That wasn't such a big problem. Or small, as things went. Though he'd spend a lot of time reaching things down for her—

Why am I entertaining this ridiculous idea?

He needed a better argument. "You are always trying to fix other people's problems. That's what this is actually about, isn't it?"

She stuck out a stubborn chin. "It's a gute idea for both of us, even if solving our problems is the reason I thought of it."

As all Amish did, Joshua tried to not take pride in himself. Gotte must've thought he needed an extra lesson. Being proposed to only because the girl had problems to solve, even if some were his, wasn't exactly flattering.

"Joy . . . that's not a reason to marry."

"But it *could* be part of the reason."

"Nae—"

"Listen." She leaned closer, her face a study in earnestness. "We are wonderful gute friends. We get along well. I like you just as you are, and I think you like me, too, even when I'm trying to help others. In fact, I'd say we understand each other better than most couples. We respect each other." He hitched an eyebrow at that, and she chuckled. "Most of the time. But more than that, I think we would be great partners. We would . . . balance well. Work well together."

Part of that made a tiny bit of sense. Joy had always been a part of his life, and she was right. He genuinely liked her, too, but this was another of her ideas that would probably only land him in trouble. The kind he couldn't get out of either. Marriage was forever.

"Wouldn't you want to work with horses the rest of your life?" she pressed.

That did give Joshua serious pause. A way to serve both his family, do his duty by his parents, and yet still pursue his own dream.

I could take over the Yoders' horse farm one day.

Except . . . he'd be marrying without love. Without romantic love at least. Was this Gotte's plan in his life or his own selfish heart wanting things it shouldn't? He'd been so certain staying in the shop was the right thing to do.

Nae. We'd be foolish to jump into this.

"Think about the marriages you would want to model your own after," Joy said, interrupting his thoughts. "For me, if I can't have what Mammi and Dawdi had, then I'd choose my parents' marriage. My mamm and dat were arranged."

Joshua startled. "I didn't know that."

She nodded, strangely solemn for Joy. "Not officially, but they were childhood friends, like us. Their parents realized that they would be a fine match and sat them down to recommend they marry. They've made a fine marriage. A strong partnership that has stood the test of time."

"And that's what you want?" Joshua asked slowly.

With her big heart, he'd always assumed Joy wouldn't

settle for less than the "over the moon" kind of love, as she used to call it.

Then again, there had always been a certain practicality to her. In fact, that side of her was why she, more often than not, managed to pull him into her adventures.

"I don't know why I didn't see it sooner." Her dark eyes grew wider as she shook her head at herself. "And if it means that you work with the horses . . . maybe take over from Dat one day . . . And I can maybe do more with my quilts through the shop while working with your family . . ." She reached out and took his hand in hers, and he was struck again at the softness of her skin. Such an odd thing to notice in this moment. Joy's mamm didn't let her do much with the horses, but he knew she worked hard around the house and garden. Skin this soft shouldn't be possible, but suddenly Joshua was oddly grateful for that fact. He lifted his gaze from their hands to her big brown eyes. Kind eyes.

And somehow, as always happened with Joy, the hope and optimism practically bubbling from her like a natural spring was too enticing to say no to. Not immediately at least. *Could* they do this?

"We don't love each other . . ." he said.

Plus, she was nothing like the quiet, biddable wife he'd pictured, not that he'd hurt her feelings by sharing that.

"But we *do* love each other. Even if it's friendship," she countered. She was right about that, too. But she was also . . . Joy. The rest of his life was a long time to spend with a woman simply so he could work with horses.

"I—"

"Don't say no," she rushed to stop him.

He closed his mouth slowly.

"Don't say anything yet . . ." she insisted, then bit her lip.

He'd never seen Joy so uncertain of herself. Other than the sinking boat incident. She'd gotten in, he'd pushed, and immediately the boat had started to flounder.

She looked then like she did now . . . wide-eyed, lost, and yet so sure he'd come to her rescue.

"Oll recht. I will think about it," he found himself saying. "I'll pray that Gotte shows me what the right path is."

After all, marriage was a huge step to be taking on a whim.

Joy's face lit up as though he'd said yes. "Wunderbaar." She bounced in her seat.

Then she let go of his hand and turned to face front. She'd said what she'd come to say and was ready to be taken home. Trying to fight back the sudden urge to laugh, Joshua shook his head. If he said yes to this, to marriage and a life with Joy, he'd definitely never be bored.

That was the *only* thing he was certain about now.

JOY SAT IN her grossmammi's old rocking chair as she worked on another of her quilts. She'd gotten to the part she loved best, the stitchwork. This was to be a gift for Eliza Ebersole's new baby, and she wanted it to be perfect. Only her mind kept wandering.

A week. One whole, entire, unending week had passed since Joy had proposed to Joshua Kanagy, and had she heard anything from him? Nae. Not a peep. At this point she'd take anything, even a rejection. The not knowing was awful.

How long did it take to make up his mind after all? What was he doing, exactly, to *think* about it? Perhaps he needed reminding that she'd asked. She'd resisted approaching him until now because she hadn't wanted to push. If their marriage was to work, he needed to come to it willingly. Wholeheartedly.

But a week should be more than enough time.

Joy glanced down to find that she'd messed up her stitching yet again, which she *never* did. With a huff of irritation, she carefully pulled it out, then set everything aside for later.

Time to do something about this marriage situation. She needed an answer. One way or another.

"Mamm," she called out.

"Upstairs and don't yell."

Joy didn't bother to point out that Mamm had yelled, too. She knew from long experience that argument got her nowhere. Instead she made her way in the direction of where her mother's voice had come from to find her in the boys' room on her hands and knees dusting the baseboards.

"Would it be okay if I took the buggy into town?" Joy asked.

Mamm stopped mid-swipe to raise her head. "What do you need?"

Joy already had thought of a reason, one she'd already planned on. She was just going to do it sooner than she'd been thinking. "I'd like to get material for a quilt."

"From town? Don't you usually get that from Mary Hershberger at the farmer's market?"

"Jah, but A Thankful Heart has yellow fabric that would be perfect for the next one."

"What about Eliza's quilt? Are you already finished?"

"Almost. Another day or so. I thought I'd make one to donate to the fundraiser event for the Peachys' medical bills."

Mamm's expression softened. "Jah. Your quilts are always lovely. I'm sure that would help raise a lot of money."

Joy grinned. "Denki, Mamm."

She hurried to her room to put her pin money in a pocket. Wanting that material hadn't been a lie. Hopefully the Kanagys' shop hadn't sold it yet.

Glancing in the mirror, she adjusted her prayer kapp and made sure she was presentable. As she turned away, movement outside caught her eye. With a frown she moved to the window, studying the activity going on. Dat was in the small paddock with the two-year-old colt he was starting to break . . . and Leroy Miller was with him, arms akimbo, and standing well back as though not quite sure where he needed to be standing.

"Mamm," she called out without turning her head and tried not to let panic enter her voice. This was bad, though.

"For the last time," her mother's voice came from down the hall, getting nearer with each word. "Do not yell. If you want me, come find me. You're too old for this, Joy."

"Sorry." She turned her head to find Mamm standing in the doorway.

"What do you need?"

Joy pointed. "What is Leroy Miller doing with Dat?"

The self-satisfied smirk that spread over her mamm's face sent Joy's worry level cloud high. Anna Yoder came to stand beside her at the window, peering out over the scene. Then gave a happy nod. "Your dat needs help, especially with Joshua no longer able to. Leroy agreed to give it a try."

Joy opened her mouth but only a squeak came out. Was it too late already? Had Mamm just given Joshua's job away to Leroy Miller so she could matchmake?

"But Leroy knows nothing about horses," she managed.

"Nonsense." Her mater reached out to tuck a stray strand of hair into her kapp. "They may live in town, but he is Amish. The Millers own a horse and buggy like all of us. Of course he knows about horses."

"But not about training them," Joy tried to point out.

The warning ridges of a scowl appeared between her mamm's brows. "He can learn. I expect you to treat him as you would any guest in our house." She tipped her head, the dark eyes Joy had inherited studying her dochder's face. "In fact. Get him to help you hitch up the buggy."

No use arguing when Mamm got that look in her eyes. "I will." Trying to arrange her features in a neutral, uncaring, not worried way, she walked without haste toward the stairs.

"And be nice," her mamm called after her.

She scrunched up her nose but didn't comment back. She was *always* nice.

Granted . . . maybe she'd been toying with the idea of scaring Leroy off, but he didn't deserve that. The only way to get rid of him and save Joshua's job with her dat was to get engaged.

Right now.

Chapter Four

JOSHUA STOOD INSIDE A Thankful Heart, arms crossed, staring out the window at the busy street while he waited for the customer he was helping to make up her mind. Unfortunately, this process was taking not a short amount of time.

Summer was always one of the shop's busiest seasons but especially on a Saturday. They were in the heart of Indiana Amish country of the Elkhart-LaGrange counties and drew tourists and outsiders for various reasons. Especially their historic downtown with its quaint shops and places to eat lining the main street.

Charity Creek, Indiana, bustled with cars and people on foot as well as several buggies passing by. The town itself was small enough where locals recognized most anyone—both Amish and, to a certain extent, Englisch—who lived in the area. Everyone was in everybody else's business, especially within his Amish community, though that came with benefits. Everyone took care of each other as well.

But just now he didn't see a single person, car, or buggy pass by, lost in thought the way he was, also only vaguely aware of the willowy woman standing beside him debating over her choices. Joshua's mind was miles away and centered on a certain dark-haired, dark-eyed girl who'd upended all his thinking with one little question.

He'd avoided Joy all week as he'd swung wildly between telling her no, telling her yes, and telling her maybe. All for a hundred different reasons. Practically each hour he'd argued himself into a different corner, only to argue his way back out of it the next hour.

"I don't know," Alice Schrock murmured, interrupting his obsessing.

She stared at two different quilts, debating which would look better on her son's bed. Apparently, some kind of situation with a dog and mud and irreparable destruction had made his current quilt unusable.

"This one doesn't feel like Bartholomew."

Joshua winced. Not that there was anything wrong with the name, but the child toting that unfortunate moniker was sickly, underweight, and undersized. Saddling the poor kid with Bartholomew . . . that just sounded like an extra burden for him to try to lug around.

"What do you think?" She turned to blink at him through wire-rimmed glasses. This was the fourth time she'd asked.

The two quilts she was debating between were blue, both with starburst patterns, a description he only knew from working in the shop so long. One had a bit of pink in the pattern and was perhaps more flowery. That was the only discernable difference to him.

"I like the one without the pink," he said. For the fourth time as well.

Alice pursed her lips, brows beetled as she stared between them some more, and Joshua had to physically keep himself from sighing loud and long. How hard could it be to pick a blue quilt, between two blue quilts, for one small boy?

He was fairly certain Bartholomew Schrock wouldn't care either way. Unless the dog incident had been on purpose.

"What color was his last quilt?" Joshua asked slowly.

Alice's smile was tinted with sadness. "Pink. Such a bright and cheery color, don't you think?"

He passed a hand over his mouth, hiding a grin. The dog most definitely had been on purpose. "Maybe Bartholomew is ready for a . . . stronger color," he suggested.

"Oh, no. He loved the pink. He was so sad about his quilt being ruined. Buckets and buckets of tears."

Joshua nodded solemnly, now secretly impressed with Bartholomew's acting abilities. Mental note to tell the teacher to put that kid in the lead role for the Christmas play this year.

"I'll take this one," Alice said after another round of debating. To no one's surprise, she chose the one with the pink in it.

Sorry, Bartholomew, he silently apologized to the absent child. *I tried.*

Joshua pasted a polite smile to his features. "Wunderbaar," he said. "I'll take this in the back and have Mamm wrap it up nicely while I ring up the sale."

He moved quickly to the back of the shop and through the curtains. Off-limits to customers, this section held their extra inventory, a small kitchen, and a table for taking their noon meal and sometimes dinner, particularly in the summers when they extended their hours with the extra sunlight.

"Here, Mamm," he said. "Please wrap it up for me?"

"Of course." She smiled over the quilt. "This is one of my favorites. Who is it for?"

"Bartholomew Schrock."

Though Mamm's expression didn't change one whit, she did blink several times. "Oh."

He shot her a grin, only to have her bat his arm. "Now, now," she said. "Maybe he likes pink."

Joshua chuckled. "The dog ruined the last pink one."

Bartholomew would have to get extra creative to get rid of this one. He couldn't pull the same trick twice. Joshua knew that lesson.

In the back corner, counting inventory for the end of the month, Daniel snorted. "Remember when you accidentally closed the lace curtains in the window so that a hunk was sticking outside during a thunderstorm?"

Joshua shot his bruder a glare, surreptitiously waving a hand at him, but Daniel had his back to them, not pausing in his counting.

"Then Mamm replaced those," Daniel blithered on, oblivious. "And a bunch of moths got to the new ones?"

"Joshua Kanagy."

He winced at the tone of his mother's voice and, schooling his features into the innocent, wide-eyed expression that had gotten him out of more than one scrape as a kid, and which he hadn't had to use in several years, turned to face her. She stood, in all her tiny fieriness, arms crossed and glaring at him.

"What actually happened to that *expensive* second set of curtains?"

"I—"

"And don't even try to lie to me," she cut him off. "Gotte will know."

Joshua couldn't hide his wince this time. "They were *girly*, Mamm," he said by way of explanation, suddenly feeling all of ten years old again.

Her foot started tapping, a sure sign of temper.

At least Dat was in the front of the store and didn't have to add his own disappointment to the mix. Joshua had felt badly about those darn curtains for years.

He slumped forward. "I may have caught a bunch of moths and put them in a box with the curtains," he confessed.

Her outraged gasp was worse than he'd hoped for, so he did the only thing he could. Lifted his head and captured her hand, bringing it to his chest.

"Let me go," she demanded, tugging lightly. Only her lips had started twitching.

He stayed where he was. "Forgive me? I was young, and such things are important to buwes. How about I replace those with my own money? Or get anything else you need for the house?" He considered his options quickly. "I know you've been eyeing that quilt Joy Yoder made Aaron and Hope for their wedding."

Joy again. He couldn't seem to get her out of his head. Still, this was about Mamm. She'd gushed about that quilt for days.

The foot stopped tapping at least, which meant he was making headway. "Please, Mamm. I know it's late, but better late than never."

"Uh-huh." She wasn't buying that. "You would not have confessed if your bruder hadn't spoken up."

"Sorry," Daniel muttered from his corner, earning a glare from Mamm. Joshua didn't dare turn around.

"Please let me make up for it," he said. "After all, just the other day you were telling Anna Yoder how happy you were about the men your boys had become. Let me prove you right."

Guilt twinged in his heart. He'd brought up that moment of maternal pride on purpose. Mamm tended to go easier on them when she was reminded of her own sins. He'd learned that handy tidbit about her around the same time that he'd ruined the second set of curtains.

Finally, Ruth Kanagy gave in with a long, drawn-out sigh. "You are a charmer," she said. "For sure and certain. But jah. I *would* love one of Joy's quilts. She does the best stitching in the county."

He said nothing, not wanting to talk about Joy—the woman he might or might not marry.

"Denki, Mamm. I truly am sorry about the curtains." He released her hand and kissed her cheek.

"Ach," she said, batting his arm again, but playfully this time.

As he pulled back, she put her hand to his cheek. "Are you unwell?" she asked softly. "You haven't been yourself this past week."

Joy's fault. That and truly missing the work with the Yoders' horses. He gave his mother an easy grin. "Right as rain. I'll go ring up Alice."

He could feel Mamm's gaze follow him back out to the front of the shop and tried to put his worries aside as he moved to the computerized register—approved by the bishop for use in the shop only. Even carefully entering the sale into the computer didn't do much to make those thoughts, running circles in his head like a dog with string caught on its tail, of marriage to Joy stop.

Could he spend the rest of his life with her? She would be fun, a loving mater, and according to Anna Yoder at least, an excellent housekeeper, too. A hard worker. He knew, from the treats at frolics, that she was a gute cook. At least, when she wasn't running around helping others.

But marriage was a serious consideration. He should enter into it for the right reason—because Gotte had led him to that path.

Was that what was happening here? Gotte opening his eyes to possibility?

The bell over the door rang, announcing a new customer. "Welcome to A Thankful Heart," Joshua called out without lifting his gaze from what he was doing. "We'll be right with you."

"Oh, wunderbaar," his mother sang out. "I was just talking to Joshua about you, Joy."

He jerked his head up to encounter dark eyes, pinched with surprise and a wariness that sat uneasily on her usually open face. She stared back at him, not glancing away to his mother. "You have?" she asked faintly. "About what exactly?"

UNACCUSTOMED HEAT FLARED into Joy's cheeks as she stared at the man she'd proposed marriage to only a week ago. Had he been talking to his parents? Asking their advice? What if they talked to her parents? What if he said no and that had happened?

She'd be appalled, was what.

"Joshua is going to commission you to make me a quilt," Ruth Kanagy chirped.

Joy rested a hand on a jar of pickled onions to steady herself as relief rushed through her like a river breaking its banks. Clearly, his mother didn't know. If he was going to reject her, she'd rather it be without anyone else knowing what a fool she'd made of herself. Joshua might be a tease, but he was never mean about it. She trusted him to keep it to himself and move on with their friendship, if no was the answer.

"Oh." She swallowed, then rallied with a smile she hoped appeared interested rather than relieved. "I would love to, for sure and certain."

"Lovely. But actually, before you do that, I have a customer who has commissioned three quilts and Ruby Jones can't do it, which puts me in a tight spot. Would you be interested?"

Interested in selling her quilts? It took everything she had not to shout the "yes" bursting through her. Mamm wouldn't like it. Joy paused, then reasoned she wasn't working officially if she was doing Ruth a favor. "I would love to."

Ruth's smile grew. "Come on back and we can discuss the patterns and colors she's requested."

Joy cast a glance at Joshua, who paused, then sent her a crooked grin and a "what can you do" shrug. He had to know she was here to speak with him.

Hiding a groan at the interruption—she'd built up her courage all the way here and come in ready to demand an answer—Joy followed Ruth behind the curtain.

She'd been back here lots of times, of course. When Ruth, who snagged a magazine of quilting patterns on the way by, went to sit at the small round table where they often ate their lunchtime meals, Joy hesitated, her hand on the back of the chair. "Actually, why don't you find the pages you're looking for. I need to ask Joshua a quick question, if that's oll recht."

Ruth, already poring over the glossy pictures, waved her hand. "Take your time."

Phew. Because, as much as she loved quilting, and this was a wonderful opportunity to start her business if she married, Joy was fairly certain sitting here discussing quilts would be akin to torture while everything inside her was waiting for a certain answer about her future.

Rushing back into the storefront, she was pleased to find Joshua out from behind the counter and unoccupied, no customers in the store right then. Snagging him by the wrist, she tugged him toward the door. "I'll have him back in a jiffy, Joseph," she tossed at his father. "It can't wait. Very important. It shouldn't take long. You have things handled in here, jah?"

She didn't wait for answers before scooting the both of them through the door to the jangle of the bell. Had it gotten louder since she came in?

"Joy. What are you—"

"Not yet," she insisted. Then she proceeded to drag him around the corner, down the small alleyway between shops, and into what had once been his brother Aaron's carpentry space where he made toys for the shop. Unfortunately, with the warmth of the summer day and all the windows closed up tight, she started sweating the second they were inside.

"Nae," she said, turning right around and pushing him back outside. They'd just have to risk being overheard.

"Joy, you are the most confusing girl in the entire world," Joshua muttered, but let himself be maneuvered into the cooler outside air.

Joy turned to face him squarely. Only when she looked up, her gaze connected with laughing dark eyes that carried enough exasperation that her own lips twitched in automatic response. They'd always been able to laugh together, and she hoped that would bode well for marriage.

If he said yes . . .

She sobered suddenly. "Mamm has Leroy Miller working with Dat and the horses," she said quietly.

Every trace of humor deserted Joshua's eyes, his expression turning serious, lips pressed flat. "But he doesn't know horses," he said, confusion drawing his brows down over his eyes.

He had nice, thick brows, straight and strong. They went well with the strength of his features. *Why am I noticing his eyebrows right this second?*

She grimaced. "Mamm says Dat can teach him."

"That'll take more time than Mervin has."

Joy waited for the other shoe to drop.

Joshua glanced away and ran his hand over his chin, the rasp of his skin against the close-shaved stubble there suddenly extra loud to her. Apparently, in crisis, her ears turned sensitive.

She held still, though hopping from foot to foot was tempting, and waited for him to think. Long familiarity told her Joshua couldn't be rushed. He had to reach conclusions on his own or they didn't stick. Look at that time when she was ten and she tried to convince him to find her a handsome frog to kiss and turn into a prince. He hadn't wanted to, but eventually gave in to her needling, and ended up bringing her Isaiah Ebersole to kiss instead, insisting he was close enough. Neither Joy nor Isaiah had been thrilled about that.

Finally, his dark eyes turned her way, searching her face. Was he trying to decide if he could live with seeing it every single day for the rest of his life? Maybe he didn't find her pretty? She was probably getting the better end of the deal when it came to that. Joshua was one of the handsomest men in the county. Not that the outside mattered. What was on the inside was more important.

"Are you sure?" he asked, his voice turning softer, deeper, the way he spoke to the horses. Soothing.

She knew what he was asking. Was she sure she was ready to take this monumental step, and with him?

She didn't dare tell him that once the idea had occurred to her, all the other men whom she might consider for a husband had suddenly become . . . less interesting wasn't right, but less. Just less. Every day that he'd taken to think about her proposal, her heart had shrunk a little more at the possibility that he'd say no in the end.

She inhaled, her heart suddenly lifting. "Gute and sure," she said, equally solemn.

He nodded, almost as though to himself, his gaze never leaving hers. "In that case . . . Joy Yoder, will you be my wife?"

Happiness starburst inside her, filling her to the brim with glowing joy, and spontaneously, she flung her arms around Joshua's neck with a laugh. He caught her, his own deep laugh rumbling against her ear. "That better be a yes."

She chuckled and pulled back to grin into his face. "That's a yes."

He took a deep breath and let it out in a rush. "We're getting married, jah?"

"Jah."

"We'd better tell my parents," he said. "Then I'm thinking we should go and tell yours, before Leroy takes my job."

Usually they would ask the bishop first, but nothing was conventional about this marriage anyway.

His eyes crinkled and she took it as a sign of confidence. Meanwhile, butterflies the size of buggies took up immediate residence in her stomach, beating away a bit of the delight of the moment. Ach du lieva. What were her parents going to say to this?

Chapter Five

THE WAY HER body tensed, practically buzzing like a humming bee beside him, her gaze shifting around, Joshua got ready in case Joy bolted for her buggy. He was *not* doing this on his own. Not that he blamed her. His entire body may as well have been plugged into one of the Englischers' light sockets, jolting him with an electric current.

He hadn't known, until the instant he asked her, that he was going to say yes to Joy's proposal. Not even when she'd told him about the Leroy situation. She hadn't had to explain that if they didn't act fast, there would be no job for Joshua to take.

He'd prayed, then and there, for the answer, but only the breeze had stirred in reply, catching the ends of the loose ties of her kapp. He'd stared into her dark eyes and decided that marrying Joy was the right thing to do. What he wanted to do. For many reasons.

So he'd asked. Because a man had to do things the right way.

Strange, the flutter of nerves as the words had come out of his mouth. What if she changed her mind right then? What if after getting a "yes" from him, she realized she couldn't do it? Not that she had. Joy's spontaneity was one of the things he could count on. She went fearlessly through life, always expecting the best outcome.

Taking her hand in his, so she couldn't get away, he led them back inside the shop. "Dat, may we speak to you in the back?" he asked.

His fater's eyebrows slowly rose, but he nodded. As they walked behind the curtain, Dat said, "Daniel, go work in the front."

Daniel didn't even bother to turn around. "I'm not done with inventory yet."

"Go," Dat said. Seriously enough that Daniel paused in what he was doing.

How did Dat know this was important already? Joshua glanced at Joy, who had tucked herself close to his side, one hand in his, the other wrapped around his wrist so tight, she was making his arm tingle.

With a frowning stare at Joshua, who said nothing, Daniel scooted past them and out onto the shop floor, his quiet bruder's least favorite place to be.

Meanwhile, his fater went to his mater's side, putting a hand around her waist. "I think we know what this is about," Dat said.

Joshua couldn't control the shock that tried to contort his face into something that probably looked like a cat he'd seen once, all squished up like it had run into a wall too hard.

"You do?" he asked slowly, exchanging a quick glance with Joy.

How could they possibly?

His mater sent another bolt of shock through him as she nodded. "Of course. You've both been acting so strange this past week, even Anna and Mervin commented on it the other day."

When had their parents seen one another this week?

Mamm shifted her gaze to Joy. "Only I'm sorry, but we won't go against your mater's wishes and let Joshua teach you about horses so that you can help your dat."

That's what they thought? *Oh, sis yucht.* They were in for a surprise.

Joy's grip on him tightened and he glanced down into eyes suddenly filled with a fear the likes of which he'd never seen from her before. Joy was light and ease and maintained that Gotte would work everything out in his due course as long as they walked in faith to the best of their ability. Fear wasn't part of her makeup.

"Actually . . ." Joshua raised his head, giving her hand a squeeze. "I have asked Joy to marry me, and she has said yes."

Neither of his parents moved. Not even a blink between them. And he was fairly certain that they'd both stopped breathing.

"Ach du lieva," his mother whispered.

Joshua couldn't tell if that was a good or a bad use of the words.

Then she turned her head to stare at Dat, who managed to clear his throat. "When did this happen?"

Joshua's turn to clear his throat. He refused to outright lie to his parents, but he wasn't going to tell them the entire story either. That was between him and his future wife.

My bride.

Suddenly the reality of what they were doing struck with the force of one of Aaron's hammers on a nail head. Joy was going to be his fraa, his wife, his helpmate through life.

A feeling that might be happiness expanded inside his chest. Hard to tell around the attack of nerves determined to make every muscle in his body string tight.

"We've been close since childhood," he said. "But only recently Gotte has opened my eyes to how we've both grown up. I've always shared my life with her, and now I want that to be true for always."

True. All true words.

"I see . . ." His parents exchanged a long look, communicating in that silent way they often did.

Then his mater gave the tiniest of nods, and together they turned, smiles in full evidence. "Ach, we have been praying for such a match," Mamm said as she hurried forward.

Before he could get over yet another jolt of surprise, she snatched Joy from his side and hugged her tight. "I've always thought of you as a dochder, and now you really will be."

"Me too," Joy said faintly, returning the hug, and looking at him helplessly over his shoulder.

Dat clapped him on the back, grin broad and sincere. "We've long thought Joy would be the right wife for you. I'm so glad you were smart enough to see it."

Where in heaven's name was all this coming from? "Why didn't you say something sooner?" Joshua asked.

His mother snorted. "You always did have to make up your own mind. Even as a child."

"For sure and certain," Joy murmured.

This hadn't been his idea, though. He had to clamp his teeth shut to keep from telling his parents how it truly happened as proof that he *could* let others lead. "Oh, really?" He cocked his head at her, eyebrows raised.

She clearly got the message because she rolled her eyes before turning her back on him. "Would it be possible for Joshua to come home with me, so that we might tell my parents as well?"

His dat turned a frown on him. "You haven't talk to the bishop?"

"I intend to, Dat. After we talk with the Yoders," Joshua assured him.

"I should think so. My sons will be proper in how they find wives."

Not wincing was a challenge he almost failed. Joy did fail, only she pretended something was in her eye.

"Don't cry." His mistaken mother pulled her in for another hug. "I know your parents will be thrilled." She paused. "Though Anna might be disappointed about Leroy Miller."

"Mamm," Joshua said. "I am just as fine a prospect for Joy as Leroy Miller."

His mater patted him on the cheek. "Of course." She bit her lip. "All the same, you'd better get over there soon. I think Anna wanted to hire Leroy to help Mervin with the horses so that he'd spend time with Joy."

Joshua found himself hustled out the back of the store. Without Joy, who stayed behind while he got the Yoders' buggy ready. Already Mamm was thrilled to be deep into talk of quilts and wedding plans and where he and Joy would live after they were married.

That was a wonderful gute question. He had no idea. Which brought up another one for him . . . perhaps they should be married soon. Otherwise, when would Joy start to work in the shop?

Not that they had brought that topic up with his parents. That was for later. One shock at a time.

"Need any help?"

Joshua jumped at the sound of Joy's voice. He'd been so caught up in his thoughts, he hadn't seen her come outside.

"Nae," he said, sounding grumbly and he knew it. "Hop in. I'll be right there."

JOY COULDN'T KEEP her knees from knocking together as she sat beside Joshua in the buggy. Neither of them said a word as he turned the horse down the alley behind the storefronts that lined the main street of Charity Creek.

More and more Amish were leaving farming behind as their numbers grew and land became a scarce commodity, turning ever more costly as well as limited in availability. Some had started small businesses. The Troyers, one of the first families with a storefront in town, had had the excellent Amish sense to purchase an open field that backed up behind the shops. All the other Plain folk now turned their horses out and parked their buggies at one end of the field, for a small fee to cover taxes and other expenses on the land.

Halfway home, Joy slid a glance sideways to where Joshua handled the reins with the casual confidence of long use. Mervin always talked about Joshua's soft hands with horses. Gentle on the reins, and yet firm enough to be obeyed. Hopefully he would be the same as a husband and fater.

"Are you nervous?" he asked suddenly.

For an inexplicable reason, the tension making her shoulders climb up around her ears eased, because she suddenly realized she wasn't doing this alone. "Jah. They might say no."

Rather than grin her fear away, as she'd semi-expected, Joshua just nodded.

She peered closer, finding no hint of humor, only solemnity. "Do *you* think they'll refuse?"

He flicked her a glance before directing his gaze forward. "I hope they will be happy with the arrangement."

Mamm might be disappointed. "They *do* love you," she said slowly.

Finally out came the crooked grin. "Of course. What's not to love?"

Joy batted his arm, suddenly feeling lighter, as though he'd taken the burden of her worry onto his strong shoulders. Because this was how it should be. Easy.

The silence between them the rest of the way to her home wasn't strained. It just sort of . . . was. Both of them lost in their own thoughts. No doubt similar thoughts. Joy wouldn't be easy until after her parents gave their blessing.

Pulling her buggy around to the side of the house where it always went, he brought them to a stop. But he didn't get out. After a long beat, Joy turned her head to search his face, shadowed under the brim of his hat and the shade from the house.

He seemed so . . . earnest. Was he going to change his mind?

"I think I should kiss you," he said.

Joy about fell out of her seat. Doing her best to compose the astonishment out of her face, she managed to limit herself to only a raise of her eyebrows. "Um . . . why?"

"Joy." He tossed out her name as though the reason should be obvious.

She pursed her lips. "I'm serious. Why?"

An almost pained expression flitted across his face before the somberness was back. "That's what engaged people do. We don't want our first time to be in front of your parents or mine. It will be . . . awkward enough." He lifted his dark gaze, searching her face. "Jah?"

Oh, sis yucht. She'd never been kissed. Not once. Only he made a gute point. "What if I'm bad at it?" she whispered.

Joshua's face softened, his gaze warming. "We'll take it slow."

Slow.

"Okay." Joy closed her eyes and leaned toward him, lips pursed, waiting.

Nothing happened.

Lips still pursed, she frowned, then cracked one eye open to find him trying not to laugh out loud.

With a disgruntled hiss, she jerked away, back ramrod straight. "Never you mind, Joshua Kanagy."

"No." He tried to sober, only he couldn't.

"You had your chance." She hopped out of the buggy, stomping toward the house, not sure if she was angry that she was right—she *was* bad at kissing—or angry at him for laughing about it.

"Joy." He caught up with her. "I wasn't laughing at you."

"Could have fooled me."

"I thought you were sort of adorable. Like a little girl told to let her grossmammi pinch her cheek."

"Uh-huh." She didn't stop moving.

Joshua tugged her to a halt her with a hand to her arm, then took her by the shoulders to turn her around to face him. "Is it that hard to think of kissing me?"

Joy twitched her shoulders, glancing away. "No."

"Then what?"

She couldn't seem to pull the answer from under the

depths of her mortification. A gentle finger under her chin tipped her face to his. "Have you never been kissed?" he asked.

How did he know? After a pause, Joy shook her head, the movement so small, she didn't even dislodge his hand.

A slow smile that about stole the breath from her lungs spread over Joshua's handsome face, lighting his eyes something wonderful. "Gute," he said in a voice gone strangely deeper.

"Close your eyes," he said.

And Gotte help her, she did.

The softness of his kiss, when it came, surprised her the most. Like butterflies over her lips. She gasped and he pressed closer, a hand at the small of her back keeping her steady. He kissed her once, twice more, and her heart might as well have been a bird, taking flight with each precious touch.

Who knew kissing could be so—

"Joy Yoder! *What* do you think you are doing?"

With a yelp, Joy jumped away from Joshua and turned to face her mamm, who was standing at the corner of the house, hands on her hips, and madder than Joy had ever seen her. If she glowered any harder, her face would start to look like cabbage, all bumps where there should have been eyes and a mouth.

"And Joshua Kanagy." Mamm put a hand to her mouth when she realized who was kissing her daughter. "Shame. Shame on you."

She turned her glare back on Joy. "Get inside right this minute."

Joy almost took a step in her direction, except Joshua's hand suddenly wrapped around her own, tugging her to his side. "Anna, I have just asked Joy to marry me, and she accepted," he said, grave and suddenly proper. "We have come for your blessing." He grimaced. "I had hoped to ask Mervin first, of course. I am sorry for that."

Seeing her mater, who was never at a loss for words, search for them now like a fish in a pond, mouth opening and closing, should not have been so satisfying. What kind of dochder was she to enjoy seeing her formidable parent put on the wrong foot for the first time maybe ever?

Joy turned her face into Joshua's shoulder and hoped it appeared as though she was snuggling with her fiancé and not attempting to bottle the laughter that wanted to bubble out of her.

"If you laugh, I'm going to laugh," Joshua muttered at her out of the side of his mouth. Which only made her want to giggle harder.

But she managed to suck in a long, fortifying breath, then lifted her head. "Mamm?" she asked.

Her mamm dropped her hands to her sides in a gesture that looked like resignation, her face a study in nothing. Only the words that came out of her mouth were, "Ach vell, it is about time."

Chapter Six

JOSHUA EYED THE Stoltzfuses' side yard from where he stood in the back, waiting for Joy to appear with her parents. Her bruders had already sprinted around the corner, so he knew they were coming.

For some odd reason, he felt as though he should prepare himself to see her.

In the dash of getting engaged, he'd clean forgotten the frolic that was taking place much of the day. He and his family had planned to close their shop early to join in helping. Susan and Moses Stoltzfus, newly married and newly moved to Charity Creek in search of work at the nearby factory, had bought a house that needed to be painted inside and out. The community was coming together to share the work.

The frolic was already in full swing when he'd arrived, and Joshua had jumped right in, painting the small shed in the backyard so that it would match the rest of the house—which was being turned from dingy white to a bright yellow that should weather the Indiana winters well—once it was finished.

At least, that's what Joshua vaguely remembered his mamm murmuring as they drove up. She was inside now, helping all the women prepare to feed everyone working. Meanwhile, Daniel was up on a ladder painting the siding of the house. Aaron and Hope were here, too, also inside.

Hope had squealed at the news of his engagement to Joy before he could shush her. After all, they hadn't talked to the bishop yet, which meant no announcement to the community.

"Ach du lieva. I have hoped and prayed for this," she'd lowered her voice to declare. And Aaron had clapped him on the shoulder, grinning from ear to ear.

Hoped and prayed for what? That Joshua find a bride? Or that he marry Joy?

Because this was the third person, out of the only three groups to be told, to say something along those lines, and Joshua was starting to feel like he'd missed something. The way that sweet kiss affected him gave him the same pause—

"I think that spot has plenty of paint."

Joshua dropped the brush as Joy suddenly appeared at his side, dark eyes sparkling with her usual humor.

"Joy Yoder—"

"Soon-to-be Kanagy," she supplied, tipping her head with a smile.

Joy Kanagy. It had a nice ring to it. Much better than Joy Miller, which she'd be if she wed Leroy. Joshua pushed the oddly distasteful notion aside. "You surprised me."

"I wasn't trying to. What were you so deep in thought about?"

Kissing her, actually. Not that he was about to admit that to himself, let alone to her. Kissing Joy had been . . .

Nice, he told himself. *And that's all it needed to be.*

He disregarded how the word didn't sit right, even inside his own head. Not quite enough to describe what that kiss had been. As it should be since he was marrying her. He could set that worry aside now.

"I was thinking about where we should live after we marry," he said instead. Not entirely a lie. He'd been thinking about that last night.

"Come to any decisions about it?" she asked. As though wondering politely about a new display in the store or the weather or what treat his mamm brought today . . . and not where she'd be living the rest of her life.

He shook his head.

Her gaze slid away from his, her cheeks warming. Maybe she wasn't as casual about it as he thought. Was she thinking about the kiss they'd shared, too? They'd been interrupted and so busy answering questions and celebrating with her family after that, neither had had a chance to digest that it had even happened.

Had *she* liked it?

It had been ridiculous of him to feel so pleased that he was the only man she'd ever kissed. Strange, too. As though suddenly Joy had become a different person to him.

Which, in a way, she was. He just hadn't anticipated how fast things would change. Maybe a foolish part of him had pictured them going on as they always had—laughing together, chatting, him getting her out of trouble when that happened—only in the same house and with her going to the shop and him out to the barn with her dat.

He picked up the paintbrush and cleaned it off before dipping it back in the paint.

"I'd . . . better go inside and help," she said after a second. She paused, but he didn't lift his head.

If they were going to keep things as close to the same as they could, he wouldn't be bothered with where she happened to be during the frolic.

Joy walked away without another word. Only Joshua couldn't let her go. "Joy?"

She turned back, her expression both slightly wary and curious at the same time, which pinched, because he'd put that look on her face. Now he wanted to fix it.

"I'm . . ." How did he go about putting his feelings into words when he wasn't clear yet what he was feeling? "I'm glad we are getting married," he said finally.

The smile she gave him, slow and sweet and pure Joy, told him he'd said the right thing. "Me too," she murmured, then headed inside, leaving him to wonder at the warmth filling his heart in her wake.

It must be Gotte telling him they were making the right decision.

Joshua blew out a long breath then turned back to the shed, only to pause. Joy was right. He'd been painting the same spot over and over. At this rate, he'd be here until the rooster crowed at dawn. With a shake of his head at himself, he dipped the brush again and purposefully started on a different spot.

Even with his determination to focus on his task, he was already regretting choosing to work outside. Now his head was elsewhere, wondering at what was happening inside the house without him.

"We've come to help," Daniel said from behind him. He must've finished what he was doing on the house.

Joshua turned in time to catch Aaron's snort. "I've come to escape all the talk of weddings."

"Jah." Joshua shook his head, then turned back to his task.

For some strange reason, Joshua didn't wish to discuss marrying Joy with his bruders. Maybe because they'd ask too many questions. This marriage was clearly blessed, given how many people apparently saw this coming or had been praying for such an event. He wished they'd leave it at that.

"So when did it all happen?" Aaron asked, his voice disconnected as he worked on the other side of the shed.

See . . . They couldn't even wait two minutes to start in on him.

"What?" Joshua asked back.

Aaron popped his head around the side. "Falling in love with Joy. Mamm could've knocked me over with a feather when she told us the news."

"Jah. You should've seen your face." Joshua grinned at the memory. That alone had made all this worth it.

"You should've seen yours," Aaron shot back.

His grin disappeared at that. "What does that mean?"

"Aaron," Daniel said from the other side, his low, quiet voice a warning.

Aaron grimaced. "It's just . . . nothing you or Joy have done lately showed any signs that you even liked each other . . . that way."

Daniel pulled a face that was impossible to interpret, though it came close to disagreeing with what Aaron had said.

Joshua ignored them both. "Joy will make an excellent fraa—she is fun and hardworking and kind. She loves kinder, and . . ."

He paused. Maybe he shouldn't say anything about the store yet.

"And . . ."

"And she knows me better than anyone, except maybe you two, and likes me and I like her."

Daniel came around from his side at that. "You do make sense."

Exactly.

"So long as you're both happy, we're happy for you."

Joshua gave his bruder a shoulder bump, since his hands were covered with paint. "Thank you. I think we will be."

"As long as this isn't another fence," Aaron tacked on, echoing Daniel's words.

Lifting his gaze to heaven, silently asking for patience, Joshua turned to face a stern expression. "Not this again."

"Yes, this. *You* weren't the one who paid the price," Aaron pointed out.

When he'd been ten, Joshua had organized all the boys who lived closest to their house to swap chores by using chores like money. If you didn't want to mend a fence, swap that for a different chore, or even a few chores, that another buwe didn't want to do.

It had worked a treat until Mamm found Micah Miller weeding her herb garden. For Aaron. His bruder had got an earful, along with a month of weeding every day by himself as punishment despite the fact that he'd already finished mending that darn fence he'd swapped Micah for as payment.

"I helped you weed the garden every single day," Joshua pointed out. Not for the first time.

"But you never told Mamm whose idea it was."

Actually, it had been Joy's idea, but he'd never told anyone that. Ever. Not even his bruders. "What would that have fixed?"

"Maybe she would have made you weed the garden instead."

Joshua ground his teeth together. They'd been having this argument for twelve years now. "Do you want me to go confess to Mamm right now? Would that make you feel better?"

"You're missing the point."

"What is the point yet?" Joshua flung out an arm in exasperation.

"Hey!" Daniel protested.

He and Aaron both turned and burst into laughter at the sight of yellow paint splattered across their bruder's face. Daniel pulled out a handkerchief and mopped at it. "The point is you don't always think through consequences or own up to your mistakes."

"When I was ten maybe," Joshua said. "But I've grown up since then and have been for a decent while. Though you two seem determined to ignore that fact."

Daniel kept going as though he hadn't spoken. "In this case, many other people would be affected if it goes wrong."

Joshua froze, every part of him locking up with anger. It took him a full thirty seconds to tamp down hurtful words. "You think marrying Joy will go wrong?"

Daniel shook his head. "We think that it has happened too fast, and there has to be a reason for that."

"I've known Joy all my life."

"And never once acted as though you thought of her as anything but a sister."

After that kiss, he wasn't so sure that was right anymore. "I am entering into this marriage in faith, with every hope and expectation that it will be as blessed as Mamm and Dat's."

Aaron set his feet and crossed his arms, staring Joshua down. "So you're not doing this to work with the Yoders' horses instead of in the shop?"

Oh, sis yucht. Joshua said nothing. He wouldn't lie, but this was also more complicated than just the horses.

"That's what we thought," Daniel murmured with a grimace.

Joshua shook his head, then shook it again before pinning Aaron with a hard stare. "Just because you fell head over heels for Hope doesn't mean that's the only way to find yourself a solid marriage," he said.

"I know that—"

"This marriage is between me, Joy, and Gotte. If you can't support us, then give your concerns to Him, instead of me."

He dropped the brush in the bucket of paint and stomped away.

"Joshua—" Aaron called after him.

"Let him go." He caught Daniel's quieter words. "He's right."

Joshua trudged his way around the side of the house. Halfway to the road, he swung back around and instead walked into the house from the front and right to Joy's side.

JOY BLINKED AS Joshua suddenly appeared and stopped close enough that she could smell the sunshine on his clothes. Her cheeks were starting to ache with holding her smile—because brides were supposed to be excited—in place. Not that she wasn't. She was. Everything was going exactly to plan with the way their families and now their community had embraced the idea of her marrying Joshua. However, having this many curious eyes on her was . . . a lot.

"There he is," Bishop Miller boomed, a tad too jovially.

Joy turned her smile to Joshua. "The bishop has been admonishing me that we didn't come to see him first."

She blinked again, because a heartbeat before he pinned

his own smile to his face, Joshua's expression could have curdled fresh milk. She would swear that he was angry. But why?

"I am sorry," Joshua said to Jethro Miller—Leroy's fater. "It all happened so fast, and we just told our families. I'm afraid the excitement got away from us."

Jethro nodded his head, glancing between them both. "I expect you to visit me this week. Jah?"

"Of course," Joshua agreed.

Joy wanted to take his hand and squeeze it, because the tension radiating off him could give them all sunburn. What on earth had happened to him while painting the shed? It wasn't that big that he would have struggled to do it all on his own.

"And I guess you'll be wanting Leroy's new job back for yourself," Jethro continued.

Well . . . there went that cat leaping out of the bag with a loud yowl.

Beside her, Joshua stiffened so much, she could've shattered him with a glance. Which meant she didn't dare look at him. Nor at her mater, who she could feel burning holes into her skull with a single sharp stare.

"That explains it." Joy caught the whispered words off to her left and turned her head to find Katie Jones at the sink washing berries. Was Katie talking about something else? She had to be. Everyone knew that Katie was only kindness itself. The perfect Amish girl.

Forcing her attention back to their parents—and Joshua still silent at her side—Joy was left to try to navigate this. "We haven't discussed it with our families yet," she said.

Only instead of cutting that line of talk off at the knees, it apparently triggered a flood.

"Why would Joshua want a job with Mervin?" Joshua's dat asked, gaze swinging back and forth between them.

Ruth Kanagy rolled her eyes. "Ach, Joseph. You can be blind when you want to be."

"What?"

Joseph Kanagy's expression would've been comical if her mamm hadn't stepped in then. "Who would help in the store if Joshua were working with the horses?" she asked.

Ruth's eyebrows rose in gentle surprise. "Joy, of course." She shot her an encouraging look. "Hope and I would be wonderful happy to have her there."

Joy didn't dare say a word, because now her mamm's eyes had turned to sharpened butcher's knives. If she got any hotter, steam might start rising from under her kapp.

"But what about when the boppli come?" Mamm insisted.

Oh help. They were already talking babies. Gotte willing, He would bless them later down the road, after she had time to settle in the shop and get her quilting idea running. Which she still had to speak with Joshua about.

"I managed to work in the store and mind my own boppli, Anna Yoder." Now Ruth was offended. This discussion was going awry quick.

"Joshua is going to take over the shop with Daniel." Joseph Kanagy was still hung up on that, though everyone else had seen the writing on the wall.

With each new comment, the discussion was growing louder, drawing more attention.

"Do something," Joy hissed at her silent fiancé.

Joshua crossed his arms, which she knew well as a sign of stubborn temper from him.

Joy swallowed a sigh and cleared her throat. "Of course, we would want to talk to both our families before we decide what's best."

Both sets of parents bit words off mid-sentence and appeared to realize that they'd stirred many curious gazes inside the home with their discussion. With comical speed, expressions were rearranged to pleasantness. "Of course," Mamm said. "Plenty of time to decide."

Joy knew that expression *and* especially that phrasing. She'd heard it her entire life anytime she asked for or wanted to do something that her mother wouldn't allow. If Mamm didn't say no outright, she simply bided her time. Kept putting that something off until it was too late or Joy lost interest. "Plenty of time to decide" meant *never*.

Which meant Joy would need to act fast to push the issue her way.

"Actually," Joy said. Finally she risked a glance at Joshua, daring him with her eyes to contradict her and receiving a frown at whatever he saw in her face. "We were thinking we might be married at the end of the month."

Given that they'd discussed no such thing, he did an admirable job of hiding his reaction. After a slow blink and slight widening of his eyes, he stepped closer, his broad shoulder against hers, and faced down both their families. "Jah," he said. "After all, we've known each other forever. No need for a long engagement."

And luckily they didn't live in one of the communities that set weddings for after fall harvest and not before.

"So soon?" Ruth gasped. "That's hardly time to plan."

Mamm, Joy had no trouble seeing, said nothing. She couldn't around lips pressed so flat they disappeared. Not that she could say anything against it outright. After all, she was the one who'd been pressing Joy to get married and have all those boppli as soon as possible.

Joshua leaned over to whisper in her ear, "That's set a fox in the henhouse."

Whatever temper he'd been in before, it must have disappeared, because his voice shook with laughter.

Ruth turned to Anna. "We'd better get word out to our friends and family out of town so they can make plans right away."

Joy's mamm paused, then gave a snappy nod. "Jah. Maybe an announcement in *Die Botschaf* would be fastest."

In the weekly newspaper serving Old Order Amish communities everywhere? Joy opened her mouth to protest that they wished to have only a small wedding, but Joshua tugged on her arm to get her attention, then shook his head.

He was right. They had enough hurdles to cross, no need to borrow trouble. Let their mamms deal with the wedding preparation.

"I think we should go now," Joy whispered back.

"Jah. Quick." He straightened. "Mamm, I'm going to drive Joy home. We have a lot to talk about."

Ruth Kanagy waved a distracted hand, still in conversation with Anna about getting a wedding done that quickly. "We'll get a ride home with Aaron and Hope," she told Joshua.

"Let's go before anyone stops us," he said to Joy.

Given her mater's narrowed gaze on her, Joy had to agree. Amazing how fast one could take their leave of the hosts and say a lot of goodbyes and accept well-wishes on their engagement if one wanted to. Somehow, Joshua hustled them out of the house in under ten minutes without one or both sets of parents stopping them from leaving.

In the buggy, Joy turned around to watch the house get smaller and smaller. When finally it disappeared, blocked by the gentle roll of a hill and a copse of tall trees, she sat forward, waited a beat, then burst out laughing. Not because she thought it was funny, but all the emotions of the day had bottled up inside her and had to get out one way or another. Her choices were either laugh or cry, and laughter was nicer.

Joshua's low rolling rumble of a chuckle sounded beside her, lifting her spirits, filling in the gaps with relief.

"We did it," she said, exhilaration filling her with a bubbling sense of accomplishment.

They'd gotten engaged, and everyone—well, mostly everyone—supported that decision, were overjoyed for them, in fact. The biggest hurdle had been cleared. They'd figure everything else out as they went along. This was really going to work!

Beside her, Joshua grunted an agreement of sorts. "What was that business about getting married at the end of the month?" he asked.

"Did you see Mamm's face? She's not happy about the working in the shop idea."

His brows lowered over his eyes. "So what if she's not? We're not doing anything wrong."

He was right. Of course he was right. The Amish frequently married for practicality and prayed that Gotte would bless the union with love later. And they did love each other, if more as friends. Still, she considered that a stronger foundation than some of die Youngie who married a person they hardly knew. "She'll think that I've only done this to get around her rule of not working."

Silence greeted that statement, then he flicked her a glance. "*Is* that why?"

"Nae," she rushed to assure him. "Not the only reason at least. All the points we've talked about are true."

After a brief pause, he nodded.

"It's just . . . I can see Mamm delaying the wedding and hoping I'll end up with Leroy after all, so I don't end up working in the shop. That's why the fast wedding."

He sat upright so hard, she winced for his poor back. "She would do that?"

Joy shrugged. "Mamm likes to have her own way. Especially when she thinks her way is the best way for me."

He grunted again, and she didn't blame him. Hearing that your future mother-in-law would rather her dochder married another man couldn't be easy. Beside her, he remained upright as though strapped to a fence post. A clear sign he was still upset. Speaking of which . . .

"Joshua . . ."

"Hmmm?"

"Why were you so angry when you came in from painting the shed?"

Another grunt. Joshua using grunts instead of words was starting to concern her. "No reason," he finally said.

She turned to face him. "Yes, there was."

But he shook his head. "Nothing worth worrying over."

She was tempted to press harder but could see in the set of his jaw that he wasn't ready to talk about it. Deciding to let it go, she had a more difficult question on her mind anyway.

"Joshua?"

He flicked her a raised eyebrow, amusement tugging at his lips now. "What?"

"If your parents don't let you leave the store . . . we should call off the engagement."

Chapter Seven

JOSHUA WAITED FOR the knock at the door that he knew was coming. He tried to be subtle about it, but he'd already got a pointed elbow in the ribs from Daniel once as they ate breakfast. Mamm had looked at him sideways when he'd grunted, but he'd shoved food in his mouth, and she'd gone back to cooking.

"These might be your best pancakes yet," he'd offered.

"Charmer," she'd said, though her smile had been pleased all the same.

This Sunday was an off week for Gmay, which meant they didn't have a church service to get to, but the shop was still closed. They'd agreed yesterday after the frolic at the Stoltzfuses' that Joy should come over and they would talk to his parents together about the future, and particularly the shop.

The problem was, he couldn't get Joy's words out of his head. That they shouldn't go through with the wedding if he didn't get to work with the horses.

Where on earth had that come from?

Actually . . . he knew why she'd said it. After all, that had been the biggest reason to spur the entire idea. They were being logical, making an important decision based on facts with Gotte's guidance. A partnership, she'd said.

So why did the thought of breaking it off sit like a rock, spiky and heavy, in the center of his chest?

"What is with you this morning?" Daniel muttered under his breath.

"Joy's coming over," he whispered back.

His older bruder frowned, just the tiniest change in expression, but it may as well have been a scowl, given his usual stoniness. Daniel was never one to share his emotions. Why a scowl? Joshua had a fair idea of how this conversation was going to go. Mamm would be for it, Dat against. Was Daniel concerned that their dat would be hurt by this, his second son to want to leave the family business in the hands of his new wife?

Joshua was already worried enough. He didn't need to pile on Daniel's concern as well.

All last night, he'd lain awake in the room he used to share with Aaron—which felt so empty now without his bruder in it—staring at the ceiling or out the window as the stars marched slowly across the night sky. He'd prayed. Prayed that Gotte would direct all the hearts and actions of those involved. Prayed that if he and Joy were doing the right thing, then the job situation would figure itself out.

When he'd dropped her off at home, Joy had looked at him with those dark eyes so full of faith that this would work out. Faith in him. Only her words still sat wrong, like clothes he'd outgrown that had become too tight.

The knock at the door sounded when he wasn't ready, and Joshua actually jumped. Both his parents stopped midbite to stare at him, eyebrows raised.

He cleared his throat. "That will be Joy."

His parents glanced at each other, sharing some opinion impossible to interpret. "Ach vell, go let the girl in," Mamm said.

Right.

Joshua jumped to his feet and hurried to the front door, taking a second to instruct his heart to stop flipping around like jumping beans. This was only Joy, after all.

As he swung the door open, all his tumbling thoughts quieted. He frowned. "You look different," he said.

She did.

Joy's eyebrows shot up the same way his parents' had a moment before. Then she glanced down at herself as though taking stock of her appearance. Not that anything had changed, truly. She was wearing a yellow dress and her prayer kapp as usual, dark hair for once neatly tucked underneath and not a stain or tear in sight. "I look exactly the same," she said, lifting a confused gaze.

Only she didn't. He just couldn't describe how.

No use arguing about it. "Kumme," he said, stepping back and opening the door wider.

"Denki." As she stepped inside, Joy's expression suddenly turned from her usual openness to curiosity. "Did you think of what to say?" she asked in a low voice.

They'd both agreed that they would individually do the talking to their own parents.

"Jah." Sort of.

"That makes one of us." She scrunched up her nose.

The expression was so Joy, a laugh rose up, moving around the lump forming in his chest. He flicked the end of her nose. "Let's get this over with."

"Oll recht."

Moving down the hall with purpose, he paused when

she cleared her throat. Turning, he found her still standing beside the door. "What?" he asked.

Joy silently held out a hand.

Oh.

Amish were not much for any kind of public physical affection, but they were a surprisingly romantic bunch in private. His parents especially. "Gute idea."

With a shake of her head, belying the twinkle in her eyes, Joy moved to his side and he took her hand in his.

The same sensation that had kicked in when he'd kissed her hit all at once. Warmth radiated from where their hands were clasped, her skin soft against his own, her hand tiny in his. The strangest urge to make sure she was always taken care of followed on the wave of warmth. Not that Joy needed to be cosseted or protected from anything, but suddenly she seemed . . . delicate . . . to him. As though that sunshine, anything-is-possible personality hid a tender heart easily bruised. One worth watching over.

But he'd already known that. Hadn't he been watching over her most of his life?

Joshua pulled his shoulders back and tugged her into the kitchen, where his family had miraculously managed to finish eating and clean the kitchen in the few minutes he'd taken to let her in. They were finishing up as he and Joy appeared.

"Joy," Mamm said, and hurried over to give her a hug. "What a lovely surprise. Joshua didn't tell us you'd be coming over today."

"He didn't?" Joy's wide-eyed act of innocence had Joshua swallowing back a chuckle. They'd agreed not to warn their families. Best to tackle these tough talks without giving their parents time to think first. She turned to look at him and *tsk*ed.

Joshua grinned. He couldn't help it.

Mamm rolled her eyes. "Would you like something to drink, Joy? I have fresh-made punch."

"Sounds lovely."

At a none-too-subtle hitch of Dat's head at Daniel, his bruder mumbled an excuse about needing to tend to his bees and left the house out the back door. Joshua pulled out a chair and seated Joy beside him at the table. As soon as they all had their drinks, his parents joined them.

"Mamm . . . Dat . . ." Joshua winced. Not the best start. "We wanted to talk to you—"

"About what changes need to happen after your marriage," Mamm finished for him. "Your fater and I have already discussed it."

Uh-oh. He exchanged a glance with Joy, who said nothing for once, simply reached for his hand under the table.

"You did?" he asked.

Mamm took his fater's hand in hers, a sign of solidarity between them. "Dat and I are in agreement. If the Yoders wish you to take on Mervin's business with the horses, and Joy would like to take your place in the shop, we are both happy to have her."

"You are?" The words popped out before he could stop them, searching Dat's face for any clue as to how he truly felt about this. His own happiness wasn't worth breaking his fater's heart.

Dat leaned forward. "I won't deny that I pictured handing A Thankful Heart over to all three of my sons, but your mamm is right. Hope and Joy are both more suited to the work and they are, or will be . . ." He shot Joy a smile. "Kanagys, yet. And when the boppli start arriving, one day this shop will still be handed down within the family."

Mamm reached over and patted Dat's hand, a small

show of affection and support, and Joshua had no idea what to think. Was he a bad son to have put his fater in this position? Having to give up his own dreams.

"Are you sure?" Joy asked quietly beside him. Subdued. Not Joy's usual effervescence. "We wouldn't want to get in the way of a family legacy."

But Joseph Kanagy shook his head. "Nae. Ruth is right. Gotte has blessed Joshua with a skill and a passion for horses, and this marriage is a blessing for all of us."

Beside him, Joy let out a long, silent breath that only he noticed because she was still squeezing his hand, the pressure letting up slightly. She'd been nervous? At least he wasn't alone in that.

"Denki," he said to his parents. "This means the world to both of us."

"Are you sure you want to take on the shop, Joy?" Mamm asked.

Joy's smile was back to normal. "For sure and certain! I think I would love it." She paused as though unsure if she should say more. "Erm . . . Especially if we can do more with my quilts after I get settled in the shop."

Mamm straightened, beaming. "Of course. Your quilts will be wonderful popular."

Joshua had no idea why that statement sent pride puffing him up. He did his best to stamp it out. "Pride goeth before destruction, and an haughty spirit before a fall," as the Bible said in Proverbs.

"Denki," Joy murmured, lowering her gaze humbly. "I do enjoy the quilts, and I enjoy talking with people, so it seems . . ."

"Perfect," he murmured beside her.

How had he not come up with this solution himself a long time ago anyhow? He must have been blind as a field mole.

"As to living situations," Mamm continued.

Joshua and Joy both straightened, her grip on him tightening even more. They hadn't got past discussing getting engaged and the situation with the shop and horses.

"We would like to offer you our Dawdi Haus," Dat said. A shadow passed over his features. "After all, no one is using it since my dat passed."

Joy turned her head to look at Joshua and he looked back, waiting for her reaction.

"Really?" she squeaked.

He couldn't tell quite what the squeak meant. Was she happy about this?

Ruth and Joseph nodded, smiling at each other in parental contentment. "Joy could ride with us to the shop in the mornings while Joshua goes to the Yoders' to work with the horses."

Joshua had assumed they'd try to find a house of their own nearby, still in the same church district, but this was better. Close to family and convenient, but still with room of their own. He was still watching Joy. "Is that what you wish?"

She blinked at him, and the sparkle in her eyes banked slowly. Then she offered him a sunny smile. "Why don't we talk about it on the way to talk to my parents?" she asked.

"Smart," Mamm said, and stood.

A signal to them all to get moving apparently. Joy had, somewhere during the discussion, finished her entire glass of punch. Joshua had been so focused on the situation, he'd managed to miss that. Meanwhile, he hadn't touched his. He grabbed the glass and drank it all down in one long swallow.

"We'll be back later," he said, moving to the sink to rinse the glass out.

"Take your time." Mamm waved her hand. "You've hardly had any to yourselves. Maybe after speaking with Mervin and Anna, you should take your lovely new bride on a date."

Now they were going on dates yet? Why did everyone have the notion this was a romance? Not that they'd done anything to correct that, but still . . .

Joshua forced his suddenly stiff features to relax. "That would be nice. Don't you think, Joy?"

"It would?"

He pinched the back of her arm and she jumped, then cleared her throat. "Of course it would. Maybe I'll make us a picnic."

"We just ate breakfast," Joshua pointed out.

"A snack picnic," she amended quickly.

That, at least, would give them privacy to discuss their future together. "Wunderbaar."

His parents smiled again, and Joshua could feel the tension oozing from his shoulders and back. Another hurdle cleared, now for the tougher nut to crack. Joy's mamm.

JOY ENTERED THE house ahead of Joshua. He'd followed her in his own buggy so she wouldn't have to drive him back later.

"Mamm?" she called.

"In here."

Joshua stepped into the house behind her, his big shoulders filling the doorframe. Like her, he was in his Sunday best, with the black jacket and hat. This was what he'd look like on their wedding day. Strong and fine and her partner, in everything.

Pride was not usually a sin she struggled with, but she

might on that day, marrying the handsomest boy in their district. Probably in the whole tri-county area. All the girls said so, though they said that about all the Kanagy boys, but she'd be married to one.

Not that what was on the outside mattered. Eventually their youth would fade, but even then, he'd be handsome to her, she suspected. Because of his heart.

He'd been her hero since she was a little girl.

Taking his hand, she led him through the gathering room to the kitchen, where Mamm was at the counter rolling out dough and Dat was at the kitchen table with a glass of milk. Mamm smiled—she actually smiled. "I thought you might like to take a tin of my sugar cookies to singeon," she said. "To celebrate announcing your upcoming wedding."

Soon, they wouldn't be attending the Sunday evening events that were time for die Youngie to gather together socially. They'd be married and busy with their own family.

"You'll miss those when we stop," Joshua murmured.

Echoing her thoughts so exactly that she blinked at him. Then turned a suspicious gaze on her mater. She never made cookies for Joy to bring. Why did this feel like a test?

"We wanted to talk to you about—"

Mamm waved a hand. "The horses. We know."

They weren't even going to give them time to state their arguments? She rushed into them anyway. "You know Joshua's gift with horses is a blessing. Dat could use him."

Mamm nodded sharply. "We agree."

"Dat could even expand the business with Joshua's help—" Joy cut herself off mid-word. "You agree?"

Mamm folded her hands on top of the table. "Of course. Joshua will be family and he *is* gifted. Of course he must work with your dat. It only makes sense."

Dat pulled at his beard, blue eyes twinkling, though his expression remained firmly grave.

"But . . ."

Joy almost groaned. There was always a but.

"Joy may not work in the shop until *after* you are wed." She bent a hard gaze on Joshua. "Then the decision to do so rests with her husband, not with her parents."

Joshua nodded solemnly. "It won't be long that we have to wait."

True.

"What about Leroy?" Joy asked.

Her parents exchanged a glance, and this one she had no trouble interpreting. Whatever came next was entirely Mamm's idea. Dat's pinched lips said he was not convinced. "We thought we would offer for him to continue to learn and help, in case he wishes to find this sort of work elsewhere."

"I see . . ." Joy didn't really. Leroy was sure to slow down the work, but perhaps he truly wanted to work with horses. She couldn't take that away from him.

Joshua crossed the room, offering his hand to her fater to shake. "I won't let you down, Mervin."

Dat's pinched lips eased and he glanced at Mamm, an odd light in his eyes, before turning back to Joshua. "I know. This is best for all of us."

Mamm's expression, though, was complacent, not a hint of ire or suspicion in sight.

That was it?

Joy still wasn't entirely sure this was real. Perhaps she was dreaming? After all, she'd spent all day avoiding her parents and preparing reasonable arguments in her head for every possible delay or dissatisfaction or argument Mamm might present. Instead, by some miracle, both their families had been agreeable to everything.

Too much so. This had been too easy.

Would they have been as agreeable without the marriage? If Joshua had simply asked to swap work, without proposing to her, would both sets of parents have said yes to his request anyway?

Vell . . . her mother wouldn't have. But could she have been convinced?

Joy suspected she didn't want to find out the answer to that, because where would that leave her? Being thrown at Leroy Miller's head, still. Only . . . that was a terribly selfish way to view this. What if Joshua would rather have his dream without a wife he didn't love romantically in tow?

Joy swallowed around a sudden lump in her throat. "We were thinking of going on a picnic," she managed. Because suddenly she needed to get out of the house, away from her mater's discerning stare.

"That sounds lovely," Mamm said. "When you come back, we can talk about the wedding plans."

Mamm, even in the short time before the wedding, was going to want to do everything "right." After all, her only dochder got married just once, please Gotte.

Joshua went out to the barn with her dat while she put together a quick basket with a few of Mamm's cookies, two small pieces of the cake Joy had taken to the frolic, the end-of-season strawberries, and a jug of water. Throwing one of the first quilts she'd ever made over her arm, she picked up the basket and headed out to gather her husband-to-be and find a spot with privacy.

Twenty minutes later, she spread out the quilt under the shade of a large elm tree, and Joshua set down the basket. After getting everything out and serving both of them, she took a huge bite of cake, frowning at nothing in particular as she chewed.

"That was too easy," she said.

A small leaf fluttered onto her skirt and she brushed it away. She was still worried that maybe they hadn't needed to go through all of this in the first place.

"Too easy?" Joshua asked. Then grinned around a cookie. "You wanted to fight about it?"

"Nae. Not fight, but . . ." Joy sighed. She had to say this. She had to give him the opportunity to choose. "Maybe you didn't need to marry me to have this turn out right?"

The silence could have been the dark hole of the abandoned well on her family's property. Joy kept her gaze glued to the food on her plate and waited.

"Are you having second thoughts?" he asked in a low, tight voice.

That had her yanking her gaze up in surprise. "Not *me*. I mean for *you*."

He was quiet again for a long time. Long enough that she suddenly wanted to squirm. Another leaf falling onto her plate this time gave her the excuse to glance away as she plucked it up and tossed it aside.

"Nae," Joshua said slowly. "I don't want to change my mind. I still think we should marry."

Not that he wanted to, but that they should. She took another big bite of cake, not tasting a thing, as she chewed that over. Of course . . . his parents still needed to replace him in the shop, and Joy couldn't do that if they weren't married.

Why did disappointment wrap around that realization like a tangled rope? Somewhere along the way, marrying Joshua was becoming . . . more. More important. Something she truly wanted. Or was she just so set on this course that she didn't want to turn around?

"As long as *you* still want to . . ." he said.

She fixed a smile to her face that she hoped appeared easy. "For sure and certain."

Please don't let me be making a selfish choice. She offered the small prayer up to Gotte's ears.

Something light but prickly bounced off the top of her head. Joy craned her neck, searching the ground to find not a leaf, but an entire bunch of leaves at the end of what amounted to a tiny stick. She picked it up and frowned as she twirled it in her fingers. Then realization dawned. She didn't even have to raise her gaze upward.

"Amos and Samuel Yoder, get out of that tree this instant," she called in a loud voice.

Joshua jerked his gaze up, then snorted a laugh, which he quickly swallowed as he got a glance at her expression, sobering right quick. She watched, not without a small amount of trepidation, as both boys scrambled down from the big tree. Luckily without incident.

Muttering at each other, they finally stood before her, both heads drooped and shoulders slumped. "Don't try those hangdog faces with me," she said. "I know you only do that to get out of punishment when Mamm is mad."

The two glanced at each other as though debating giving up the ruse. Then Amos shrugged and they lifted their heads. "Don't be angry, Joy. We weren't doing nothing wrong."

She wasn't about to start on their grammar. "You know after Samuel sprained his ankle last spring that Mamm said if she finds you climbing another tree, you wouldn't like the consequences."

Amos's lips twisted. "But trees are the best place to learn things!"

Uh-oh. Exactly what she'd thought. Joy popped to her knees. Hands on her hips. "What . . . exactly . . . do you think you learned this time?"

She glanced at Joshua, who was no longer hiding amusement but studying the boys more seriously.

Amos dug a toe in the grass. "Just stuff about getting married."

"*What* about getting married?" Joshua prompted.

The worst thing would be for the boys to repeat any of that conversation to either of their parents.

"Nothing," Samuel said with a shake of his head, bowl-cut curls, the bane of Mamm's mornings, flying every which way.

Amos suddenly brightened. "We heard Mamm and Dat talking about the same thing."

She exchanged a glance with Joshua. "About us getting married?"

Amos nodded eagerly. "Mamm said that they should keep Leroy around in case it doesn't work out with Joshua."

He grimaced suddenly, as though realizing Joshua was sitting right there. Probably because Joshua had gone poker stiff. He managed to school his features into amusement, but not before Joy caught a flash of hurt.

"Oll recht, you two scamps," Joshua said. "Off with you."

Only they didn't immediately scurry away, instead watching Joy with a hopeful glint.

"What else?" she said, narrowing her eyes in mock seriousness. She'd already caught the furtive glances at the tin of cookies.

"Mamm said we're not allowed to have the cookies. They're for tonight," Samuel said.

"You want cookies?" Joshua asked.

Both boys' eyes went wide and they nodded.

"Then you have to pay the toll," Joshua said.

The way her bruders' faces fell was comical. "What kind of toll?" Samuel asked suspiciously.

"Not a fun one, I'll betchya," Amos muttered.

"Ach jah. It's a hard toll to pay."

"What is it?"

"A. . . ." He glanced at Joy, who prepared herself for anything. "Tickle Joy toll!"

With a whoop and a hoot, two small bodies tackled her to the ground. Joshua's rolling deep laugh joined their higher-pitched squeals as they all attacked Joy at once. She squealed and squirmed and laughed until her cheeks hurt and tears ran from her eyes.

Then, as suddenly as it started, Amos and Samuel were gone, snatching cookies and running away laughing. Only Joy didn't notice because she and Joshua had somehow managed to end up with her lying on the blanket staring up into his smiling dark eyes as he rested on his elbow beside her.

"That was not fair," she protested, still trying to catch her breath.

"I know, but it always wonders me how you can laugh when you're tickled." He flashed surprisingly even white teeth. Nice teeth.

Would their children get his teeth? *Ach. Children.* She'd worry about that part later.

"Plus, your dimple comes out." He touched a finger to her cheek, and their eyes met.

"Joshua," she said slowly.

"Hmmm?"

"That bit about Leroy . . . It's not that Mamm doesn't want you."

The smile faded from his face. "Nae?"

"Nae. But I saw her face the other day when the shop was first brought up. She's not happy about me working, but knows she won't have a say in it once we marry, so she's . . ."

"Making sure that you'll spend lots of time with Leroy while I'm still stuck in the shop. Just in case?"

She scrunched up her nose. "Jah. I think so."

Joshua stilled, gaze skating over her features, searching for . . . Joy wasn't sure what. His very stillness brought with it a sort of shivery tension. As though she couldn't quite breathe right.

"I'd better make sure I give you something to remember me by while you're around Leroy then," he said.

Joy tipped her head, confused. "What does that—"

Joshua leaned forward and placed his lips to hers in the sweetest, softest kiss that stole her every thought from her head. The kind full of promise. Full of hope for the future. Full of dreams she didn't quite let herself believe in anymore. After all, she'd chosen the practical path. Kissing Joshua didn't feel practical, though.

He kissed her once more, then lifted his head, and a shadow of her own regret went with him.

"That should do it," he said. Then grinned and gave her an outrageous wink.

Joy tried not to scowl, hiding it behind a roll of her eyes. She would rather be kissed because he wanted to. A realization that set her head in such a spin, she hardly spoke as they packed up their picnic and he walked her home.

I want to kiss Joshua. And I want him to want to kiss me. What did that mean?

They drove together to singeon and endured more congratulations and happy hugs from friends. She sat beside him all night . . . and a sense of rightness settled over her. More than before even, only she wasn't sure what to make of that. Afterward, Joshua brought her home, walking her to her door.

"If you get a hankering to flirt with Leroy," Joshua said as she let herself in, "just remember who kissed you first."

She almost thought he might kiss her again, just to remind her, but he sauntered away instead.

Joy scowled after him. "That goes the same for you, Joshua Kanagy," she called after him.

But only got a laconic wave in return. He didn't even turn around, but she swore his shoulders were shaking with laughter.

Chapter Eight

JOSHUA GRITTED HIS teeth as the Englischer girl who'd come into the store at least a half hour before—not more than seventeen—hemmed and hawed over which toy she wanted to purchase for her younger brother.

She cast an uncertain smile his way, peeping out from under lashes clumped with makeup. "Do you have any younger brothers?" she asked.

"Nae. I'm the youngest in my family. I have two older bruders." Now why had he bothered to tell her that?

"Oh." She bit her lip. "Are they *all* as good looking as you?"

He paused. Was that what all that hemming and hawing had been about? Interest in him? Usually he was happy to flirt a bit with the girls who came into the shop. It didn't hurt anyone, after all, and helped pass the long days. Only now that he was engaged, he had stopped all that.

Even so . . . how had he missed the fact that this girl was flirting?

He cleared his throat and tucked his hands behind him, not answering. Had she been Amish, a blush might have swept into her cheeks, or she might even have apologized for being so forward. Instead, she stared at him with frank appreciation that was making him want to fidget rather than amusing him.

A flash of movement had him glancing over at where Hope was rearranging the quilts in the back of the store to display a new one. She ducked her head as he caught her eyes, lips clearly twitching with amusement, and Joshua had to stop himself from glowering. Mamm would be upset if he scared away a customer.

"Well . . ." The girl tried now. "You're a boy."

"Jah." Were all Englischer girls this observant?

"What do *you* think he would like?"

The bruder? Joshua rubbed the back of his neck, trying to relieve the bands of tension building there. "Does he like trains or cars better?"

"Both."

He dropped his hand to his sides. "Then get him both."

The girl brightened at that. "I could give him one for Christmas and one for his birthday. That's perfect."

Blowing out a silent breath of relief that she'd finally come to a decision, he led her to the counter, inexplicably happy to put that barrier between them. Joshua finished ringing up the sale then handed over the bag of goods with a perfunctory smile. "Denki. Come again."

"Oh, I will, and I'll tell *all* my friends." She paused, and her smile turned flirtatious again. "Do you always work here?"

Oh, sis yucht.

"After I marry in a few weeks, my wife will work here instead," he said.

The tragic fall to her expression was sweet if misguided.

Even if he didn't have Joy, Joshua would never turn his back on his faith, his family, or his community. So unless she was interested in converting—which happened, though rarely and often not successfully—there would be no point to anything beyond a few flirtatious words as she shopped.

"Congratulations," she mumbled before she took her bag and scurried outside.

Joshua watched her go, then turned his head to find Hope watching him again. "What," he asked, "is so funny, Hope Kanagy?"

Gray eyes twinkled, which only made him want to frown more. "It's just odd to see you so . . . reserved with the ladies now. Like an old married man. You must really love Joy."

Joshua paused. "I was perfectly nice to that customer."

"Polite, jah." She agreed with a nod. "But I wouldn't go so far as to say nice, and definitely *not* charming. Not like usual at least."

He crossed his arms. "It is only right that I save all my charming for my bride."

"Ach jah." Hope grinned. "I think Joy would appreciate that."

The trouble was, he hadn't deliberately been *not* charming to the girl. Not directly because of Joy, at least. More like indirectly.

He'd been thinking about her all day long. Her and Leroy Miller.

Leroy had been at the Yoders' already when Joshua had stopped by to help with the morning chores before coming to the shop. Joy had been in the barn, a basket full of fresh-baked muffins on one arm, offering them to Leroy of all people. And she'd been smiling. The sweet one that made her eyes light up with shared laughter.

Does Leroy make her laugh as much as she does with me?

He couldn't picture it. Although he'd bet Leroy had appreciated her cooking. Joy was a wonderful gute baker. Her treats were often the first to go at singeon or any frolics.

What if Joy spent all this time with Leroy while Joshua was stuck in the shop? What if she fell in love with him and decided to marry him instead? After all, romantic love wasn't part of their own match. It *could* happen, then he'd be stuck without the job or the wife he wanted.

"DID YOU KNOW cows can produce up to eighty-eight pints of saliva a day?" Leroy's voice sounded from the next stall over.

Yuck.

"Is that so?" Did she sound as uninterested as she felt? Leroy Miller might be the most boring person on the planet.

Joy bit her lip at the ungracious thought and sent up a small request of forgiveness to Gotte for having it. Then again . . . guilt didn't make it any less true. Who cared about cow saliva anyway?

What had Mamm been thinking, trying to match her with this boy? Picturing a life with him . . . nights spent together after the evening meal had been cleared away and they settled in the gathering room together—her quilting and him reading about cows and sharing similar uninteresting facts—she was almost asleep on her feet merely thinking on it.

Unfortunately, if anything, given how Mamm had handed her the basket of muffins and practically shoved her into the barn to offer them to Leroy, she still hadn't given up. Despite the fact that Joy and Joshua were engaged to be married.

Did she have such little faith in Joy's decision to marry her old friend?

In fact, today, rather than having Joy work in the house, she'd sent her out to the barn to help "teach Leroy" the basics while Dat had worked breaking in the new buggy horse. Mamm could be sneaky, no doubt, though always with the best intentions.

Maybe I need to be sneakier than her.

"What are you doing this afternoon, Leroy?" she asked as she shoveled fresh hay into the stall he'd finished mucking.

He popped his head up over the side of the adjoining stall, blinking at her owlishly from behind his thick glasses. Leroy, with his deep blue eyes and hair the color of wheat at harvest time, actually was handsome, and she'd always liked his glasses. They made him appear . . . distinguished.

And yet . . . the second he opened his mouth . . .

"I was planning to go to the library. They ordered me a book on—"

"Oh, but that's wonderful gute," she interrupted.

He blinked again. "It is?"

Joy nodded. "I was planning on going to the farmer's market. Maybe you could take me? You could drop me off while you go to the library, and then come find me when you're done."

"You take *that* long?" he asked.

It wondered her how long his mater must take. The weekly farmer's market in town was rather large, with many stalls and different goods. Beatrice Miller must be a speedy shopper. "Jah, but I'm sure I'll be ready to go by the time you get done at the library."

Leroy's eyes—the only part of him she could see over the wall—scrunched up. "Mamm expects me home for lunch."

Joy waved away that concern. "I'm sure we will be back in plenty of time."

"Oll recht," he said slowly, confusion and reluctance drawing his brows over his eyes.

She ignored both. He'd thank her for this one day.

Then he disappeared to continue working. Joy whistled as she did the same. If she timed this perfectly, she might put a stopper in Mamm's scheming, and hopefully make two people happy.

As soon as chores were finished, Leroy hitched up his horse and buggy and they drove into town together. Luckily, Leroy decided to tell her all about his book. Something about breeding animals. She wasn't paying him much attention, her own mind focused on what came next. Chores had taken longer than she'd expected, and with Leroy's time limit, she was going to have to work fast.

He pulled over right outside the large parking lot, unused most days, located at the far end of the main street where the market was set up in temporary canvas-sided stalls. "Be quick," he warned. "I won't take long at the library."

Again, she had a flash of what marriage to Leroy might be like, always being chided to be quick, or probably not to laugh so loud or talk so much. He definitely needed a quieter girl. Which was perfect since she had one in mind.

"You'll find me on the far side." She pointed. "Over by the small stall selling sheds and the large one that sells artisan beers." Whatever "artisan" meant when it came to beer.

"You can't meet me here?" he asked, lips drawing into a disapproving frown.

"It won't take you long to find me," she assured him. Then, seeing his lips purse on the verge of argument, she waved and walked away.

Was Leroy's mamm such a tyrant that he feared being late that much? Actually, come to think of it, Beatrice Miller did tend toward the bossy side. Anyone married to Leroy or his sister, Lovila, would need to be biddable and easygoing, for sure and certain.

The buzz of a well-formed plan humming through her, Joy hurried through the makeshift stalls, smiling broadly at those Englischers bold enough to look her in the eyes. Many turned away, though she suspected out of shyness or not wanting to intrude or rudely stare more than any malicious intent. Amish could be equally closed off or wary of others. After all, they were seen as the outsiders wherever they went. Or tourist spectacles to be viewed with an odd sort of lack of understanding and fascination.

But Gotte had said to live separate from the world, lest they be influenced by it, and that's exactly what they did, as much as they could.

Things had changed, especially since she was born, with many church districts becoming less strict. Not all Amish made everything by hand as they used to. Trips to Walmart were common, as were linoleum floors, and the use of propane to power things like their refrigerators had also changed life for many. Not to mention how jobs had changed, especially here in northern Indiana, where so many now worked in Englischer factories.

But no one bothered her or stopped her as she made her way to her favorite stall. "Hi, Mary," she called out as she skirted the last group between her and her destination.

Coming to her feet, setting her own sewing aside, Mary Hershberger smiled shyly, her gaze not quite meeting Joy's.

Although Mary was an ordinary-looking girl with unremarkable eyes and mousy brown hair, Joy had still always thought her lovely in a sort of quiet way that the boys missed. Probably because Mary was one of five girls, and her older sisters each laid claim to the type of beauty that tended toward comment. Only their hearts didn't match their outsides at all, while Mary had the kindest heart of anyone in the district.

Leroy had seen that. Joy was sure of it. The problem was he was too reserved to do anything about it, or maybe his mamm had a different girl in mind. Joy bit her lip, realizing she should find that out before she pushed these two together too much.

"Starting a new quilt?" Mary asked.

Joy hummed her agreement with that. "I've been thinking I'd make a quilt for my wedding gift to Joshua and I want to do something special," she said, and tried not to blush.

Mary reached over to squeeze her hand. "I didn't get a chance to say so at singeon the other night . . . Congratulations on your engagement." She pursed her lips. "Though maybe I should wait to say that after it's announced in church?"

Joy waved away that formality. "Denki. I think we'll be very happy."

Or at least regular happy, and that should be enough for anyone.

With what she hoped was a casual air, she picked up a stack of quilting squares held together by a beautifully tied ribbon, leafing through the different patterns of material matched together. While Mary apparently struggled with actually making the quilts, and her baking was not the best, she was amazing with materials. She had learned to make her own cloth and sold it now at markets like these as well as online, thanks to special permission. Not only that, but she would trade with others in the districts, so she often had the best selection. Her eye for which colors and materials and patterns would complement each other best in a quilted layout was unmatched.

"I was thinking blues and yellows on a field of white," she said, thinking of the idea on the spot. A wedding quilt *was* a lovely idea, even if it had only occurred to her right this moment. Maybe in a linked hearts design. Or was that too romantic for the kind of marriage they would have? Maybe they wouldn't even share a room, though she could still give the quilt to Joshua either way.

She bit her lip.

"I know the perfect thing," Mary said, apparently unaware of Joy's momentary struggle. "I saw it the other week at the Shipshewana market. I'll be there tomorrow and see if I can find it for you."

"That would be wunderbaar," Joy said. Then paused. Now . . . to introduce the topic she'd come here to discuss. With a deliberate glance over her shoulder, she said, "My ride isn't here yet. Do you mind if I sit and wait with you?"

"Of course." Mary waved at a canvas folding chair beside her own. "My sister Beth went to get us lunch at another booth. It often takes her a while."

Because Beth liked to flirt with the Englischer boys, that much Joy knew, not that she'd ever say so. It would be unkind.

"Denki." Joy dropped into the seat. "Leroy Miller gave me a ride into town—he's been learning horses with Dat and was nice enough to let me tag along. I'm not sure when he'll be here to pick me up."

"Leroy—" Mary squeaked, and her bottom almost missed the chair she was aiming for as she, too, took a seat.

She righted herself, freckles in stark relief against skin gone suddenly pale then flushed bright red before she cleared her throat. "You know . . . I thought maybe you and Leroy might marry," she said slowly. "Not that you and Joshua aren't perfect together, but I got the impression that . . ." She trailed off.

"My mamm maybe had a few ideas." Joy waved a hand as though shooing a fly away from fresh-baked dessert. "But I always knew Leroy had his eye on another girl."

"He did?" Mary asked, her expression falling.

Joy nodded and waited. Except Mary's bravery apparently didn't go as far as asking who. How did she say this without telling tales that weren't hers to share? "Not that he would ever say anything to me," she said. "So I don't know for certain, but I've noticed a few . . . glances."

Mary bent her head over her sewing. "Oh? I'm sure whoever Leroy has chosen will be a lucky girl yet."

Joy swallowed a sigh. "I'm talking about you, Mary," she said gently.

Mary's head came up so fast, the end of one of her kapp ties smacked her in the cheek. "Me?"

Joy searched her face, wanting to be certain she was right about Mary's feelings, too. "Would you be even a little interested back? I mean if I'm right that Leroy is?"

"I—" The blush that hadn't yet receded only deepened. "Are you sure?"

Joy pursed her lips. "He hasn't said anything, so I can't be positive. But yes, I've noticed how he watches you."

"He watches me?"

"The same way I watch Katie Jones's treats at frolics," Joy teased.

For a heartbeat, a sparkle akin to excitement lit Mary's eyes, but it quickly faded. "I couldn't hope to win Leroy," she said. "He's so smart and comes from a nice family, and my mamm . . ."

She trailed off, lowering her gaze.

Mary's older sisters were in actual fact her half sisters. Their mamm had died and their dat had remarried, but after giving birth to her, Mary's mamm left the faith—jumped the fence and abandoned her family.

"Any Amish man would be lucky to have you as his fraa," Joy insisted firmly.

True, some folks in the community were inclined to watch Mary carefully, as though she were a poison pill, but not those true to the forgiveness of others that their faith taught. Although . . . was Beatrice Miller one of those who had shown Mary ungraciousness? Some unkindness? Was she the reason Leroy hadn't made a move?

Uneasiness settled in Joy's stomach like a bad apple with a worm in it. *Am I being selfish and wrong to encourage her?*

"Maybe if I were better at cooking," Mary said. "Like you or my schwesters."

As far as Joy could tell, Mary's sisters were only good at looking pretty. Perhaps she was being unkind in her heart to think such a thing.

"Did your schwesters not teach you to cook yet?" she asked gently.

"Nae. Being older, most of them were married with families of their own by the time I was old enough to learn."

True. Though of the two closest in age to Mary, Ariel only married within the last three years or so, and Bethany hadn't married yet. "I would be happy to teach you a few tricks," Joy offered.

Mary straightened at that. "Really?"

Guilt suddenly pierced Joy's heart, turning it to a stone

that sank to her feet. Why had it taken her selfish need to get Leroy away from Joshua's job to realize that Mary might need a friend to show her such things? Rather than letting the other youngie speak about her terrible thumbprint cookies, she should have offered sooner to have Mary over to cook together.

"Of course! I would love to. Also, we have a frolic coming up this weekend. Are you available Thursday? You could come over and we could cook for that together. As well as a dish for singeon Sunday."

"Denki, Joy. I would love that," Mary accepted quietly, but the enthusiasm rang in her voice.

The gratefulness in Mary's eyes humbled Joy's heart even more, and she made a silent vow to be a better friend than she had. Forget matchmaking Mary and Leroy.

"Joy Yoder?" Leroy called out. Though she couldn't see him, his voice was gruff and impatient and had Mary sitting up straight in her seat, her expression closer to stricken than elated.

"Here," Joy called out, standing so that he could see her and waving a hand.

After a frown—no doubt at her overzealous antics—Leroy marched through the crowds with a solemn expression. "We are going to be late," he said as soon as he'd reached her.

Then finally, his gaze turned to the girl in the booth with her, and he froze and stuttered over several incoherent words. "Hello, Mary," he finally got out, looking almost as though he'd rather be anywhere else, his cheeks turning ruddy.

"Leroy," Mary practically whispered.

Then all three of them stood there in a sort of stunned, awkward silence.

Oh, sis yucht. These two would never figure things out at this rate.

She'd have to watch Leroy with Mary at Gmay on Sunday and think a little more on how she could help these two overcome whatever was stopping them from seeing that the best partner for life was right in front of their noses.

Hopefully Leroy would be helping Dat with the horses when Mary came over to bake. They could try out their attempts on him. That, at least, would be a promising start.

"I'll see you Thursday, Mary," she said. "Around ten?"

"Okay," Mary whispered, her gaze glued to her lap now.

With a happy wave, Joy practically had to drag a still silent Leroy back through the market. As he drove the buggy through town, she spied a familiar dark head outside A Thankful Heart, arranging a rack of clothing out under the covered walk. Joshua glanced up as she drove by, and she sent him a cheerful wave, only to get a frown in return.

One not unlike Leroy's a moment ago in the market.

Maybe he hadn't recognized her in Leroy's buggy? Or was she being too boisterous for him, too? She shrugged and set that aside, turning her mind back to the problem of Leroy and Mary.

She prayed that Gotte would direct her works and heart to help the two of them.

Chapter Nine

JOSHUA MANAGED NOT to stalk up the steps leading to the Yoders' front door, but knocking hard at least was satisfying. He'd been like this the entire rest of the day. Toting around something that felt like anger and worry all rolled into a knotted ball inside his stomach.

Ever since he saw Joy driving happily along with Leroy Miller of all people. She'd even waved at him and flashed that darn dimple. What was she thinking?

Amos Yoder opened the door. "Hey, Joshua!" The boy beamed as though Joshua had come to see him specially. "Samuel and me is going tadpole hunting. Wanna kumme?"

Joshua managed a grin and tousled the boy's hair. "I can't today," he said. "Where's Joy?"

Amos wrinkled his nose. "Ach you want to see *her*, I guess."

Dropping to one knee, he eyed the boy closer. "Jah. Is that bad?"

"Nae. But . . ." Amos picked at a scab on his hand. "Married people are no fun. Matthew Bontrager said when his bruder got married, he stopped playing with the younger kinder. All he and his wife do now is sit and stare at each other with big eyes like this." Amos batted his ridiculously long eyelashes, then scrunched up his face and made a sound of disgust in his throat.

Joshua bit the inside of his cheek to keep from laughing. "Well . . . one day when you're older, you'll understand why."

"I'd rather not grow up if that's what happens to buwes."

Joshua tipped his head. "I promise that I'll still play with you, and so will Joy."

Amos's gaze lit up for a second, but then his eyes narrowed. "We'll see." For one so young, he already understood how other things could get in the way of casually made promises, but Joshua had meant it. "Tomorrow we're going exploring. We're going to dig a tunnel."

Having done the same with his own bruders, Joshua nodded solemnly. Tunnel digging was a highlight of boyhood. "Make sure the walls are strong," he said.

"We will." He puffed up with his own importance. "Joy's in the barn."

In a blink, that ball of awfulness from earlier knotted right back up. "Denki. Have fun with the tadpoles."

All the way to the barn, Joshua tried to find the words he needed, but they weren't coming. At least not in any way that made sense in his head. What could he say that wouldn't sound like awkward, unwarranted jealousy? She was marrying *him* after all, not Leroy.

"Joy?" he called out, but no one answered.

Except Sugar Cookie, the ratty old barn cat. Massive, he sat at the door and hissed at Joshua's call, tail whipping back and forth.

Joshua ignored the thing, especially as a faint sound of female laughter sounded from outside and toward the back where the smaller paddocks were located. He walked through the cooler shaded barn and paused when the big bay brood mare in the last stall knickered at him.

"Sorry, Schatzi," he said, running his hand over her velvet-smooth neck. "I don't have any sugar on me." He eyed her bulging belly. "When is that foal going to decide to show up anyway?"

She nosed at him, as though agreeing things were overdue, and he chuckled. With a final pat, he continued out into the dappled sunshine under the trees to find Joy standing on the lowest rung of the white fencing around the small round paddock. She was watching as Mervin walked behind the yearling they were training, holding the long buggy reins so the horse would get used to the feel of them along its back and flanks.

"He's coming along," Joshua said quietly as he got nearer.

Joy spun with a gasp and lost her footing. Luckily, he managed to scoop her up before damage was wrought. Only the way the air whooshed from his lungs as her big brown gaze connected with his, she might as well have landed them both on the ground.

Strangely, he didn't want to move, didn't want to let her go and have to step back. So he didn't. She felt . . . right . . . light in his arms and she smelled amazing. Like sunshine and cookies. She must've been baking.

"I didn't mean to scare you," he murmured.

"You didn't."

He lifted a single eyebrow. "Then this is a funny new way of greeting me. Is this what all wives do to their husbands?"

A sparkle entered her eyes, her lips twitching as she casually tugged one side of his suspenders, the gesture so intimate and yet so casually Joy, the air deserted his lungs all over again. Had the reality of marrying her changed things so much? Or had this sudden . . . interest for lack of a better word . . . in her always lurked under the surface?

Joshua had no idea.

"I was testing your reflexes," Joy said, all prim and know-it-all sounding. Which only made him want to cuddle her close and laugh at the same time.

I'm going to marry her. I might as well enjoy whatever this is.

"Then I have a test for you," he said as he lowered his head to kiss her. Something he'd been wanting to do since the last time.

Her surprised gasp made him smile, but then she pushed against his chest, and that wiped the humor right off his face.

"My dat can see us," she whisper-hissed at him.

"Ahem."

The cleared throat had Joshua jerking upright to set Joy unceremoniously back on her feet and jump back. Only to encounter Mervin's stern gaze, belied by a twinkle in his eyes not unlike his daughter's.

"I'm glad to see my dochder enjoying her future husband," he said, his expression serious.

Joshua had never blushed a day in his life, but heat flooded his neck and up his face so fast, he might as well have been on fire. He needn't be embarrassed. In his head he knew that. The Amish tended to keep their romance private, but he wasn't breaking rules, and yet he still felt the weight of having done something . . . wrong.

But what? Their district, while making sure young people kept things chaste, didn't frown on an engaged couple kissing.

Mervin grinned suddenly and hitched his head in the direction of the woods. "Maybe take it somewhere where little buwes won't see, though. Jah?"

Joshua cleared his throat and glanced at Joy, at a complete loss as to what to say.

"Come on." She had mercy on him and tugged him away, around the corner of the barn and down a path the deer used through the trees.

As soon as they were far enough away that the house was hidden from them by the leaves and branches, she stopped walking and turned to face him. If she asked him about that kiss, he had no idea what he was going to say.

"I didn't expect you to come by today," she said after a moment.

The tension slid out of his shoulders a bit, only to be replaced by his earlier ire. That's right. He had come here for a reason. "I saw you driving with Leroy Miller today."

Her eyebrows rose. "I know. I waved. Didn't you see me?" She cocked her head. "I wasn't sure because you didn't wave back."

"I didn't like it."

Joy leaned back, studying him. "Which part?" she asked slowly.

Oh, sis yucht. She thought he meant he didn't like her waving. "You riding with another man."

Another blink, this one slower, longer. "Oh." Then she frowned. "Why not?"

"Because you are engaged to me." That sounded harsh, so he tried to explain it better. "It wouldn't look right. Especially when it's with the man your mamm had picked out before we decided to get married."

Joy rolled her eyes. She actually rolled her eyes. "You know, you switch from stuffy to fun and back again so fast, I can hardly keep up sometimes."

Stuffy? She thought he was stuffy? After he kissed her yet? Or was that the fun he'd switched away from? "I'm not being stuffy."

"You are. I would never betray you in any way . . ." She poked him in the chest with a finger. "And you know me well enough to have faith in that, Joshua Kanagy."

True. Except, he'd never known her in quite this way. Before all this, she'd been just a friend. Maybe his best friend, besides his bruders. Now she was . . . more.

"I don't like seeing you with Leroy Miller," he repeated, clearly enunciating each word, stuffing his hands in his pockets. Next he'd be scuffing the ground with his boot and hanging his head like Amos did earlier.

Joy suddenly grinned. What, exactly, was so funny?

"You're jealous," she pronounced, almost gleeful.

"Nae." The word jerked from him like buckshot.

"Nae?" She was teasing now.

He crossed his arms and stared her down. "What if you saw me riding through town with Katie Jones?"

Joy's smile faded in an instant, and Joshua pressed the point home. "It isn't right, Joy."

She glanced away now, nibbling at her lower lip. Lips he still wanted to kiss. They'd been so soft against his. After all, her dat expected that that was what they were doing right now.

Get your head on straight.

He held his stare instead, keeping his hands in his pockets so he couldn't reach for her. Finally Joy sighed, her expression turning contrite. "I am sorry, Joshua. You are right. I didn't think it through."

After a pause, as his earlier resentment dissolved in the face of her apology, he softened. "We're both getting used to how different things will be now."

"Jah." She sighed again, then suddenly perked up. "But maybe if I tell you *why* I was with Leroy, you'll feel better."

Uh-oh. That had a familiar ring to it. So did the glint in her eyes. "What are you up to this time?" he asked.

Her stubborn little chin jutted out. "I'm saving your job and our future, Joshua Kanagy."

"You already did that by marrying me." Soon. Maybe her announcing such a quick wedding was a gute thing. He had a feeling he needed to tie his bride down before the wind and her will swept her away on a new adventure.

"Nae. Because Leroy still works here. Only . . . I don't think he wants to."

"He doesn't?"

She shook her head. "I think he wants to be a dairy farmer."

"And what made you think that?"

"He went to the library while we were in town and I took a peek at the book he checked out. It was about breeding dairy cows, and that's all he could talk about while I helped with chores in the barn."

He straightened. "Your mamm let you help in the barn?"

She shot him a look that told him to focus on the important stuff, so he returned his thoughts to Leroy.

"But you wouldn't have known about the dairy farm book until after you drove into town and went to the library. So why were you with him?"

A familiar mischievous expression lit up her face. "I am matchmaking him with Mary Hershberger."

She clasped her hands in front of her as though she

needed to contain the excitement bubbling inside her. Meanwhile, Joshua's mind balked. Matchmaking and Mary and Leroy all swirled around in his head like leaves swept down a fast-running river. Until finally his mind latched on to one simple fact. "Mary's family run a dairy farm."

"Jah." Only Joy brushed that aside as though unimportant when it sounded like the most important part to him. "But Leroy has liked Mary for ages, and she likes him back."

Joshua eyed his bride narrowly. "Did either of them tell you this?"

"Nae. They didn't have to. It's plain as . . . well as the Plain folk," she said.

Not to him. He'd seen no evidence of anything between those two.

"So . . ." Joy continued without a response on his side. "I had Leroy drop me off at the farmer's market while he went to the library and made certain he had to come get me."

"At the farmer's market? Why would that help?"

Joy rolled her eyes again. "Mary has a booth there every week. Didn't you know?"

Nope.

The shake of Joy's head said he should have. "Anyway," she said. "I've offered to teach Mary a few baking tips. We need to get her and Leroy some alone time." Spontaneously Joy grabbed his hand. "You will help me, won't you?"

Joshua glanced down at her hand against his. Smaller, sweeter, with slender fingers adept at making those quilts Mamm loved so much. He felt himself giving in, helpless against the kind certainty and the appeal in her eyes. She was so positive that matching Mary and Leroy would be the answer to everyone's problems.

Joshua groaned. "When have I ever said no to you, Joy Yoder?"

He decided not to examine too closely the fact that her ride with Leroy had been a matchmaking scheme for another girl, and how every ounce of anger and jealousy—she'd been annoyingly right about that—roiling inside him had disappeared with that knowledge.

JOY CHECKED ALL the ingredients laid out on the counter one more time as she listened for Mary's knock at the door. She'd decided not to start with thumbprint cookies, which was what Mary tried to bring most weeks to singeon. They were terrible, always way too sweet, but starting with those seemed too obvious, and she didn't want to hurt Mary's feelings. Instead, she'd decided to start today with her two personal favorite recipes.

The tentative knock at the door had her hurrying to open it, only to pause. "Oh."

Joshua gave her a cockeyed smile. "Is that any way to greet your future husband?"

She chuckled as she waved him in. "Sorry. I didn't mean that. Mary should arrive any moment."

"What are you going to make?" he asked as he followed her through the gathering room to the kitchen.

"Fresh-baked white bread and glazed donuts."

Joshua's eyes lit like lanterns in the night. "Mmmm . . . donuts."

"Oh, no, you don't, Joshua Kanagy. These are to help Mary win Leroy over."

He reached out and tugged on her apron string, appeal shining in his dark eyes. "Maybe just one for the man you're going to marry?"

What would she do if he used his hold to draw her closer?

Given the way she'd spent a good chunk of last night lying awake in bed swinging between trying to be sensible about this practical marriage she was about to enter into, and reliving the kisses they'd shared, she knew she'd let him. Happily.

But that wasn't very sensible. The desires at odds with each other tugged her in opposite directions, and she wasn't sure what to do about it.

"Joy." A not very subtle whisper sounded from the mudroom near the back, and she and Joshua both glanced over to encounter two little boys so covered in mud, their eyes were like white dots in the center of faces covered in muck.

"Oh, help!" she exclaimed. "For heaven's sake, do not come in here. You will trail mud all over the clean kitchen, and I'm about to have a visitor."

Samuel started to move toward the back door, but Amos grabbed his hand. "We can't go back outside. Mamm just went into the garden. She'll see us, for sure and certain."

Joy propped her hands on her hips. "And you might deserve it," she said.

Joshua suddenly cleared his throat and all three of them looked at him. "They did help sneak you in the house after you ripped your dress," he reminded her, eyes dancing.

"You are no help," she muttered back.

The soft knock she'd been waiting for sounded right then and Joy's eyes shot wide, her gaze on Joshua.

He shook his head. "I'll get these two outside and hose them off before taking them up for a bath."

"Denki," she whispered before hurrying away.

"Your dat will think I'm late," he called after her.

"I'll tell him I kept you occupied for too long," she called back.

"He'd definitely believe that."

Ignoring his quip, she paused at the front door, checking her kapp and dress and taking a beat to breathe before opening the door with a wide smile.

One that dimmed, but only for a second. "Hello, Leroy," she said in an overloud voice.

The hushed whispers behind her cut off abruptly and she could just picture Joshua's face. Not laughing right then was an effort of monumental will.

"Hi, Joy," Leroy said, none the wiser. "Your dat asked that I check in at the house each day so you can send me where he is faster."

"Oh." She'd bet her best dress that Mamm had come up with that idea. "He's in the far paddock," she said. "The larger one. Today he's going to try the yearling with the buggy—not pulling it yet, just standing in the harness. I'm sure he'll be grateful for your help."

A low grunt reached her ears, one that sounded like Joshua, and Leroy leaned to the right to peer around her. "Everything oll recht?" he asked.

She pinned an easy smile to her lips. "Jah. Denki. Go on around to—"

That happened to be the moment Mary decided to arrive, the muffled clop of her driving horse's hooves sounding down the lane before the buggy appeared in front of the house.

Perfect!

"Actually," she said to Leroy. "Before you do that, could you please help Mary?"

Leroy whipped his head around so hard, Joy winced. Then had to bite her lip as his skin turned an interesting shade of purple. "I-I-I . . . don't think she needs my help," Leroy stuttered.

"Of course she does." Joy gave him a little push, then shut the door behind him and cast a prayer up to Gotte, putting the next few minutes in His hands. Clearly Leroy needed the help.

"How'd you get mud *there*?" Joshua's voice floated down to her.

When did they go upstairs? With a hiss through her teeth, Joy hurried up to find him helping Amos out of his filthy clothes in the bathroom. "Shhhh," she admonished with a finger to her lips.

"Sorry," Joshua half whispered, half growled. "But this buwe has mud in places you don't want to know about."

"Put him in the tub and let him take it from there. He can clean up his own mess."

"But Joy—" Amos cut off his whine at her sharp look, then glanced away with a muttered, "Fine."

"Where's Samuel?" she asked Joshua.

"Anna was right outside the door, so we couldn't get out. I put him in the basement to wait." He peeled Amos's shirt over his head.

"Smart."

"I have my moments," he shot her a wink. Then he paused, his stare gaining a speculative gleam. "Was that Leroy at the door?"

She eyed him narrowly. "You know it was. I sent him to help Mary with her buggy."

Joshua's expression turned almost . . . relieved. Which made utterly no sense. He was well aware of the plan he'd agreed to help her with. There was absolutely no reason to be jealous, especially given their situation.

There was also no reason for her to feel a spark of pleased satisfaction that he might be jealous. Theirs wasn't that kind of relationship. Or so she'd had to start reminding herself lately.

Another knock at the door—Mary this time for sure and certain—and Joy scooted out of the already crowded bathroom, making a mental note to be sure the boys cleaned every inch of that room once they were done bathing. Otherwise, Mamm would definitely find out.

"Have fun baking," Joshua called after her. "And no flirting with Leroy."

She rolled her eyes as she hurried back to the stairs and tried her best to ignore the concerning flutter Joshua's words sent through her belly.

Swinging the front door wide open, she smiled for the third time, only this time the person she was expecting stood there finally. "Hi, Mary. I'm so glad you could come over today."

She meant every word.

The girl was a lovely person and maybe even a special friend. The weather was gorgeous, and they had every window in the house open wide to let in the breeze. Her plan to put Mary in Leroy's path was working already. Plus . . . Joy loved to bake. Especially eating the treats after. This would be fun.

Only suddenly, she found for once she'd almost rather be upstairs helping Joshua scrub down two filthy buwes.

Chapter Ten

JOSHUA FINISHED HAMMERING a nail and paused to wipe an already sweat-stained sleeve over his brow. The Hershbergers had picked a scorcher of a day for this—the last gasp of summer trying to hang on before autumn crept in with cooler weather and colorful, crunchy leaves underfoot.

A burst of talk sounded from below where he was perched precariously on the top of the new barn being raised. The entire community had taken the time off to help. The Hershbergers's dairy farm was doing well, selling organic milk from grass-fed, pasture-raised cows, and they had decided to expand. Who knew the Englischers would eventually realize that the price of a quality product from well-treated animals was worth it? Perhaps the world was slowly turning back to a Plain life?

"Would you like some punch, Joshua?" a feminine voice called from below.

He glanced down through the open rafters to find not Joy but Katie Jones standing there, hand shading her eyes.

"Nae, denki," he called.

She smiled and moved along.

Joshua watched her go, frowning a little. There was a time when Katie had been the ideal of the kind of Amish girl he'd thought to set his sights on. Pretty and pleasing, she cooked like a dream, was kind to all the kinder, and respected her elders. She never talked out of turn or got into messes that needed fixing, was always the first to offer a sweet word or helpful hand, and her faith was her foundation.

Funny how things worked out.

"I would have liked some punch," Daniel commented beside him. "Why didn't she ask me?"

Joshua ignored the question.

"Amos and Samuel Yoder!" Joy's shout carried. Not that the sound needed to go far. She was standing outside the beams of new construction crawling with Amish men as they worked.

"Get down here this second," she ordered.

Sure enough, out of the rafters, the two buwes climbed down, then slumped over to their schwester, who walked them away, scolding them in hushed tones that still managed to carry. He watched her shoo them away from the construction. Then she tipped her head back, lips twitching, and happened to glance up to catch him staring.

Feeling caught out, Joshua froze. Except then she smiled—one meant for him alone, like sharing a secret—and all he could do was smile right back, suddenly feeling as though they were the only two people out here. Granted, he was allowed to stare because she'd soon be his wife. Even so, the moment warmed his heart and clenched something inside him that might be . . . longing.

"This barn isn't going to build itself," he muttered to get

himself moving. He returned to his hammering, trying not to frown over how looking for Joy was becoming a new hobby.

"Why the scowl, little bruder?" Daniel asked beside him.

Of his two brothers, Daniel might be the quiet one, but he also noticed the most. Joshua couldn't very well tell him he was scowling over the fact that he'd rather be down there with Joy right now than up here. Because that would sound . . . verhuddelt.

"Sun's in my eyes," he said. Then tugged the brim of his hat lower for good measure.

Daniel didn't call him out on the lie, hammering away. "You know . . . when you first announced your engagement to Joy, I thought maybe you were marrying her to be able to work with the horses, instead of in the shop."

Joshua missed the nail and came darn close to hammering his thumb instead. "I know. You and Aaron made that clear."

"Not that there would be anything wrong with that," Daniel continued blithely on as though he hadn't spoken. "Marriages are partnerships, and I think you and Joy have always made a fine team."

"Ach jah?" Joshua did raise his gaze at that.

"Jah." Daniel didn't look up still, though his lips curved. "She gets in trouble, you get her out, and the other way around."

Joshua chuckled. "I hope we've grown up a bit, though."

Daniel's nod didn't show agreement or disagreement, but then he stopped his work to cock his head at Joshua. "But I've seen the way you look at her."

"I don't—"

"You *do*," Daniel insisted.

Joshua had no idea what to say to that . . . or how he felt

about it. Because this wasn't supposed to be a love match. This was an arrangement. Joy didn't feel that way about him, and until the day she'd proposed, he hadn't thought about feeling that way about her. A small voice in his head reminded him of those odd little moments—like appreciating her wide smile from across the volleyball net or noticing how she'd grown up as she leaned around the door of the barn—moments when he'd pause and appreciate. But he'd shaken them off each time.

Did those add up to feelings that had already been there?

He honestly couldn't say for sure, but Daniel wasn't wrong about lately. Joshua couldn't seem to stop himself from searching for Joy's face in gatherings or walking past the shop window or wanting to tease her until she laughed or wanting to kiss her again. Especially that. Even focusing around the horses had been harder lately, and usually they were all he thought about.

But her lips, her smiles, her laughs were turning into a fascination.

Was that sinful? They were to be married, so he didn't think so. Still, that wasn't what Joy had asked for.

"It's proper to want your wife in . . . that way." Daniel grimaced then got back to work.

"Jah," Joshua muttered. His brother really did see too much. Instead of denying it all, which wouldn't serve a purpose, he got back to work himself.

A small murmuring sounded from below. Probably Anna Yoder after Amos and Samuel again. Beside him Daniel lifted his head.

"Vell, I'll be . . ."

Joshua stopped what he was doing to see where Daniel was looking. "What?"

"I think that's Faith Kemp. The girl standing on her own holding the baby."

It took a second for Joshua to pick her out, then he narrowed his eyes, not sure. "It could be Mercy."

Daniel shook his head, though how he would know, Joshua wasn't sure.

Either girl would be cause enough for the murmurings and the looks she was getting. Twin girls who'd been Joshua's age, Mercy and Faith Kemp had both jumped the fence when they were only eighteen, leaving their community and joining the Englisch. Their parents, who had stayed behind, heartbroken, never talked about them, clearly having shunned their own dochders.

Except the older couple walked around the corner a second later and moved to stand beside her. Whichever Kemp girl had returned, she was dressed like the other Plain women here. As was the babe she was bouncing in her arms.

"It wonders me if one of them has decided to return," he said.

Daniel made no comment, and Joshua watched his brother watch the girl across the yard. "I hope that she feels welcomed," Daniel murmured.

Not all in their community would receive her back with open arms. More than likely, the stricter families would balk, not inviting her to frolics or stopping by to visit, but many others *would* offer forgiveness. After all, if she'd come back to Gotte's ways, like the prodigal son returned to his family, that was worth celebrating.

"I'm sure she'll be fine." Except Katie turned and walked away right that second. Maybe she hadn't meant to. He perked up at the sight of Joy making her way over to the small family, her bright smile effortless and kind as ever. "There, see . . . Joy will take care of them."

His Joy truly did have a heart for others.

"Jah." As though realizing his interest wasn't needed, Daniel seemed to force himself back into the work, and they both returned to their hammering.

A few hours later, they stopped with the barn half finished. All the men climbed down to enjoy the spread the women had laid out for lunch. Joshua was one of the last down and was walking through the shade inside the half-finished structure, the ground littered with tools and wood planks, when his ears caught a tiny squeak of distress.

Automatically, he glanced up, then bolted as Amos Yoder lost his grip on the ceiling beam he'd been clinging to.

Joshua didn't get there fast enough, though he managed to get under Amos, breaking the child's fall. He took a boot to the face for his effort, pain exploding around his eyes before he found himself in a heap on the level, packed earth that would be the barn floor with Amos a tangle of limbs on top of him.

Stunned and winded, he lay there trying to gather his wits. A heartbeat later, Amos groaned, and a heartbeat after that a screech sounded nearby.

"Amos!" That had to be Anna Yoder.

"Are you oll recht?" Joshua managed to ask the boy, gritting his teeth since talking wasn't easy with a weight tightening his chest and the pain radiating in his face.

"I . . ."

"Merciful heaven." Anna's gasp was directly overhead, and Joshua tilted his head backward to find her standing over them.

Then she moved in a rush and more people piled in through the doorframe, all murmuring sounds of distress.

A weight was lifted off him, and suddenly Joshua could breathe easier.

"Joshua!" This was Joy's gasp.

Someone dropped to the floor near him, then his head was lifted up and placed in a soft lap. "Are you hurt?" she cried. "Talk to me, Joshua."

Instead he kept his eyes closed, savoring the moment.

"What happened?" This from Joy, too, but voiced as though she wasn't asking him.

"I fell off the rafter and Joshua caught me," Amos said in a voice half contrite and half stubborn need not to admit any wrongdoing. Brave to own up to it that way, knowing he'd get in trouble.

"Joshua." Joy leaned closer now, her lips near his ear, her voice a whisper that sent a glow of contented warmth through him. He could lay here all day happily. "Please be okay."

Joshua cuddled into her lap. "Jah. Just . . . give me a minute."

Silence was followed by an outraged snort. "Joshua Kanagy, you fiend." He was shoved unceremoniously out of her lap so fast, his head hit the ground with an audible and painful thump.

Grinning, he came up on one elbow, giving the back of his head a rub. "I could have been seriously injured," he pointed out, eyeing his fiancée's outraged scowl.

"I thought you were," she snapped. "Given the blood coming out of your nose."

"Blood?" He moved his hand from the back of his head to the front and came away with a hand covered in bright red liquid. "Oh, sis yucht."

"Here." Joy shoved a clean handkerchief at him.

Putting it to the bleeding, he tipped his head back. "Does my nose look broken?"

"Worried about your pretty face? If this is an attempt at sympathy after what you just—"

"It's not," he said. "Amos kicked me in the face on the way down."

A sound of frustration escaped her, then the handkerchief was taken gently away as she got closer, examining his nose. Suddenly he found himself arrested by her eyes—such a deep brown and soft like the hearts of pansies but with a caramel-colored ring around her pupils.

"Does this hurt?" she asked, unaware of his regard and pressing at a spot.

Joshua winced, a grunt popping out of its own accord. "Not too bad."

"Uh-huh." She shook her head, then glanced over her shoulder. "Amos looks to have broken his arm. He has to go to the hospital. You may as well come yet."

"Nae. I'm sure I'll be fine."

She turned her head, studying his nose. "I don't *think* it's broken," she mused. "But that lump in the middle might be more than swelling."

"What?"

She raised her teasing gaze, only it tangled with his and they both sort of . . . stopped.

If there weren't so many people around, he'd kiss her right this instant. Could she see the urge in his eyes? The way her lips parted on a silent inhalation, he thought maybe she did.

"Wouldn't want to ruin that pretty face before I marry it," she murmured, humor sparking at him again.

Disappointment surged. Maybe she didn't feel it.

Joy studied him closer, then leaned into whisper, "Don't worry, I'll protect you from the big, bad hospital."

Which made him snort a laugh and then grunt at the throb of pain that caused.

She was well aware how he'd hated the hospital ever since he was eight and had been kicked in the shin by a horse. Luckily, it hadn't broken anything, though to this day he still had a small knot against the bone. But the hospital, with its humming lights, bustling people, and machines that beeped everywhere, had scared him then. Which was ridiculous now that he was a grown man, but . . .

"Fine," he said reluctantly. "I'll go."

Satisfied, Joy got to her feet, then offered a hand to tug him up.

JOY STOOD WITH Joshua and her fater facing the direction the nurse had taken Amos along with Samuel and their mater. She'd stayed back, not wanting to be in the way. Joshua had been looked over already and told he was just bruised. No permanent damage, thankfully.

An unfamiliar nurse came out the double doors and slowed, then smiled over Joy's shoulder. "Hello, Mr. Yoder," she said. "Have those exercises been helping?"

Joy swung, wide eyed, to find Dat giving the nice lady a brusque nod and avoiding all eye contact.

"Wonderful." The nurse nodded and bustled away.

Dat still wouldn't look at her.

"What was that about?" she asked.

He sighed. "I didn't want to tell you this way."

He'd been at the hospital enough for the nurse to recognize and remember him? And now he didn't want to tell her? Joy snuck her hand into Joshua's almost without thinking about it. "Tell me what, Dat? You're scaring me."

"Nae." Her fater shook his head. "No need to be afraid. I have something called rheumatoid arthritis."

That didn't make her feel better. "What is it?"

"Mostly it means my hands hurt."

His hands? Small memories suddenly made sense in her head—the way he gingerly held his knife at dinner, or how it had been taking longer to hitch the buggy. "How do you fix it?"

"Ach vell . . ." He ran a hand over his beard. "It can't be fixed."

"Oh, Dat . . ."

"Not to worry. I'm managing it with some medicines and the doctor gave me exercises to do that help. Although eventually I'll have to change the ways I do certain things with my hands."

That didn't sound . . . horrible. "Is it very painful?"

"Sometimes. But not all the time." His gaze slid to Joshua, then back to her. "I'll need to stop working with the horses, though. Sooner than I thought I might."

Joshua's hand gripped hers tighter, probably because the same bolt of realization was hitting him that had just struck her. Was *this* why Mamm had hired Leroy? Not just because of Joy and wanting her married, but for Dat?

"I'm glad I'll be able to help you with that," Joshua said slowly.

Dat smiled. "Me too."

"Joy, look at my cast," Amos interrupted as he emerged from wherever they'd taken him to treat what had ended up being a clean break. He was sucking on a lollipop and all puffed up on the extra attention he'd been receiving.

Samuel also happily sucked on his own lollipop, quietly following his bruder around with wide eyes.

"They said people could sign it," Amos said, his bony arm, covered in white plaster and held in a black sling around his neck, wiggling as though he couldn't hold it still.

Trying to put Dat's news out of her head, Joy propped her hands on her hips. "Well, I, for one, will not be doing any such thing," she declared.

Amos paused, as did everyone else in the waiting room.

She pointed at Joshua. "You are lucky, Amos Yoder, that Joshua will only suffer two black eyes and a bloody nose and not a worse injury."

Her younger bruder frowned and turned his gaze to Joshua, whose eyes weren't swollen shut, thank goodness, but were going to be black and blue within the next day or so. He looked like a raccoon to her already.

Amos tipped his head then scrunched up his nose. "Maybe people can sign his face like my cast," he offered.

A coughing sound came from Joshua before he got down on a knee to address Amos. "I don't think my mater . . . or Joy for that matter . . . will appreciate that for our wedding day," he said gently.

"I hope his eyes aren't still green and yellow by then," Joy tacked on.

"Oh, the wedding." Amos shrugged that away, clearly not worried about the business of adults.

Mamm sucked in sharply through her nose, a clear sign that he'd managed to stir her earlier frustration right back up, and Amos flicked her a cautious glance before his shoulders rounded. "I'm sorry I hurt you, Joshua," he muttered, then flicked Mamm another glance to see if that had fixed the problem.

Anna Yoder bent a glare on him that meant punishment was definitely headed his way, no matter what he said right now, and Amos's chin took on the long-familiar, entirely stubborn hardness that meant a battle of wills was about to commence between mater and sohn.

Joshua cleared his throat, attracting Amos's attention. "I'm less worried about the wedding than I was about you."

"Me?" Amos lifted his arm as much as the sling would allow. "But I'm fine."

Joshua nodded. "And if I hadn't been there? You could have been more seriously hurt. You realize that, don't you?"

"I guess," Amos said slowly, doubt rife in his voice.

"What would your family do if they had to stop everything to care for you?" Joshua's gaze was both firm and gentle at the same time. "In fact, I think, once you get the cast off, you should work off the hospital bills that now have to be paid."

Amos's eyes went wide at that. The Amish didn't have insurance like the Englischers did. They negotiated a pay-by-cash system with the hospitals, which did help reduce the bills. If bills were high enough after that, like with the Peachys recently, the community came together to raise the funds. Even Amos understood how expensive hospitals could be.

"But that will take *forever*," he said, horror in his voice. The first show of true regret passed over his features before his chin started to wobble.

Joshua didn't give in, though, merely nodded. "Yes, but would you force your family to take that burden for you? After all they do for you?"

Amos opened his mouth to argue, but then glanced at Joy, then Mamm, and Dat, even Samuel, who, for once, didn't offer him a way out. Her bruder's small shoulders rounded for a second before he drew them back, addressing her parents. "I will help work off the bills," he said.

Joy caught her bottom lip between her teeth at the sight of a boy perhaps realizing what it would be to become a man one day. To shoulder the responsibilities of caring for those around him, providing for them. All because Joshua showed him the way. Not with yelling or condemning either, but with kindness.

Suddenly, she could see so clearly the fater Joshua would be to their own kinder, and her heart swelled with . . . not pride . . . but a sort of deep-seated happiness that settled beautifully inside her.

Contentment. Maybe more than contentment even.

She suddenly looked forward to her marriage as more than a means to an end for both of them, maybe more than a partnership. She'd chosen well.

Joy shook herself out of her thoughts as they exited the hospital. They had had to call rides from the Hershbergers' house in order to reach the hospital quickly, Joshua's family saying they would bring the Yoders' horse and buggy back to their house for them. That meant the need to call another ride to take them home. With six of them, they had to call two cars, and this time, Joy and Joshua ended up in the back of one of the cars by themselves, despite Amos saying he wanted to ride with Joshua.

"You're being awfully quiet," her fiancé murmured to her after ten silent minutes of watching the rolling green pastures and fields of densely treed forests flash by her window. The speed of riding in a car was something she usually found exhilarating, but for once she wasn't paying all that much attention, her mind focused instead on the discovery that raising kinder with Joshua suddenly seemed like a wondrous thing for her to do. Maybe the best adventure of her life.

She pulled her gaze away to face him, tipping her head

to examine his poor, battered face, seeing him through . . . different eyes. And a tiny bit scared by that change.

"Is your dat worrying you?" he asked.

She blew out a breath. "A little. I doubt he'd tell me if the pain was unmanageable. I don't like that I didn't see it before."

"But now we're getting married, and he has me," Joshua assured her. He reached over and squeezed her hand.

"Jah." It was all she could think of to say.

"Maybe it's Amos you're worried about, then?" he asked, a small frown tugging at his brows. "Because something's bothering you."

She shook her head. "I think you got through to him," she said. Then offered a tentative smile, because she wasn't entirely sure how to act around him all of a sudden. He wasn't "just" Joshua like always. He was . . . more. But more how? "You were wunderbaar with him."

Joshua hitched a shoulder. "I was a buwe not that long ago. I remembered the first time I realized that my actions might impact the people I loved."

"When was that?" she asked, curious.

"When you almost drowned in that boat."

Joy blinked. "But . . . you jumped in and carried me out before it got too bad," she said. "And the water was hardly deep enough to drown in. I could have stood up in it."

"I know . . . but you couldn't swim yet, and you were so small and so scared. I've never been so terrified in my life. Before or since." He turned his gaze out the front windshield of the car. "I knew then that I needed to make sure you stayed safe."

What had been a glow of happiness, coming out of that strange contentment that had started at the hospital, dimmed like a lantern on the last of its oil.

"Is that why you always go along with my plans?" she asked slowly.

He nodded, turning to face her again. "Somebody has to keep you out of trouble," he teased, grinning wide, eyes sparking with amusement.

Joy did her best to grin back, though her chuckle sounded stiff in her ears. Because realization had struck with all the force of Amos's foot to Joshua's face, leaving her feeling just as bruised on the insides.

Maybe he was marrying her only because this was what he always did. He kept an eye on her. He went along with her plans. He stepped in to fix things if he had to.

Not that he'd had to in a long time. Didn't he realize that?

Joy suddenly felt cast adrift, as she had in that silly sinking boat, only now the waters were as deep and stormy as the Sea of Galilee before Jesus calmed the storms. Was this a question of needing stronger faith, like the disciples had that day? Or by marrying him, was she going against Gotte's will for Joshua's life? For her life?

Oh, help.

She needed to find the answer and quick. Before the wedding. Before they got too far down the path to turn back.

Joshua suddenly reached out and squeezed her hand, ducking his head to catch her eye. "My face will be all healed before the wedding, if that's what is worrying you," he offered.

Dutifully, Joy forced another stiff chuckle, shaking her head. "I'm just glad your nose isn't broken," she said. "Even if you did tease me by playing possum."

He chuckled as well, seeming to relax, no longer watching her so intently. "I *was* winded," he told her.

"I don't doubt it."

The car pulled up, and Joshua handed cash to the driver before helping Joy out. Her family must've arrived before them by quite a bit because there was no sign of them. "I'll go get the buggy to take you home," she said.

Only Joshua reached for her hand, tugging her to a halt. "You know . . . I've heard that kisses help wounds heal faster," he said, dark eyes suddenly warm, sending an answering, breathless sort of warmth through her.

A kiss? He wanted to kiss her again. Now she was even more confused. Unless he meant a kiss like a mater would give. Like a sister would give.

Ach du lieva.

"Of course," she murmured, and took his face in her hands, then went up on tiptoe and kissed each eye, trying to be as gentle and as sisterly as she could in the action, despite the thundering of her heart. Could he hear it this close? She released him and hopped back with a cheerful grin. "There," she said. "Guaranteed to be all better."

A flash of an emotion she couldn't put her finger on flitted across his features before he replaced it with an answering smile. "Denki."

Then he glanced over his shoulder at the road. "Don't worry about getting the buggy out," he said. "I think I'll walk home."

Oh. Disappointment tugged at her heart, trying to sink it in that tossing storm she still found herself in. "If that's what you want," she murmured.

He nodded, but didn't move to walk away, standing there, in the middle of the dirt drive of her home, staring at her, as though trying to divine her thoughts. Then he gave her his easy grin, the one that meant she shouldn't worry, only she did. "I work at the shop tomorrow and the next day," he said. "I guess I'll see you Sunday."

"Actually—" She cut herself off. Joy had been about to say that most engaged couples would spend Saturday evenings together, usually at one of their families' houses, but maybe that was only romantic couples.

However, now he'd raised his eyebrows and was waiting for her to speak. So she cleared her throat. "I think Mamm would expect you to come over Saturday nights," she said.

There, that way it wasn't her doing the asking; it was expectations.

Joshua stilled. "Of course. I should have thought of that. Dinnertime?" he asked.

"Jah." Joy didn't know what to do with her hands. "And please tell your mamm I'll have the first quilt ready for her tomorrow."

Those thick eyebrows hitched again.

"The ones I'm making for that customer," she explained with a shrug.

"Oh. Right." He seemed at a loss for a second. "Sei gut, Joy."

Her heart hopped a bit. She'd forgotten how he always used to say goodbye that way when they were younger. Words that basically meant "Be good." And no wonder if he thought he always needed to rescue her from her own follies.

On that, he turned on his heel and started walking down the lane.

Joy watched after his departing form, biting her lip again, then quietly let herself into the house, the sounds of Mamm in the kitchen preparing dinner not as comforting as she usually found. She wandered to the quilt she was working on as a wedding gift to Joshua, fingering the soft fabric.

Joy sighed deeply.

What am I supposed to do? She sent the prayer up to Gotte's ears, but no answer came back. Maybe she needed to listen harder and have patience.

Not her best quality. For Joshua's sake, though, she would try.

Chapter Eleven

JOSHUA MOVED AROUND the store, getting things ready to open up. Today was Mamm's day to be home. They each had an assigned day to stay back and work on different chores while the others worked in the shop. Joshua wished today were *his* chore day because then he could go over to the Yoders' as soon as he was done.

Something about the way he and Joy had parted yesterday still sat funny with him. Not a worry, really. More like a vague sense that she'd been acting strange. He'd teased her, hoping for a kiss, and he'd gotten one. Two, in fact. Though not exactly the kind he'd been angling for. Joy wasn't so naïve that she might mistake his intentions, was she? Or maybe, as a proper Amish girl, she was shy about such things? Or his previous kisses made her uncomfortable?

Maybe, a small voice in his head piped up, *she doesn't see you in that light.*

Amish didn't speak about intimacies between a mann and fraa, but when he was still in school, Daniel had come home one day even quieter than he usually was, a sure sign that he was upset. It had taken time and a lot of needling, but eventually Joshua had dragged from his older brother the fact that Caleb Blank, whose own older brother had recently married, had explained to Caleb how babies were made, and Caleb had then shared this piece of dubious wisdom with Daniel.

Joshua, all of nine or so, had had a hard time not laughing.

"Ach vell, of course," he'd said, puffing up with his own knowledge. "I've helped Mervin Yoder with the mares and stud horses lots of times."

Actually, he'd been too small then, but he'd been the one to bring the mare out to Mervin. Still, that was helping. Either way, Joshua had figured everyone knew how babies were made. After all, horses weren't the only animals to give evidence to this truth. Cows, pigs, bunnies . . . These were just facts as far as he was concerned.

Now that he and Joy were to be married . . .

Maybe she didn't know? Harder not to these days when many of die Youngie owned, or snuck, cell phones—having to give them up when they were finally baptized. The world had intruded more into Amish lives than ever before. Still, he'd heard stories of girls going innocently to their wedding nights, unaware of the way things worked.

Joy had spoken of a partnership, and building a solid marriage on friendship, but if she could hardly bring herself to kiss him . . . babies would be. . . .

Ach du lieva.

No way was he about to bring up such a subject with her. Not until their wedding night at least, and hopefully her mamm would explain things before then. Besides, others had worked through arranged marriages and managed to figure out how to have kinder together. He and Joy would, too, in the end. He had to trust Gotte in this.

"Laying out those pickles must be tricky if you have to think so hard about it," a feminine voice full of teasing laughter jerked Joshua out of his thoughts.

He spun, still crouched before the canned and pickled section of the store, to stare up at the object of those deep thoughts.

"Joy?" he asked.

Her smile widened. Probably because he looked so verhuddelt.

"What are you doing here?" he asked.

The smile dimmed and he immediately wanted to take back the words, because if anything, the day had brightened with her in it. She indicated a quilt draped over one arm. "Remember? I told you to tell your mater that I would finish it today," she said.

Right. The quilt for the customer. She wasn't here to see him, just drop off her wares.

Joshua plopped the jar of Dorcas Troyer's pickles on the shelf and rose from where he crouched to reach out for the quilt. This one was smaller and maybe baby themed in shades of the softest pink. For a baby girl.

If he and Joy had a baby girl, she would have dark hair and eyes like both of them, but Joshua hoped she got Joy's smile.

Stop thinking of boppli.

He cleared his throat and lifted his gaze to find Joy watching him with raised eyebrows and an air of vague concern while his head was in the clouds.

"Are you oll recht?" she asked softly. "Does your head still hurt you?"

Suddenly she stepped closer, right into his space, bringing the scents of sunshine and cookies with her. "I mean, I understand that a nasty strike to the head can cause damage . . . inside. Do you have a headache? Maybe you should go home?" The words were pouring from her now, and bemused, Joshua waited for her to wind down.

She scowled fiercely. "It wondered me that those doctors hardly glanced at you and didn't run any tests, only flashed that light in your eyes. What could that tell them anyway?"

Joy reached up, gently feathering her fingers over his bruised cheekbone. "Where does it hurt?"

Joshua froze under her touch . . . at the concern in her eyes and how she wasn't afraid to be near him. Maybe he had gotten it all wrong?

"Do you like kissing me, Joy?" the words tumbled out, though softly, for her ears alone.

Her fingers stilled against his skin and her gaze flashed to his, surprise widening them before she dropped her hand and took a halting step back. Away from him.

Not what he was hoping for.

"Joshua Kanagy, what a question to ask."

She glanced around them, and he became immediately aware that they were discussing this in the middle of the shop. Luckily, the place was empty right then, if he didn't count Daniel in the back corner putting out new leather goods from Eli Bontrager. His brother's back was turned and he didn't appear to have heard. Still . . .

"Kumme," Joshua said.

Taking the quilt from her unresisting hands, he laid it haphazardly over another one hanging from pegs that would swing apart for easy browsing, then bustled her out of the shop and around to the alleyway, affording them a small amount of privacy.

"What in heaven's name has gotten into you?" she asked, having to jog to keep up with his long strides.

He stopped and turned her to face him.

Only before he could open his mouth and ask the question again, because he intended to have his answer—if kissing him was at least enjoyable to her, then he wouldn't worry any more about the rest—Joy propped her hands on her hips. "I think you got hit in the head harder than the doctors thought," she said. "We should get you home. You are not yourself—"

"I'm fine," he cut her off. "But this is important. We are to be married."

She crossed her arms now, eyeing him sideways as though trying to determine if she needed help getting him home. "I know we are to be married. It was my idea."

He was determined not to be distracted. "Do you like kissing me, Joy?"

Her cheeks turned a delightful pink and she glanced away. "Why are you asking this?"

A fair question, one he had no intention of answering directly. He'd scare her into breaking the engagement if he jumped right into the realities of marriage. Instead, he skirted the issue. "Our marriage is based on friendship," he started slowly.

Her brows lowered slightly, not following, but not stopping him.

"But it seems to me, that a mann and fraa . . . kiss."

"Jah."

"And if you . . . don't like kissing me, that could be a . . . problem."

If anything, the color in her cheeks surged. Joy swallowed, her gaze flicking around the alley at anything but him, as though searching for an answer there.

His heart sank, pushed down by his expanding lungs. "If it's this hard to answer—"

"Jah." The word burst from her, and she cringed, glancing over her shoulder to the street. Then she turned back to him.

Only he was still confused. "Jah, it's hard to answer? Or jah, you like it?"

She tipped up her chin as though facing down the consequences her mater might be doling out, staring him in the eye. "I like it."

The breath he was holding whooshed from his lungs, and his heart bounced back into place. Except . . . "You're not only saying that so that I'll still marry you? Are you?"

Joy rolled her eyes. "Nae."

"Maybe we should make sure?"

Her lips parted, but no sound came out. For once, he had the rare fun of seeing Joy shocked into silence. Stepping closer, he lifted his hands to frame her face, marveling at the softness of her skin as he stared into trusting brown eyes.

"Gute?" he asked quietly, hoping she wanted this as much as he suddenly did.

She swallowed, then nodded her head. Just once.

Slowly, never taking his gaze from hers, Joshua lowered his head. He brushed his lips over hers softly, savoring the even softer skin and the sugar scent of her. She trembled the tiniest bit.

"Don't be afraid," he whispered.

"I'm not," she whispered back.

Then Joy sighed, sort of sinking into him, and Joshua almost lost his head at the rush of rightness. The warmth of the sun on his shoulders, and the warmth of the response of the woman in his arms. Where had Joy Yoder learned to kiss like this? After all, he was her first. She'd said so, and she kissed him with an innocence, a pure trust that he would take care of her, and his heart swelled at that trust.

A faith he should honor.

With a groan, he took her by the shoulders and set her back from him. She stood with her face tipped up to his, eyes closed, for a long second, giving him time to absorb the picture of her that way.

She blinked her eyes open, the dark pools slightly dazed and confused.

"We . . ." He had to pause to catch his breath. "We should stop."

Before things got out of hand . . . or someone caught them. After all, he'd assured the bishop that they were honoring the Ordnung.

Joy's rosy cheeks turned rosier, and she stepped back. "Joshua?" she asked.

Uh-oh. He knew that twinkle in her eyes. "Jah?"

Her lips curled mischievously, her dimple playing hide and seek with him. "Do you like kissing me?"

A laugh huffed from him. "Jah. I like kissing you, Joy." Actually, "like" was a tame word for the way his heart was pounding.

"I guess that's gute . . . since we're to be married."

They stood there, in the middle of the alley, grinning at each other like fools. This was going to work out after all.

JOY LET HERSELF into her house through the mudroom after putting up the horse and buggy, her mind entirely on what had just happened with Joshua, and her feet walking on air, because she definitely wasn't feeling the hard ground. That had not been the way a man would ever, ever kiss a sister. Joshua might not be in love with her, but at least she had got that concern all wrong.

"Joy? Is that you?" Mamm called from the kitchen.

She rounded the corner, only to stumble to a halt at the

sight of Hope Kanagy and Mary Hershberger in their kitchen . . . and Mamm's growing frown of disappointment. All three of them sat at the kitchen table with glasses of lemonade, half-drunk already, which meant they'd been here awhile.

"Did you forget you'd invited Mary and Hope over to bake, Joy?"

Only after Joshua had kissed her so nicely.

"Nae, Mamm," she said. Then moved to her friends. "I am so sorry. I went into town to get an ingredient we were out of, but it took longer than I thought."

She held up the brown paper bag Joshua had put the maple syrup in for her. Guilt pinched at her heart. The maple syrup wasn't a lie. They did need it for the recipe she was going to teach Mary. Hope had learned about the lesson via Joshua telling Aaron and asked to join in. Always having liked the other girl, even more so now that she would be her sister-in-law, Joy was happy to include her.

Still, the maple syrup had been an excuse. She'd deliberately chosen a recipe she was missing an ingredient for that would take her into town so she could drop off the quilt. Mamm didn't know about the quilts yet. Joy wasn't entirely sure what she would say, especially now with the engagement and everything.

Best not to rock the boat. After all, technically she wasn't doing this for the money but to help Ruth out of a tight spot.

Mary's solemn face relaxed at her explanation. "I would have gone with you."

"I'll remember that next time." Joy set the bag on the counter and started pulling out the other ingredients they'd need. "I thought we'd make a pecan pie. Mamm said I could share her secret ingredient as long as you promise to keep it secret."

Mamm's earlier expression eased. "Have fun, you three," she said, and disappeared outside, no doubt to tend the garden. She was turning the soil over to remove the summer crop residue and weed growth and get ready for fall plantings.

"What's the secret ingredient?" Mary asked once they were alone.

Joy pulled the maple syrup out of the bag and held it up with a flourish. "I add more than Mamm does, though," Joy confessed in a conspiratorial whisper. "I always double the best part of the recipe."

Immediately, Hope whipped out a leatherbound book of what appeared to be blank pages and wrote that down. As soon as she was finished, she slowly lifted her head to find both Mary and Joy watching, curious.

Color swept into Hope's cheeks. "I'm . . ." She chuckled. "I'm sure you've heard that I am a terrible cook."

Joy had avoided Hope's offerings after her first burnt casserole experience but didn't want to say so. Neither apparently did Mary, and they both kept quiet.

But Hope laughed. "It's okay. I was awful, but Aaron figured out that my problem wasn't the cooking. I just couldn't remember all the steps and ingredients. So he started me writing down the recipes in detail with all the hints."

She held up her journal, showing them a few neatly written pages.

Mary brightened. "Ach, that's a wonderful gute idea. I'll have to get a journal, too."

Hope laughed. "I'll bring you one from the shop next time." She paused, her gaze moving to Joy. "I mean, if we do this again."

"Of course!" Joy said at once. "I love to cook almost as much as I love to quilt."

"How are the quilts coming for the shop?" Hope asked—too loudly.

Joy glanced to the window, which was open to allow in the whisper of a breeze, hoping Mamm didn't overhear that. "I dropped off the first one when I picked up the maple syrup," she said, though quietly, hoping the other girl would follow her lead.

"The baby blanket?" was the next question, not hushed, though.

Eager to get off this topic, she nodded.

But Hope was still going. "The Englischer who ordered these said the baby quilt would be perfect for her new kinskind. A granddaughter. Her own dochder is due any day now."

Joy needed to turn this conversation to other topics. After she and Joshua were married, Mamm would no longer have a say, but right now, Joy would rather not find out what her thoughts might be.

"Let's get started." She moved to the small writing desk in the gathering room and pulled out paper and a pencil, handing them to Mary. "So you can take notes today, too," she said.

Together they jumped into baking a pecan pie from scratch, starting with the crust, a recipe Joy knew the other girls could use for almost all their other pies, and even recipes like chicken pot pie. Rather than do the actual work, to give Mary and Hope the chance to learn on their own, Joy pulled a chair into the kitchen and sat, working on yet another quilt while guiding her friends through each step.

Hope tipped her head at the material in her hands. "Is that another one for the shop?"

Trying not to wince, Joy shook her head. "This is a wedding gift for Joshua," she said. Then described the design.

Both her friends lit up. "That's perfect for the two of

you," Mary said. Then sighed. "I hope I fall in love with and marry a friend," she said. "It's so romantic."

Sitting back down, Joy ducked her head. Falling in love . . . it did sound romantic. Maybe . . .

"I was so sure Joshua and Katie—" Mary suddenly cut herself off, biting her bottom lip.

Joy's nimble fingers paused in their work, but she forced herself to not even glance up and instead kept working. "Katie Jones?" she asked, proud of how casual her voice sounded.

The same girl who kept offering Joshua a drink at the barn raising the other day? The same one he'd taunted her with about being seen out riding in a buggy together? Perfect Katie Jones, who was the best cook, best housekeeper, sweet to everyone, quiet, and never in trouble. Never even a raised eyebrow in her direction. That Katie Jones?

"Oh." The relief in Mary's voice was palpable. "You already knew about that? I'm so glad. I would hate to hurt your feelings, Joy."

Yup. That Katie Jones. Oh, help. Knew about what exactly? She glanced at Hope, but the other girl was intent on whisking the wet ingredients together for the pie.

Mary paused, then brightened. "Then again, Joshua proposed to you, not Katie, so of course that wouldn't be a problem."

Not visibly wincing was turning into a new hobby for Joy. "I hope Katie wasn't . . . errr . . ." How serious was it after all?

"Well . . ." Mary nibbled at her lip. "A few weeks before you announced your engagement, she had told me that Joshua had driven her home from singeon."

He had? How had she missed that?

"And he'd gone to her place a time or two, I think." Mary's eyes went wide. "But it must not have worked out."

Which told Joy a lot and not very much all at once. Joshua wasn't one to lead a girl on. Had it been serious? Had Joshua kissed Katie, too? While she and Katie had never been particularly close, she would hate to have broken the other girl's heart with her actions. She'd believed Joshua to be unattached and heart whole when she proposed.

Comparing herself to Katie, meanwhile, was futile. Joy would come out looking worse every time. Not at all quiet or docile. Was that the kind of girl Joshua really wanted? The needle slipped and Joy hissed, yanking her hand back from the white of the quilt to suck on the small pinprick beading with blood.

"Maybe Katie was the one who broke it off," Hope offered. Until now she'd been unusually silent.

Joy shot them both what she hoped appeared to be a complacent smile. "Katie's so nice, and so gute at everything. She'll find the right husband for her soon, I'm sure."

Mary and Hope's shoulders both dropped slightly, as though relieved, although Hope continued to cast little searching glances in Joy's direction. Which meant, rather than entirely enjoying her day with friends, by the end of it, Joy's face ached from pinning happiness to it. Being cheerful had never been such a chore.

One thing was certain—at Gmay and singeon on Sunday, she'd have to watch Joshua and Katie closely. If she detected even a hint of heartbreak . . .

Well . . . she'd figure it out then.

Chapter Twelve

JOSHUA PRESSED AT the center of his chest, where the strangest sensation had settled. Like pressure. Not indigestion. At least he didn't think so, but maybe he'd eaten something that had gone bad without realizing it. He stood outside with the other young men his age, waiting for the church service to start.

"Stop watching for Joy," Aaron teased beside him. "Anyone would think you're in love."

The confused pucker pulling at Joshua's brow was real. "I'm *not* watching for Joy."

Or he hadn't realized he was. True, he hadn't seen her more than a glimpse or two when he'd been over at the Yoders' to help with the horses the last few days. Trying to do more to help ease Mervin's workload and give his poor hands a break. Now that he knew about the arthritis, he could see how his almost-father-in-law moved slower or winced often.

Thank goodness things had worked out between him and Joy. Gotte's doing, no doubt.

At least, he thought things were worked out with her. Except she hadn't even come down to the barn to tease him or chat with him, though she'd sent Mary down with treats for Leroy several times. Hope, too, had brought goodies home to Aaron, who'd been happy to brag about it when they got together Friday night for a family dinner.

Meanwhile, Joshua hadn't gotten any treats. Not a single sugar cookie for him. Unless you counted dessert last night, which he didn't. She'd made that for everyone. Wasn't a bride supposed to want to spoil her groom? Or was that only if they were in love?

After that kiss, he'd thought . . .

Actually, maybe he hadn't thought too hard about what would change by kissing her. Nothing apparently. Maybe it had affected him more. He frowned over that, too.

"Joshua." Jethro Miller, the bishop of their community, blocked his view of the arriving buggies with broad shoulders and an even broader midsection. "I believe after the service, before the meal, would be an excellent time to have a talk."

Joshua tried not to grimace, though he must not have been successful because the bishop chuckled. "Don't worry. I keep these talks brief."

"I'll find you after service," Joshua agreed, and received a smiling nod, before Jethro moved on to greet others.

"It's not bad," Aaron said. "In fact, I found much of what Jethro and I discussed to be helpful. He's a solid man of faith."

Which was no doubt why Gotte had chosen him to be one of the leaders of his flock. As with all Amish, ministers were selected by lot. A tradition from the earliest of Christian churches, all baptized members—both men and women—nominated married men for an open position of a minister or bishop. Then they left the decision in Gotte's hands by lot. Those chosen took the position as a weighty responsibility, adding it to their own work, never paid for it. None more so than Jethro Miller, Joshua was of the opinion.

Gotte was wise in all things.

The rest of the time leading up to church service, Joshua tried not to watch for Joy. In the end it didn't matter, because he still missed her arrival. Which was why, after filing into the benches, which had been set up outdoors today under the shade of a massive oak tree, his first glimpse of her was when the women filed in.

She was sitting right beside Katie Jones with Mary Hershberger on her other side. She happened to glance up and catch his eye, but rather than smile—not appropriate during service, though this *was* Joy, who never could help herself—she simply gave him a barely noticeable bob of her head. That was it. Disappointment wormed its way into his heart and sat there like a lump. Though he had no idea what he'd expected otherwise.

After service, of course, Jethro was waiting for him as they all filed away. "Let's take a walk while the meal is being set up?" Jethro offered.

This time, Joshua did catch Joy's gaze on him. At her raised eyebrows, he gave a small shrug. Tucking his hands behind his back, he fell in step with the bishop and they wandered around the back of the house, past the vegetable garden, and toward a small stream that ran through the property.

"I've known you all your life, Joshua," Jethro began. "And I've been pleased to see you grow into a strong, steady young man of faith."

Joshua lowered his gaze, not wanting to be prideful. Despite Anna Yoder trying to pair Joy with Jethro's son, Joshua admired this man greatly. Jethro, tall and wide shouldered, spoke the same way he walked—in a slow, measured cadence. His mind seemed to work in the same fashion, both methodical and wary to make judgment. Never the first to cast stones.

"You are already baptized and a member in good standing with the church, as is Joy, which is a needed starting point, as you both understand and have devoted yourselves to our ways."

"Jah." Not much else to say to that.

"I have a few questions to ask you, though I'm fairly certain I already know the answers."

"Of course."

"Have you been . . . pushing fences . . . in any way?"

Breaking the rules of the Ordnung under which their community operated, the bishop meant. "Nae. I try to live my life to Gotte's will." Joshua paused, thinking about those kisses. However, kissing once one was engaged was deemed acceptable in their community of Amish, though not in some of the Plainer communities.

"Excellent. As I said, I wasn't expecting any different." Jethro paused.

Long enough that he gave Joshua time to think. Probably a technique the bishop had learned a while back. He'd been selected as a minister as a young man, so he had lots of practice with young couples.

"May I ask you a question?" Joshua said.

"Of course."

"Joy and I . . ." He paused to gather his words, suddenly extra aware of the sun beating down, even through the material of his Sunday hat. "We didn't fall in love," he finally said. "We decided that as the best of friends, we would make the best of partners."

Jethro nodded along but said nothing.

"Many Amish make practical marriages," Joshua continued. "But as this wasn't arranged by others, was our idea, I want to make sure . . . we're doing the right thing."

"Wise to want to be certain," Jethro murmured thoughtfully. "I made a practical marriage myself."

"That's why I wanted to ask you."

"I've found that both kinds come with their own special challenges and their own special benefits. In the case of a more arranged marriage, you know that you're not entering into such an important and lifetime commitment based on a rush of emotions that might burn out after a few months or years. I have personally also discovered that love—maybe not the giddiness of young love, but something deeper—came with time. The challenge is to be true partners. Caring and consideration aren't always front of mind when the romantic kind of love isn't there, if you see what I mean."

Joshua stopped walking and turned to face him. "I will always put Joy's needs first," he said. "As the husband, as the head of our household, I consider that my special responsibility."

Jethro clapped him on the shoulder. "And Joy is kindness herself, so you should be fine to go on with."

Why did talking it out make him breathe a little easier? He had already thought he'd been taking the right step for the right reasons, but now the ground was even more solid under his feet than before.

"Any other advice?" he asked.

Jethro pursed his lips. "My usual advice to a couple entering marriage is to turn to Gotte first, and always be honest with each other."

Honest. What would Joy say if he told her that he was starting to wonder if friendship was the only reason he'd accepted her proposal? Did he dare tell her, or did he have faith and patience that Gotte would work it out?

Jethro passed a hand over his beard. "Yours is a more specific question, so I'll say this. If you build your marriage on faith, honesty, and forgiveness, you will always find your way through any situation or question facing you."

Joshua held out a hand to shake. "Denki."

"I'm here anytime you need me." He suddenly grinned, looking like a much younger man. "Despite the fact that we had nurtured hopes of Leroy pairing off with Joy."

Joshua chuckled as he knew he was supposed to, even if he wanted to growl like a riled dog instead. "Joy thinks that Mary Hershberger might be a match for Leroy. She has this notion that he is interested in becoming a dairy farmer."

Jethro's eyebrows rose slowly. "Is that so?"

"It's what Joy thinks anyway." Joshua started them walking back toward the gathering.

"I appreciate you sharing. I plan to speak to Joy after the meal. Maybe I'll ask her about that." Jethro clapped him on the shoulder and inhaled. "I don't know about you, but I'm starving."

Joshua wasn't so sure he could eat. He wouldn't have a chance to speak with Joy until after the meal. She'd be too busy serving at first, then eating with the other women. The problem was . . . suddenly, he needed to reassure himself that they were still both fully committed to the path they'd chosen to walk.

Or maybe he'd know after the bishop spoke with Joy.

JOY LAY IN her bed, hand tucked between her cheek and pillow, and stared at the moonlight moving across the wall opposite, unable to sleep as she tossed the day over and over and over in her head like a salad.

After the service, the bishop had first spoken with

Joshua, who'd given her a nod that everything was fine as they'd returned. Then, following the meal, Jethro Miller had taken her aside separately.

A slightly awkward, but ultimately easier-than-expected, conversation. The only surprise was when he'd asked if she thought Leroy and Mary should be encouraged. Had Joshua told him of the plan to get those two together? She'd been honest about her own observations, but nothing else, and he'd listened thoughtfully, not pressing for more. She'd always liked Leroy's dat.

Joy had nodded at Joshua the same way he had at her. Then bubbles of emotion—something eager that she wasn't ready to pin down—had struck as he ducked his head, hiding a large, what appeared to be relieved, grin. Only now that she was remembering it, that grin had been confusing yet. Marriage was a serious, solemn, life-long step to take, and Joshua, once he put his mind to something, was always fully committed. So of course he'd be relieved.

But would he have been . . . excited . . . if she'd been Katie, or another more traditional Amish girl, he was engaged to instead? As opposed to being just relieved that their plan was working out?

Joy had tried to get Katie talking as they'd worked side by side serving the meal, but they'd been too busy. Then Hope had waved her over to sit with her and Mary. So she was no closer there. Joshua hadn't attended singeon in the evening—wanting to keep an eye on Schatzi, who was set to foal any day now. The rest of Joy's time was taken up working in her bedroom on the quilts for Ruth Kanagy's customer. She was starting to get behind on them because of the way she was sneaking around, hiding them from Mamm. Ruth would expect the next one soon, since they'd agreed on a schedule.

A small snick of sound, like a bird tapping at her window, had her stopping all her muddled thinking and listening with a frown. No trees were near enough to her room to make that noise. Another one had her up on her elbow, watching the window nearest her. Sure enough, a second later, something small struck the glass.

Getting to her feet, she cautiously moved to the window and inched the curtain back to peer outside.

Who knew hearts could jump so hard? Joshua stood in the shadows, face upturned. As she watched, he tossed something at her window again. This was Joshua. No need to get all worked up. Trying to ignore the sudden return of those bubbles from earlier in the day, she pulled the curtain back and opened the window. "What are you doing?" she whisper-hissed at him.

"Come down," he beckoned with a wave and a grin that reminded her of younger him.

Pinching her lips around a smile, she shook her head at him. Incorrigible man. "Wait there."

His grin flashed in the dark as she turned away from the window. She tried not to let those bubbles be about anything more than a fun adventure. What could he possibly want at this hour?

In a rush of silent movements, she dressed—after all, she'd promised the bishop only today that her behavior was all it should be. Getting caught with Joshua in the middle of the night in her nightgown seemed like asking for speculation and doubts; fully dressed was clearly better.

Sneaking down the stairs, she avoided all the squeaky steps—after all, this wasn't her first midnight escapade, though it had been quite a while—then slipped out the back door. She was watching her feet on the steps and not looking up, so she ran right into Joshua, who caught her with a muffled *oomph*.

"Careful there."

Her breath snagged at his nearness, the warmth of his hands on her arms, the flash of even white teeth in the dark. He and his brothers had been blessed with excellent teeth. Carefully, she stepped back. "Sorry. I thought you were going to wait around the side of the house."

He shook his head. "No need. Your dat sent me."

Of all the things in the world that she thought this was about, her dat was definitely not one of them. Every semi-formed romantic notion of a moonlight stroll to celebrate the bishop's blessing, or half-formed ideas along those lines, disappeared in a poof, and the excited bubbles popped, leaving only a soapy film of disappointment in their wake.

Which was *ridiculous*, she wanted to yell at herself. This was *just* Joshua. But just Joshua was becoming something else to her, something more that she was maybe too scared to acknowledge was happening.

"My dat?" she asked slowly, trying not to let her emotions show on her face.

"Schatzi had her foal finally. He sent Amos to fetch me here to help a few hours ago. We thought you'd like to see her."

Doing her best to perk up at the news—Joy loved the baby horses more than anything except maybe Mamm's chocolate cake—she turned her feet toward the barn. "How thoughtful."

She tried not to grimace at the trite words. Had this happened any other way, she'd probably be tripping over her feet in excitement. Instead she walked. Or maybe, she was weighted down with dashed hopes. Dumm hopes, foolish hopes, ones that she shouldn't have considered in the first place.

Joshua fell in step beside her but didn't speak.

Joy scoured her head for anything to break the silence, which suddenly turned as heavy as her heart and feet. "Why not send Amos to wake me up yet?"

A deep chuckle curled around her in the night. "He's fast asleep in the next stall."

"Oh."

They hurried into the barn where a single battery-operated lantern cast a buzzing blue light over the stall where her dat stood, gazing over the top of the closed stall door. Pulling up beside him, Joy went up on her tiptoes to peer over as well and, as always happened, was caught up in the sheer beauty of new life.

Schatzi, a pretty bay-colored mare with a black mane and tail and a queenly personality, was already on her feet in the clean straw, standing over a tiny version of herself. A colt, still damp from birth, boasted a lighter-colored coat that would darken over time, the wisp of a black mane and tail that would grow out, a white blaze down his nose, and four white socks.

Her dat wrapped an arm around her shoulders and squeezed her close to his side, though she noticed he didn't use his hands to squeeze. He didn't use his hands for a lot of things, she'd started to realize since she found out about the arthritis. She tried not to worry on that, focusing instead on the moment. She and Dat had always loved sharing these times together ever since she was little. "This one will be a new buggy horse for you and Joshua," he whispered into her hair. "My wedding gift to you."

Joy turned to face her fater, who smiled at her with such tenderness, tears suddenly stung her eyes. How had she been so blessed to be born to such parents? She bit her lip to prevent the tears from welling over. "Denki, Dat."

He squeezed her again, and together they turned back to the horses.

Schatzi nosed her brand-new baby, and the foal lifted his head, his long ears flicking back and forth, only to put his head down again as though to say, *I'm tired. Leave me alone.*

Come on, little one. Joy kept the words to herself. This was all up to the foal and to his mother.

The colt lifted his head again and the muscles in his flanks twitched, a sure sign he was readying himself to get to his feet for the first time. Dat stepped away, murmuring to Joshua, but she couldn't pull her gaze away from the miracle happening right in front of her to listen.

The colt appeared to gather himself, then pushed up, but only managed to get three feet under him. One of his front legs was bent, and he still balanced precariously on one knee, back legs sprawled wide. Another heave and he was up on all fours, but sort of tilted back to lean his backside against the wood of the stall walls. He looked as startled as anyone that he was standing, and Joy giggled.

A hand snuck into hers, strong and rough and capable, and she glanced at Joshua, who turned his head to look back, dark eyes shining, lips tipped up, sharing in her delight. Contentment settled around her heart, lifting the weight from earlier.

At Joshua's side felt . . . right.

A rustle had them both turning to find their new foal ducking under his mother's chest, stretching out his neck, clearly aiming for food, which was at the other end. The colt had braced his front legs and was moving his back legs as though that would make him walk, but he wasn't going anywhere because he was stopped by his mother's bulk.

Joy chuckled.

Finally, after a few more stops and starts, the colt figured out how to get all four feet moving and make his way around Schatzi's bulk to her side, though he stumbled a bit along the way. Then he moved right under his mother, unerringly to the milk waiting. Bending underneath, the tiny horse took his first meal.

"They always know exactly what to do," Joy whispered. Unlike human babies, who were so helpless . . . for years even.

Leaning her chin on the hand not already being held, Joy sighed. "After we are married, will you always wake me for the birth of new foals?" she asked. She could never get tired of watching these first few moments of life.

Joshua was silent long enough that she tipped her head to find him watching her, a smile tugging at the corners of his mouth, and a light in his eyes she'd never seen before and didn't know quite what to make of, except an answering rush of giddiness told her she liked it.

"Always," he murmured in answer to her question.

He squeezed her hand and they both turned back to watch the foal, that contentment swelling inside her again. Was it selfish to wish they could be like this forever?

Chapter Thirteen

DESPITE THE LATE night, and very little sleep, Joshua woke up bright-eyed. It helped that he wasn't working in the shop today. He'd get through his chores at home this morning, then hurry over to the Yoders' to see how the new colt was doing.

Their new colt. His and Joy's.

Everything was moving along exactly as it should, and Joy had gazed at him last night with a new kind of happiness in her eyes and her smile. He'd seen it. More than that, an answering warmth had bloomed inside his own chest. He didn't know for sure what that had been—growing affection or a sort of contentment with his choices—but he felt it promised good things, regardless. No need to question further.

Popping out of bed, he washed and dressed and hustled downstairs to find Mamm laying a heaping platter of pancakes on the table. He kissed her cheek, which made her chuckle and swat at his arm at the same time.

"Ach, get on with you," she said.

"Where are Dat and Daniel?" he asked.

"They went to meet Adam at the shop early. He's bringing more of his metalwork to sell."

The gruff ferrier had been difficult to persuade to sell through them. "Wunderbaar."

Mamm didn't seem to notice the off tone in his voice, and Joshua was already kicking himself for being bothered at all. It was just . . . until now, his parents had shared everything to do with the shop with him. With the whole family. But not this morning. Like Aaron had, he was leaving, and soon. Maybe they saw no need.

He wouldn't be part of that anymore.

As excited as he was about the path he was taking, it suddenly struck him that his life was about to change forever. No more of Mamm's pancakes in the mornings or discussing who would be doing what for the family business. No more debate over a new ware they were considering adding to the inventory for the shop. He'd grown up spending his life with his family all together in one place most of the day, and soon, he would hardly see them on a daily basis.

He cleared his throat. "Mamm?"

"Hmmm?" She didn't turn away from more pancakes bubbling away on the stovetop. Though goodness knew who she thought would eat them with Daniel and Dat away. She was still cooking as though she had three hungry, growing buwes to feed every day.

"Since I have you alone, I want to ask you something."

She still didn't turn. "What's that?"

"I need you to be honest with me." Not that his mater would even contemplate otherwise, but she might not tell the entire story if she thought to protect his feelings.

Ruth Kanagy turned dark eyes on him, the same color as his and Aaron's, searching his face. "Let me finish these. Then I'll sit down and listen."

He nodded and a few minutes later sat facing her.

"What is it?" she asked, concern marring her brow.

"Is Dat . . . is he heartbroken that I want to leave the business?" he asked, not quite knowing what he would do if she said yes.

But the question had to be asked. He had to be certain his choices weren't causing his family pain.

After a long pause, Mamm reached across the table and patted his hand. "I can see this worries you, but don't let it. Dat wants your happiness above all else."

That did not answer his question.

"But—"

"I think the best person to ask would be Dat. Don't you?" She gave his hand another pat, then got busy smothering her pancakes in maple syrup, the conversation over as far as she was concerned.

Joshua made himself a promise that he'd get a private moment with his fater as soon as he had a chance. After all, the bishop would announce his and Joy's engagement officially during the church service in two Sundays and they'd be married the Thursday following.

Three weeks. Less than. In less than three weeks he'd be married to Joy.

He tried not to let anticipation hurry him through his work. After all, a job half done would only have to be done twice. Finally he was able to make his way to the Yoders'. He walked since both buggies were taken by his family. But . . . instead of going straight to the barn to see the colt, he found himself on the front porch of Joy's house before consciously deciding to go there first. Hat in hand, he knocked then waited with a sudden . . . not uneasiness . . . but something nervous twisting in his gut.

The door swung open, and Joy stared at him for a second before breaking into a smile that knocked the nervousness . . . and all the air . . . right out of him, leaving him struggling to breathe properly. He'd always liked her smiles before, appreciated how sweetly and easily she doled them out, but they'd never done that to him in the past.

What if he went through life struggling to breathe around his wife all the time? That didn't sound proper to him. Maybe kissing her had been a bad idea. It has started a lot of ideas.

When he didn't say anything, just stood there and stared, Joy's eyebrows rose slowly, a spark of amusement glinting in her eyes. "Do you need something?" she asked. "Dat is already in the barn."

Why had he come here again? Ach, he remembered. "Do you want to come visit the colt with me?" he asked. "He should have a name."

Pleasure lit his fiancée up from inside, over even such a small pleasure as naming a tiny newborn horse. "Mamm," she called behind her. "I'll be right back."

She didn't wait for her mother to answer, stepping out and closing the door behind her. She stood near, and the scent of her—sunshine and cookies—had the same impact it had had the night before when he'd stood beside her in the barn, settling inside him as though he'd come home.

Together they meandered down to the barn, not talking, but not needing to as they simply enjoyed the warmth of the sun on their heads, the soft breeze, and each other.

"Dat?" Joy called out as they entered the barn.

No answer from Mervin, though several horses knickered and Joy chuckled. They stopped at the stall where

Schatzi and her baby were housed comfortably. The tiny horse was lying down taking a nap while mama watched over him protectively.

"If he gets his sire's height, he'll make a fine buggy horse," Joshua said in a low voice, not wanting to disturb them.

"Jah. That's what he was bred for." Joy nodded, not taking her gaze from the animal.

"What should we call him?" he asked.

She pursed her lips, studying their first wedding gift. "Star?" she asked, waving vaguely at her own forehead.

Joshua shook his head. "Too many horses named Star."

That tugged a grin from her. "Are you calling me unoriginal?"

"In naming a horse, maybe," he teased.

"Ach vell . . . What are your ideas, Mr. Creative?"

"Hmmm . . . He's a gift. What about something like Bounty or Present?"

Joy tipped her head, studying the foal. "I like Bounty okay."

"But not quite right?"

Dark eyes flashed at him, but she didn't bother asking him how he knew. He just did. Without arguing, she gave a small shake of her head.

"Joy . . ." He stopped and started over a question that loomed larger by the day.

"What?" she asked, turning to face him fully.

He studied her upturned face—with her wide, dark eyes that always seemed to be laughing, lips turned up at the corners, unblemished skin that turned rosy when she blushed, and a pert nose that he hoped their daughters would inherit from their mother. Looking at this face every day for the rest of his life would be no hardship. And yet . . .

"Are you nervous?" he asked.

He almost expected her to laugh off the question or be genuinely confused by it. Instead, she nibbled at her lower lip. "More nervous than about anything I've ever done in my life," she owned quietly.

"Even when you walked through the woods at night without your parents' permission to bring Naomi Wingard soup when she was sick? How old were you then?"

"Ten, and that was terrifying." She chuckled. "But this might be worse. Knots around here"—she indicated her tummy—"seem to have become permanent."

Joshua sobered. "Jah. Me too."

They studied each other quietly. "I will be a true husband to you, Joy. I promise."

That drew a chuckle from her. "I have no doubts about that," she said. "You are one of the best men I know, Joshua Kanagy. A bit bossy, and a little full of your own opinions, but I can handle that."

"Hey," he protested.

Her eyes crinkled. "But you are hardworking and kind, gentle when you need to be and strong in the same way. Look at how you are with the horses." She nodded at Schatzi and her foal. "Gotte is foremost in your thoughts and you walk in faith."

Unaccustomed heat rose in his face at all the compliments yet. From Joy in particular, who, all his life, had been prone to making sure his pride didn't get out of hand. "Are you sure we're talking about me?"

"For sure and certain. I'm not saying you're perfect. Only Jesus was perfect. You like to have your own way too much and tend to think you know better than everyone else, and you are terrible at describing quilts in the shop."

"What?" He pulled up at the last one. "I sold a yellow quilt the other day without any trouble."

"Uh-huh. I heard that your mamm had to step in when you didn't know if it would fit the bed."

"How should I know what size bed they have?"

Joy rolled her eyes. "You could tell them what size the quilt was made for. It's on the label."

He blew out a grunt of indignation. "Well, you're not perfect either, Joy Yoder."

"Jah. I know that." She wrinkled her nose. Then considered him with narrowed eyes. "Anything you can't live with?"

Joshua gave that more consideration than maybe her lighthearted question warranted. "I do feel blessed that I'll have a wife who can cook better than anyone else in the district. And I love the way you sing when you work."

"Not very well," she murmured.

"Off-key, jah, but it makes the work pass pleasantly." He cleared his throat. "And you have a true heart of mercy and kindness. You see others' needs I think often before they see for themselves."

"That's nothing special." Joy waved it away.

He took her chin between his thumb and index finger to be sure she knew how serious he was. "Your heart for others is a gift, like my way with horses is a gift."

Joy stared at him, eyes wide and mouth slightly parted, as though she hadn't really thought he'd noticed or even cared. Only his fingers warmed, the sensation spreading through the rest of him, so he let go before he did something verhuddelt, like kiss her again.

She cleared her throat. "Mamm is always saying I'd give the clothes off my own back if I thought someone needed them, and then be left with no clothes."

He knew what Anna Yoder was getting at with that. "Your heart is always in the right place, and that's what's important."

Tension visibly eased from Joy's shoulders. Had she been worried that he'd think the same thing?

"I've been saving you since we were little," he said, trying to reassure her. "It's no hardship to continue once we're married."

"Me?" she hooted. "*I'm* not the only one who needs saving."

Joshua narrowed his eyes. "That time I took your bruders ice fishing doesn't count."

"Amos fell through the ice because it wasn't thick enough," she reminded him.

Not that she needed to, he still felt wonderful bad about that. Amos might have gotten sick from the cold; only Gotte's hand had kept the boy well.

"But you have to admit that I save you more than you save me," he pushed.

"Maybe . . ." she allowed. "Or maybe, you think you're saving me when really I don't need it."

How had the conversation spiraled out of control like this? Feeling underappreciated for all those times he'd helped, he crossed his arms. "Like when?"

"It doesn't matter. Regardless, I'm *not* a baby anymore, Joshua. I hope you see that."

She didn't need to tell him. He'd noticed how she'd grown up all on his own just fine.

"Rather than saving me," Joy continued. "What if you supported me instead? Or discussed your concerns openly?"

"I thought that's what I was doing by marrying you," he pointed out.

Except her face sort of fell, as though he'd said the exact

wrong thing. He started forward, reaching for her hand, except a female voice called out a greeting from the entrance to the barn, and Joy turned her attention that way.

"Gute dag," she answered back.

It took Joshua a longer second to turn his head and take in the fact that Mary was there again, but this time, instead of Hope, Katie Jones had come along.

Ach du lieva.

"I'd better get to work," Joshua muttered at Joy. Then nodded at the two girls. "Mary. Katie."

"Kumme," Joy said, ushering them away.

Katie paused, glancing over her shoulder at him, but Joshua turned his back on her. Their own greetings to Joy followed him out of the barn, where he found Mervin already at work in the nearest paddock. Leroy Miller was right there beside him, doing all the things that required hands, his expression behind his glasses one of total concentration, even though they were only walking the horse. Joshua swallowed a sigh and tamped down on the sudden sense that his position in the world, his path, wasn't as set in stone as he'd thought. Maybe his job and Joy were both up in the air.

He sent a silent prayer to Gotte to show him the way to keep this path straight.

JOY DIDN'T KNOW if she was coming or going. Those kind things Joshua had said had burrowed right into her heart, filling her with feelings she'd had no idea were there. She also had no idea he thought that, and those two situations made her react . . . badly. Mostly because she'd wanted to hug him, lay her cheek on his chest, and sink into whatever was happening to her when she was around him. Which scared her, because that wasn't the plan.

So instead she'd ruined it.

Then her friends had shown up. She'd secretly studied Joshua's face when he'd seen Katie, waiting for any sign that he was heartbroken over the girl. After all, when Katie had hinted that she'd like to join one of her baking sessions with Mary, that was partly why Joy had happily agreed.

Only Joshua had got out of the barn as though the hay loft had gone up in flames. At the same time, he hadn't looked any way but how he normally did at the sight of the other girl. Which meant Joy knew nothing different than before.

"Is it two cups or three?" Mary asked uncertainly, holding a heaping scoop over a large mixing bowl.

"Two," Joy said. "But you want to flatten the top."

She moved to Mary's side and showed her.

"Like this, Mary." Katie helpfully held up her own leveled cup of flour, although her smile was more piteous than kind.

Joy had to stop from scrunching up her nose. Maybe Katie meant well, but the way her subtle tone and overhelpful manner were coming across were clearly upsetting Mary. Her friend had been confident and smiling the other occasions they'd baked together, but now she was acting nervous and unsure of herself, asking questions she hadn't needed to ask the last few times they'd met.

Swallowing her frustration, Joy pointed out the next steps, then resumed her seat, working away at one of her quilt projects. She owed Ruth Kanagy this one and one more. Soon. Only she kept running out of time in the day, hardly making any progress as she went along.

After all, she needed to sew her wedding dress and one for Hope, who had happily agreed to stand with Joy on the day. Amish didn't have bridesmaids and groomsmen like the

Englischers, but they did have two couples to stand with them. Joshua had already asked his bruders. Joy was thinking of asking Mary as well, which meant another dress to sew for her friend. Mamm had been buying stacks and stacks of celery, part of the traditional wedding meal for after the services. She'd also been cleaning like mad. Not just the surfaces. She wanted every nook and cranny perfect, assigning Joy what seemed like a hundred more chores every day.

Soon, Joy wouldn't have time to go to church on Sundays if things kept up this way. But she decided not to worry about it. Things always had a way of working themselves out. She could only do her best every day and put the rest in Gotte's hands.

"And the sugar?" Mary asked now. "Do I flatten that, too?"

Katie cleared her throat softly to herself. Joy had to bite her tongue, tempted to remind her of the Christian charity she should be showing, the rebuke sharp and needling on her lips. Instead, offering Mary a kind smile, she got up again, laying her quilting to the side. Clearly, she wasn't going to get to it during the baking.

"Like this." She showed Mary again how to tap the cup so that the sugar settled and you got a precise amount.

Her own mamm baked on instinct—a little of this, a lot of that—but Joy always found it easier, once she'd mastered a recipe, to always do it the same after that.

"How are the wedding plans coming?" Katie asked.

Even though the question was quite normal, tension wound around Joy's heart like the old barn cat who would wind around her ankles before he tried to take a nip out of her calf.

"Wonderful gute," she answered. She didn't want to rub Katie's nose in her luck if the other girl was still nursing a sore heart.

"What color did you choose for your wedding dress? Blue?"

Katie's interest had Joy relaxing a bit. Maybe she really was fine. Blue was the traditional color for a wedding dress—which would become her nice church dress afterward—but their district didn't restrict the color, similar to how they didn't restrict the date as other districts did. "I decided to go with yellow," she said.

"Yellow?" Katie's pursed lips left no doubt about her opinion.

But Mary acted enthused. "You always look so lovely in that color. It makes your dark hair shine, and it's bright and cheerful, just like you."

Right then and there, Joy decided to ask her to stand up for her with Hope. She'd try to get Mary on her own before she and Katie left.

"When I get married," Katie murmured, "I'm going to wear blue to match my eyes." She blinked those eyes, which were one of her best features. Katie really was lovely. And proper. Never coloring outside the lines. No wonder Joshua had been interested.

"That will be perfect," Joy said, and received a beaming smile in return.

"I think . . . I'll wear blue, too," Mary said. "It's traditional."

Katie tipped her head to the side. "Maybe not with your coloring, though."

Despite silently agreeing—Mary's slightly mousy coloring tended to turn sallow when she wore blue, as she was now—Joy wanted to pinch Katie Jones right in the arm.

"You know what color would be beautiful on you?" Joy asked Mary instead.

Mary shook her head.

"Green. Like a spring green. It would bring out the color of your eyes and the hint of red in your hair."

Mary's hands stilled as she considered it. "I've never had a green dress before."

No. That didn't surprise Joy. Anyone with half an eye could see Mary got the hand-me-downs from her sisters, so she'd never had a chance to see for herself.

"Ruth Kanagy got in a swath of a beautiful material for a dress in their shop. It's what made me think of it. Maybe we could go later this week and see." Joy was already thinking she might make Mary's wedding dress out of that.

Usually, the attendants wore the same color as the bride, but she'd already decided to make Hope a pale pink dress. Beside their yellow and pink, the green would be pretty. Still Plain, of course—she would start her married life in a proper Amish way—but it might make Mary happy, so a small deviation wouldn't be bad.

"Where are you going to live after you're married, Joy?" Katie asked next, clearly bored with the talk of dress colors.

"The Kanagys have a Dawdi Haus," Joy said, trying not to show how uncomfortable she was with such a question.

"Ach, that will be nice to be so close to family," Mary said.

"Mmm . . ." Katie pursed her lips. "Personally, I think starting life in my own home is what I would prefer. It gives you more of a chance to figure things out for yourself. I mean, what if his mamm is constantly interfering?"

"I don't see Ruth being the type," Joy murmured.

"True. Still . . . when I was courting—" Katie suddenly cut herself off, covering her mouth with her hand and staring at Joy with wide eyes. "I'm sorry. I shouldn't have said anything."

But Joy could see she'd meant to all the same. Maybe Katie wasn't so perfect after all. Had Joshua seen that?

Or am I being critical? Uncharitable?

Still, she'd invited Katie over to find out exactly this, so she wasn't going to let the sudden burn in the center of her chest stop things now. Instead, she did her best to appear blandly interested. "I had heard you had a beau."

She didn't dare glance at Mary, who'd gone stiff as the fireplace poker beside her, hands suspended over the bowl she'd been whisking. Seeing as she was the one who'd mentioned Joshua and Katie to Joy in the first place, a small pinch of guilt struck her in the heart. Too late to take it back, though.

Katie lowered her own hand slowly, pausing in what she was doing. "Jah. He is a wonderful gute man. If I hadn't been so silly, maybe . . ." She paused, then shrugged, her expression tragic. "But it doesn't matter anymore."

She offered Joy what appeared to be a brave, selfless smile, and Joy smiled back, not sure what to make of any of this. Katie had a habit of blowing things out of proportion. A small grass snake became a poisonous serpent that almost bit her arm off, a brisk wind was a tornado trying to tear down the house, and a small cold became life-threatening pneumonia. Also, she hadn't mentioned Joshua by name.

But who else could she be speaking of?

Joy knew better than to believe every word, but still . . . Katie wasn't a liar either. It would go against her faith, against her practice as Amish. A nugget of truth could always be found in her stories. Trying to hide her thoughts as she moved to the counter to help Mary knead the dough for the sugar cookies they were making, Joy determined to do what she should have done in the first place . . . put this in Gotte's hands.

If Joshua was nursing a broken heart for Katie, or didn't

want to marry Joy anymore, then he would say so. Time to grow up and stop being so silly. He would be her husband soon, and she trusted him to do the right thing in the end. As she should.

Giving herself a mental nod, Joy determinedly put all the questions behind her.

Chapter Fourteen

JOSHUA ROLLED THE die across the game board, then scowled as Joy tried to cover up her chortle beside him. He'd rolled a one. Again. That had to be the twentieth time he'd rolled that number in this game.

After going home to clean up from working with the horses, he'd come back at Mervin's invitation to join them for dinner and games. Joy cooked the meal that night, which was probably why the invitation, seeing as today wasn't Saturday, which was the traditional night to spend at a fiancée's home with her family.

I'm probably going to have to let out my pants after our first year of marriage eating her food.

"Gute" was a small word for what she did in the kitchen. "Appeditlich" was better—so delicious, he'd had seconds even though he was full. Now they all sat around the kitchen table playing Clue.

Watching Mervin try to pick up the small pieces with his painful hands without offering to help was a silent awfulness. How had Joy's dat stood the pain so quietly? Joy's own concerned winces were almost as painful to see. But the Yoders clearly hadn't told the boys yet, and Joshua wasn't going to do it for them, so he didn't say anything.

With a not entirely playful huff, he moved his piece on the board one square, barely closer to where he was trying to get.

Scooping up the die in her hand, Joy arranged her face in an overly solicitous manner, pursed lips and all. "That was too bad," she said.

Given that he was essentially racing her to the end of the game, jah, too bad was right. "You're not at all sorry," he accused.

"Nae," she said on a laugh, dimple in full view. "Not even a little bit."

After a dramatic show of shaking and blowing on her die, Joy laughed and rolled a number that got her into the room they'd been heading to already. And Joshua tried not to groan. He was pretty sure she was about to win . . . again. She *always* won this game. He knew for sure the culprit was Colonel Mustard in the Library, the room on the board she'd just entered, but he hadn't figured out the weapon yet. If he'd got there first, he was planning to guess.

Joy straightened in her chair, mischief playing around her eyes as she held her own cards in front of her face, peeping at each of them with narrowed eyes. "Who could it be?" she asked in a cackling voice, which sent Amos and Samuel into hoots of laughter—like it had every time Joy had her turn.

Mervin rolled his eyes. "Get it over with, liebchen."

Joy scrunched her nose at him. "Fine. I accuse Colonel Mustard, with the candlestick, in the Library," she announced with a flourish.

"Can I look, Joy?" Samuel asked shyly.

She paused, her hand already reaching for the small envelope with the answer, then picked it up and handed it to him.

Not for the first time tonight, Joshua noted that she was going to make a wunderbaar mater. She'd be just the right combination of fun and proper, teaching her kinder kindness, mercy, and living up to her name with joy. It probably meant more of the discipline would fall to him, but he was fine with that.

"Go ahead," she begged, practically climbing over the table for a peek. "Am I right?"

With eager fingers, Samuel pulled the cards out and studied them.

"Vell?" Amos prompted.

One at a time, the younger boy laid each card on the table face up. "Colonel Mustard. With the candlestick. In the Library. Joy wins!"

Joy jumped up with a cheer while the rest of them groaned, except Samuel, who danced around with her.

"If it wasn't against our ways to bet," Joy teased, "I'd start trading chores for wins."

Anna Yoder snorted. "No dochder of mine—"

"I was *joking*, Mamm. I would never do that." The angelic smile she tried on didn't fool Anna any.

"Huh," Anna huffed, eyes narrowed at Joy, but her lips were twitching.

Anna was a tough nut to crack, but Joshua had learned years before that for all her gruff talk and strict rules, she was a marshmallow on the inside when it came to her children. She loved them fiercely and protected them the best way she knew how.

Which was probably why Joy loved her so much back,

even when she strained against those rules, chomping at the bit like one of Mervin's horses. Getting up, Joy moved around the table and hugged her mamm, who swatted at her, uncomfortable with the show of affection even as she hugged her back.

"Go on up to bed," Joy said. "Joshua and I can put this away and make sure the boys brush their teeth."

After a pause, Anna gave in. "Denki," she said to both Joy and Joshua, who waved them off, glad to be of help.

In short order, they had the kitchen put to rights, then made their way upstairs to the buwes' room. "Did you say your prayers?" Joy demanded, hands on her hips, suddenly a replica of her mother.

"Ach jah," Samuel said, curly hair flopping in his eyes as he nodded.

"Gute. Now, let me see those teeth," Joy said.

Amos and then Samuel gave her gruesome, tooth-filled grins, and she leaned in to inspect closely. With a satisfied grunt, she waved them to their room. Then, obviously out of long habit, both buwes got into bed and Joy tucked them in one at a time, giving them a kiss on the forehead. "Gute nacht," she said.

It wasn't right for a man to melt at the sight of a woman with her bruders, but here he was, practically a puddle on the floor.

After closing the door behind her, Joy led the way downstairs and out onto the front porch, where the air was starting to turn crisper. Fall was almost upon them, Joshua's favorite time of year, when the world and the farms started to slow to the pace of winter. Not that there weren't always a thousand things to do, but after harvest, which was coming up soon, the rush of the spring and summer eased.

They both paused on the porch before moving down the

stairs, only Joy's steps led her toward the barn. She'd promised to drive him home after dinner, but he couldn't let her return on her own in the dark. He'd stayed too long, and dusk's long shadows had since been replaced by a clear and star-filled night.

He snagged her by the hand and tugged her the other way. "I'll walk home."

"But it's miles yet, and dark."

"I don't mind."

She must've recognized the stubborn set to his chin, because she gave in and moved to walk with him down the drive to the road. Even though he should have let go, which was what a proper Amish man would have done, Joshua didn't want to. He liked holding Joy's hand, tucked into his, small and slender and sweet.

She didn't tug to take it back either, though, so he let himself enjoy this one moment.

"Joshua?" Joy asked in a voice that he'd never heard from her before. Tentative. Unsure.

"Hmm?"

"Is there another girl you would rather be marrying?" she asked.

Joshua pulled up sharply at that and used his grip on her hand to bring her around to face him. "What a thing to ask," he said, studying her face. Only she wouldn't look at him. "What brought this on?"

She hitched a shoulder. "I don't know. It just occurred to me that maybe you'd had someone else in mind before I . . ."

Joshua scoured his mind and landed on the answer. Katie Jones had been baking with Joy and Mary today.

Maybe he should tell Joy about Katie. About how, for half a second, he'd thought she was the kind of girl he was looking for. But he hadn't even thought of her when Joy proposed to him. Not even a twinkle of an idea. Funny that he was only realizing that now.

"Nae, Joy. There is no other girl, and—" He cut her off, holding up a hand as she opened her mouth with another question. "I'm not leaving another girl with a broken heart either."

Finally Joy looked him directly in the eyes, searching his gaze as though to assure herself he was telling the truth.

"Have I ever lied to you?" he asked.

"Nae. Never."

"I don't intend to start now. So . . . how about we put aside this silly thought. Jah?"

After a second, she gave a low chuckle. "Jah. I guess I *was* being silly."

"Joy," he said softly.

She stilled, gazing back with the kind of trust she'd always shown in him.

Joshua squeezed her hand. Part of him wanted to ask if her worries came from a deeper set of doubts about marrying him, but he must be a coward, because he couldn't make the question come out of his mouth. "Not long until we're married, then we can get to the business of settling down. These questions will go away, then."

Joy lit up with amusement. "Settling down might be a lot to ask of your new wife."

He laughed with her. "I guess so."

"But finding our footing as a married couple, jah. I guess we can do that."

Joshua lifted a hand, brushing his fingertips along the curve of her obstinate chin. "I'd like to—"

A flash of movement coming from the house caught his attention, and Joshua cut off what he was about to ask right in time to see the backs of two little buwes sneaking away from the house and running quickly in the direction of the barn.

"Like to what?" Joy prompted, unaware of what had distracted him.

Joshua sighed and dropped his hand to his side. Gotte apparently wanted him to wait. "Your bruders just ran into the woods."

JOY WHIPPED HER head around to stare in the direction Joshua hitched his chin toward. Sure enough, she caught the flash of a white nightshirt and a blond head as her bruders disappeared into the trees like tiny, fast-moving ghosts.

"Ach du lieva. What are they up to now?" she murmured.

Joshua's low chuckle cut off as she turned to face him.

"You find this funny?" she asked.

"Nae." Only he had to pass a hand over his mouth to hide his grin. "You just sound like your mater."

"Ach vell, ha ha ha." Here she'd been hoping not to be quite as immovable as Mamm when she had her own kinder. "I'd better go get them."

Without waiting for Joshua, assuming he'd go on home, she made a beeline for the woods where Amos and Samuel had disappeared. Only, he followed her, his long strides eating up the ground so that he reached the tree line first. There he paused and waited for her.

"I'm pretty sure they went in here," he said.

Without a quibble, she let him take the lead. Now that darkness had fallen, the woods were harder to negotiate without a flashlight or a lantern, so she put a hand out, grasping a hunk of Joshua's white shirt, and no doubt wrinkling it something terrible. He paused, holding a branch back so it didn't whack her in the face after he passed by.

Thanks to the thick undergrowth, they had to do a lot of changing direction and even backtracking until suddenly they burst into a clearing Joy recognized from her own childhood exploring these woods. Right in the center of the large field stood a massive maple tree, still green with summer, in which a rickety and somewhat lopsided stack of wood she suspected was supposed to be a tree haus balanced precariously.

"Merciful heavens," she whispered, grasping on to Joshua tighter. "They're going to break their necks when that comes down."

"Jah," he said, his mouth a grim slash and his eyes a hard glitter in the moonlight. "Don't startle them, just in case."

She barely swallowed back her shout, then nodded. Making their way to the base of the tree, trying to rustle the grasses loudly, they got to where the boys had nailed boards as ladder steps up the trunk. "Amos?" she tried to call softly. "Samuel?"

Silence greeted her, so Joy cleared her throat and called their names again louder. This time a shuffling that reminded her of the time rats got into their cellar sounded along with a hushed whisper of boys thinking they couldn't be heard as they discussed what to do.

Joy propped her hands on her hips and glared above her head at the entrance cut into the floor of the tree haus—a solid twenty feet above her head. How on earth did they get all that wood up that high? And where did they get the neatly sawed planks in the first place?

"Answer me right this minute," she demanded in a stronger voice.

Another shuffle, then Amos's head appeared in the

opening, hair flopping into his eyes. "Don't be mad, Joy. We've built a wonderful gute fort. Just like Dat showed us when we helped him make the birdhouse for Mamm."

The birdhouse? *That* was the experience they used to get up there? Especially when Amos still had his cast on. He shouldn't have been climbing, let alone building. She exchanged a glance with Joshua, who didn't bother to hide his own horror.

Samuel must've moved, because the structure gave a terrible groaning protest and leaves dropped down on top of their heads. Fear lodged in Joy's chest like the stone rolled in front of Jesus's tomb, trapping her pounding heart inside. How had the thing not collapsed before now?

"We're just finishing the last bit," Amos assured her, acting oblivious to the creaking.

"Nae," she called out, doing her best not to sound panicked. "Come down here, please."

"Ach vell, it'll just be a second." Amos's head disappeared, but she'd caught the flash of stubborn determination in his jutted-out chin. He wasn't going to come down without persuasion, for sure and certain.

"I'll go up and get them," Joshua said.

Only when he stepped on the first ladder rung, a simple board nailed into the tree, it gave under his weight and he lurched against the bark, scraping his already bruised face against it.

Joy hissed her concern before turning him to check. Sure enough, tiny beads of blood were welling up along a long scratch down his cheek. She bit her lip. "You're going to look a sight at our wedding, Joshua Kanagy."

And all because of her bruders.

The tree house groaned again, only louder this time, and the leaves rustled and shook. The tree limbs seemed to move as though the big maple were trying to shake the boys out of her branches.

"Amos, Samuel, come down right now," Joy called, not bothering to hide the panic this time, her voice sharp and urgent with it.

"Ach, oll recht," came the reluctant reply.

Only, however they were moving inside, they must've done it at the same time, because the entire structure started to pitch sideways.

"Help!" That was Samuel's yelp.

"Don't move!" Joy yelled back.

Silence and the structure settled.

"Don't move," she repeated. "Stay as still as mice in a trap. I'm coming to get you."

She reached for the next ladder rung up, but Joshua grabbed her arm. "I can't let you do that. It's too dangerous."

"I'm small enough that these will hold me." She pointed at the broken rung. "But not you."

They didn't have time to argue. She could see that truth in Joshua's eyes as his jaw turned to stone, he clenched his teeth so hard. Then he held out his hands, fingers laced together to give her a boost up to the first working rung.

"I'll be right here," he said. "Use me as a cushion if you fall."

As though she could aim. "Not funny."

"It wasn't meant to be," came the muttered reply.

Which was the moment she realized how scared Joshua was. He'd been grim but calm up until now, but his expression suddenly reminded her of that time in the boat. Her heart managed to both swell and squeeze in her chest all at the same time. Not with fear, but with awe and thanks for this man, that he cared so much.

Not that it dispelled the fear.

Please watch over us, Lord. Deliver us safely out of this tree. She sent the prayer silently winging to Gotte.

Before she could think herself out if it, Joy scrambled the first few "steps" up the trunk of the tree. Thankfully, they held her weight without protest or movement. So she kept going carefully until she reached the bottom of the fort. Unfortunately, the way the structure had shifted, she had to lean away from the tree, gripping one rung with her fingertips in order to pop her head inside the entrance.

There she found Amos and Samuel huddled in the far corner, gripping each other tight, eyes wide and trained on her face. Samuel's cheeks were already covered in tears, though he didn't make a peep. They were seated in the area of the structure that had nothing actually holding it up—no limb underneath the flooring, no supports attaching to the tree as a base or stilts to the ground.

"Amos," she said, as calmly and softly as she could, trying not to let them hear the shake in her voice. "I want you to crawl very slowly, and very carefully, toward me. Try to stay over the part with the limb underneath."

He shook his head. "I won't leave Samuel."

"Just like a gute big bruder," she said. "But if you both move at the same time, it will be bad. So one at a time, jah? You're closest to me."

"It's okay, Amos," Samuel whispered. "Save yourself."

Her heart clenched at that—so sweet and brave. Fear churned through her, making her hands and legs tremble so hard, she worried that she wouldn't get herself, let alone the boys, out of this predicament. Yet despite all that, Joy had to hide a smile at Samuel's self-sacrificing words.

She held out one hand toward Amos. With careful movements, he inched his way across the floor, all three of them tensing and grimacing with every sound. Finally he made it to her, except there wasn't room for him to pass her on the ladder and climb down to Joshua while she got Samuel.

Joy bit her lip. No way could the tree haus take her weight, which meant she had only one choice.

"I'm going to climb down, and you follow me," she told Amos. "Samuel . . . Don't move at all until I come back. Jah?"

He gave a tiny nod, words apparently freezing in his poor petrified head. Ready to go, she was dumm enough to look down as she put both hands back on the rung and realized exactly how far up she was. The ground sort of spun beneath her horrified gaze.

"Don't look at the ground," Amos whispered. "Look at the steps."

Forcing herself to do just that, Joy gulped, then made herself take one step down, then another. She paused, to help Amos reach for the rungs, which was harder for him now that the structure had shifted away from the trunk. Not letting herself think about how he was going to climb with a restrictive cast on one arm, she grunted with the effort of keeping them both in the dratted tree.

All the way down, Joy held her breath, waiting for the tree haus to come tumbling down with Samuel inside, or one of the rungs to break and Amos to fall the rest of the way. Finally, she stepped off the tree and Joshua, waiting silently for them, plucked Amos right off the trunk when he got low enough. Their eyes met over his head, his intent on hers, his face taut with worry.

She gulped. "I have to go—"

"I know," he said. Though the tight tone to his voice told her he didn't like it one bit.

Trying to be careful and hurrying at the same time was

not the easiest thing in the world, but she made it to the top again to find Samuel still huddled in his corner. "Your turn," she said.

Unfortunately, he shook his head, his small body trembling so hard, she worried that he'd never unlock his fear and move.

"Amos is waiting," she coaxed with what she prayed was an easy smile. "And so is Joshua."

Samuel's eyes got big. "Joshua's here?" he whispered.

"Jah, and he would want you to be brave so that we can both get down safely."

"Come on, Samuel," Amos yelled below them, though the tremor in his voice belied his irritation.

"You will be fine," she said. "You're so light, this fort will hardly notice."

"I'm big for my age," he insisted, but he also inched forward.

Willing him to keep going, she tried to keep up a flow of light chatter. "That is true," she mused. "Just think what the other buwes in the gmayna will say when they hear how high up you were."

He moved forward again, except the structure shuddered and they both froze, splinters digging under her fingernails as she gripped the lip of the opening hard, as though she could physically hold it steady. After a long, terrifying second waiting for everything to collapse out from under Samuel, taking her down with it, Joy waved at him to continue. "Maybe a little faster yet."

Finally, his small hand landed in hers, and like Amos, she helped him reach the steps to climb down. The second Samuel's feet touched the ground, she was on her knees with her arms wrapped tight around both her bruders. At last able to give the fear free rein, she couldn't stop her body from shaking in reaction so hard, her teeth almost came loose with it.

"Please, please, please don't ever do that again," she whispered to them.

"Aw, Joy." Amos struggled in her tight grasp and she let them go. "We would've been fine."

A warning crack sounded above them. Moving faster than she'd ever seen him, Joshua somehow gathered all three of them up in an untidy heap and yanked them out from under the fort just in time for the entire thing to come crashing down in a loud heap of leaves, tree limbs, and broken pieces of wood, with dust flying into the air and making them all cough.

In the silence, when she finally got her mind working again, Joy found herself plastered to Joshua, one arm wrapped around his neck even as the other was somehow holding on to both boys.

"It's safe now," he said into her hair softly, stirring the wisps that had come out of her kapp in the kerfuffle.

With a reluctance that she didn't have time to examine too closely, she let go of him and helped her bruders up. Then she went down to one knee in front of both Amos and Samuel, trying to make them understand how serious that had been. "You are old enough to know better than to build something like this without an adult."

Amos stared back at her with mutinous disagreement, jutting that chin out again, but Samuel scuffed his foot in the grass. "We wanted to surprise you," he said.

Joy shared a glance with Joshua, though she kept her expression serious. "This was for me? How exactly?"

"Nae." Samuel shook his head. "For Joshua."

Her fiancé's eyebrows leapt almost clean into his hairline. "For *me*?"

Samuel nodded. "We think Joshua should take our room when you get married, Joy, but then we wouldn't have a place to sleep. So Amos came up with the idea of building us a house of our own."

Amos's bony little chest puffed up with pride. "We were almost done yet."

Joy closed her eyes. Exactly how was she supposed to encourage the selflessness of the idea and not deflate that sense of accomplishment while impressing on these two how dangerous this had been?

She took a deep breath, then another, and opened her eyes. "I love that you wanted to help Joshua and me. It shows such a big heart for others."

Both boys nodded.

"You should know that Joshua and I plan to live in the Dawdi Haus at the Kanagys'."

The little faces fell. "Oh," Samuel mumbled.

"Most married couples want a separate home for themselves if they can afford it," she explained gently.

"Jah," Amos said, suddenly full of wisdom. "Matthew Beckett says it's so the stork will bring the babies."

Joshua hid a laugh with a cough.

Joy, meanwhile, had to force the heat out of her own cheeks, thankful suddenly for the darkness. "I am also impressed that you got so much done on your own, but . . ." She paused then turned them to stare at the wreckage, aghast. "What if you had been in there when it fell?" she asked.

"We would be oll recht—"

Joshua put a hand on Amos's shoulder. "From that high up, you'd, at the very least, be back in the hospital with more expensive bills."

She took a moment to study the man she was going to

marry, suddenly realizing how responsible he'd become. Like in the hospital, his way with her bruders made it so easy to picture how he'd be with their kinder one day. If she couldn't have the kind of love her grandparents had, she wanted a true partnership, and Gotte had blessed her with Joshua. Except with that realization came another that suddenly set a sting of tears in her eyes.

She didn't deserve Joshua.

Amos's mouth twisted and he glanced at his cast, which all his friends had signed. She could practically see the debate going on in his head weighing the responsibility of those bills against the danger and the attention he'd get.

Joshua must've, too, because he bent over to address him directly. "What if it came down on top of Joy?" he asked softly.

Amos's expression fell, then he shifted his gaze to her, studying her as though trying to determine if she would have been as "oll recht" as he or Samuel in the fall. "Jah. Girls break easier than boys," he agreed.

This was not the time to argue that point. Joshua, at least, was getting through to him. "Will you ever do anything this dangerous again?" he asked.

Amos thought for a moment, then . . . "Nae." He turned to face her. "I'm sorry, Joy."

She nodded.

"I'm sorry, too," Samuel hurried to add his apology. "We won't never do something dangerous again," he vowed in a small voice.

"Thank Gotte," she murmured. Then tugged them both in for a hug. "Because I don't know what I'd do if I lost you."

"Aw, Joy," Amos muttered. Even so, he snuggled into her for a heartbeat just the same.

She got to her feet as she let them go, Joshua straightening to come to her side. "If you wanted a fort," he said, "all you had to do was ask."

Both boys lit up. "You mean we can build another one together?" Amos asked.

Joy gave her soon-to-be husband a pointed stare. Rewarding these two right now was not the way for them to learn this lesson.

Clearly on the point of saying yes, he grimaced. "Err . . . Maybe after the wedding."

Amos narrowed his eyes at them. "Do we have to tell Mamm?"

Oh, help. Dishonesty—even just by omission—was one of her mater's sticking points, but the boys already got in trouble enough. Especially Amos with the rafter stunt.

"If you promise to never, ever build without help or permission again," she said slowly, "then I think we won't worry her."

The two boys whooped. "We promise," Amos said.

"Jah. Promise," Samuel said.

"I'm glad to hear it. Now get back to bed, and don't let Mamm catch you sneaking back into the house."

With another whoop—which made her feel as though she'd made the wrong choice just then, they were way too happy about avoiding trouble with their mater—they ran off toward the house.

Joy took one step to follow, only Joshua suddenly took her by the arm and swung her around, wrapping his arms around her and hugging her tight. He didn't say anything for the longest time . . . just stood there holding her.

"Joshua?" she asked softly.

"Just give me a second to put my heart back in the right place," he said in a gruff voice into her hair. "It tried to jump right out of my chest."

With a huff of a laugh, she hugged him back. "I don't mind admitting I was scared to death."

"Me too," he said, pulling back to stare down into her face, his gaze tracing over her features as though memorizing every curve and plain. "I've never felt so helpless in my life. We should definitely pray that our kinder are more like me."

At that bit of nonsense, she smacked him on the arm, even as the thought of their children sent a swarm of butterflies to nest in her stomach. He thought about their kinder?

"I think, between the two of us, we're in for quite an adventure," she said.

"Jah," he agreed, taking her hand and tugging her back through the woods. "I hope my heart can take it."

Chapter Fifteen

JOSHUA'S HEART WAS not in his work today or, for that matter, most days lately. He was supposed to be arranging a whole new kitchen display. Mamm was trying to feature a new set of cast-iron skillets and casserole dishes along with fall-related canned goods, recipes, and whatnot. Not particularly his area of expertise, but better than what Hope was doing with a section of autumn-themed decorations for the Englischers—those too fancy for Plain folk.

He knew exactly who was to blame for his wandering mind, too.

Joy Yoder soon-to-be Kanagy.

She had almost died in that dumm tree haus, and he'd never been so relieved to see her with both feet on the ground. When he closed his eyes at night, he could still picture her balanced precariously above his head, leaning away from the safety of the tree with her head inside the bottom of the fort. He also pictured her in a heap of broken limbs and blood and shattered wood.

It had been so close. So horribly close. If Samuel had been harder to persuade to come down, or the boys had moved in the wrong way . . . he could have lost her.

But given her behavior since, a bigger worry was starting to present itself . . .

A loud, put-upon sigh sounded from behind Joshua. "What have I taught you all your life?" Ruth Kanagy said from behind him.

Joshua paused and tilted his head to study his efforts with the display, but it all looked fine to him. Though, granted, he wasn't exactly focused.

After the bishop had announced his and Joy's upcoming marriage in church Sunday, all he could think about was that and her and how he couldn't lose her.

Of course, both their mothers had now flown into a bustle of activity getting everything ready in time. Joy seemed even busier . . . not just helping them, but spending time with Mary, parading the girl in front of Leroy every chance she got, and also working on the quilts. She was always working on one or another.

Almost as though she were avoiding him, which was his new, bigger source of concern. Because why would she do that? Or was he being . . . sensitive? That wasn't like him.

"Joshua?" Mamm prompted, pulling him back to her question.

He frowned, trying to figure out what his mother was picking on with the display. "Um . . ." He had nothing.

"Put the smaller, pretty items up top—"

"And the big, bulky items at the bottom," he finished for her. He pointed a finger at the items. "I know, Mamm, but you said you wanted to feature the skillets. I can't feature them at the bottom."

"You only need *one* to display, silly," she pointed out.

He had put them all together on the largest shelf, stacked up neatly. "Ach vell, I guess so."

Mamm put a hand on his shoulder. "I know you have important things on your mind with this wedding, but we need you here working. At least for another ten days."

"Jah. Sorry."

She squeezed his shoulder, then left him to it. With a grumble he kept mostly to himself, Joshua started unstacking the heavy skillets from the display, setting them aside. The bell over the door jangled, and both he and Hope turned to greet the new customer.

"Joy?" he asked.

She hadn't told him she'd be coming by today. Standing before the sun-filled windows at the front of the shop in a pretty green dress, she had concerning dark circles lingering under her eyes, the sight hitting him like he'd fallen off a roof. Was that from working too hard or from worrying too much?

Even so, she about took his breath away, and that was when it hit him.

Somewhere along the way of protecting her and being drawn into her good deeds and everything else, he'd fallen in love with Joy Yoder.

I'm in love with the girl I'm going to marry.

Head over heels with it. Giddy with it even. Only of course he was. He never would have agreed to marrying her if there hadn't already been a deeper connection there. No wonder Katie had disappointed him when he'd tried to start something with her . . . Katie could never be Joy. How could he not have realized sooner?

Warmth burrowed into his chest in the region of his heart and spread out from there. A sheer, breath-stealing kind of happiness that wanted to burst out of him. But as fast as the sensation filled him up, it drained right out again.

Because Joy wasn't in love with him. She'd asked him for a partnership based on friendship and mutual liking, not a love match.

Ach du lieva. What do I do now?

With a smile that appeared forced to him—after all, he'd had the scales stripped from his eyes now, and could finally truly see her—she made her way over. "I finished another one of the quilts I owe your mamm," she said, holding up a bright red, white, and green one, which he'd seen her working on every day for the last little while.

"Oh, wunderbaar," Mamm exclaimed from behind him. "I had hoped you'd finish soon. The customer called this morning to say she'd found a similar one to the one she'd commissioned, and I assured her this would be done soon. She'll want the final one quickly, too."

Ruth wasn't looking at Joy as she said this, but at the quilt, so she didn't catch the way Joy flinched. Joshua didn't miss it.

"What does 'quickly' mean, Mamm?" he asked.

But Joy shook her head at him. "The last one you said all she cared about was that it be mostly white. I can do an easier pattern," she assured. "I should be able to finish it before the wedding."

"Are you sure?" Mamm asked.

Joy offered her best sunny face, bouncing lightly on her toes. "For sure and certain."

Only Joshua didn't like it. "With all the wedding preparations—"

He was waved off. "Mamm and Ruth have those well in hand. I practically have nothing to do."

Not true. She was constantly cleaning and cooking at her mater's direction. Why was she ignoring this?

His mother, oblivious, beamed and apparently took

Joy's comments at face value. Could she not see how tired Joy was? She was obviously working late into the night. As her future husband, he should be seeing to her health.

His mother wandered off to the back of the store, probably to call the customer, and Hope turned her back on them with a smile that said she was giving them what privacy she could. Except Joy didn't love him. She cared for him, but there was a difference. No need for privacy with their arrangement.

One he was suddenly questioning himself on. Could he marry her knowing he loved her more than she did him? Was that fair to either of them? Or should he trust that love would come for her in time?

She turned her big brown eyes his way. "I . . . I promised Mary I'd help her with her booth at the market today," she said. "Her sisters were busy."

Before Joshua could even glance at the clock, his mamm called out from the back room. "If you can wait long enough for Joshua to finish that display, he could go with you."

He tried not to startle. "I can?" he asked back with a glance at the clock over the register.

Hadn't Mamm just been saying they needed him working and focused in the shop? Besides, Mamm never let them go early like that, and with Dat not here for the day because he was one town over checking on an upcoming delivery, and Daniel at home for chores, that would leave only Mamm and Hope in the shop.

She popped her head out from behind the curtain. "Ach jah. It's been slow today and . . ." She paused, her gaze suddenly turning pointed, and the point was directed at him. "You two should enjoy the lovely weather."

In other words, he'd been useless around the shop and

she was getting him out of her hair with the excuse of giving him time with his fiancée. He had no doubt that was what she'd intended to say before rewording to spare Joy the knowledge that her future husband could be less than helpful.

Joshua shot his mother a cheeky grin and got a *tsk* in response, even as she chuckled.

"Ach vell, if I have to wait, why don't I help you with the display," Joy said. "I have to learn anyway."

"Better to learn from Hope," Mamm teased before disappearing back behind the curtain again.

Joy raised her eyebrows at him, tired eyes full of sudden laughter and warmth, the way they usually were, though not as much lately. "What did you do to your mater?" she whispered.

"Nothing," he whispered back. "I'm an angel and the perfect son."

Her delicate snort indicated a lack of faith in that statement, but that only made him grin. Joy chuckled as they turned together to face the display he'd been working on. He explained quickly about the kitchen and fall theme and how he was going to put one—and only one—skillet on the eye-level part of the display case but stack the others at the bottom.

Tipping her head to the side, she studied the space. "Why don't we set the skillet on its side against the backing of the shelf?" she asked and proceeded to do so. "That way it's more visible and also leaves more room to put other smaller things in front of it. Jah?"

"I can already tell I'm going to enjoy working with you, Joy," Hope commented from across the room. "We're going to have a lot of fun together."

Which earned her a grin from Joy, and a grumble from Joshua.

The setup for the display went remarkably quickly after that, the two of them working together in easy harmony, as they always did, until they were all done.

"What do you think, Hope?" Joy asked, stepping back, with her hands on her hips to assess their handiwork.

"Hope?" he challenged. "Why aren't you asking me?"

"Because you were part of the creative process," she teased. "We need an outside opinion."

Chuckling, Hope crossed the room and angled her head to view the display one way then the other. "It looks wunderbaar," she finally said. "Eye catching, but easy to access."

Joy shot him a triumphant glance.

"Joy Yoder, *what* do you think you're doing?" Anna Yoder's voice rang out with all the force of an angry hoof strike to a stall door.

Beside him, Joy jumped. Joshua almost did, too. He hadn't even heard the ring of the bell, let alone the door opening to let her mater in.

"You'd best not be working," Anna said, eyes flinty and mouth pinched. "Because you promised me that you would wait until after you married."

"I'm not, Mamm," Joy assured her, eyes round.

"It looks like work to me, organizing the shelf." Anna flicked an accusing hand at the display.

Joy tried again. "But Ruth said—"

"*Ruth* is not your mater," Anna cut her off.

"She wasn't working," Joshua stepped in, or tried to. Only Joy put her hand on his arm, giving him a warning squeeze followed by a tiny shake of her head.

Hating to have to leave her on her own, he still did as she wished, clamping his mouth shut.

"Mamm," Joy said in a voice gone unusually quiet. He'd heard her do that once or twice with her mother. The same way he spoke to a spooked horse, actually. "Ruth said if Joshua finished this display, he could go to the market with me to help Mary. So I was helping him get done faster."

Anna crossed her arms, toe tapping as she considered this. "I see. Are you done here?" She waved at the display again, only softer this time.

"Jah." Joy tugged on his sleeve the way she used to as a little girl. "Kumme, Joshua."

They hurriedly exited the shop together out the front and headed down the covered walkway that lined the main street shops of town, moving in the direction of the vacant parking lot where the market was always set up.

Joy, for once, was quiet, all of her usual chatter hidden behind her thoughts.

"She's not mad," he felt he needed to point out.

She blinked. "I know. I just . . ." She bit her lip in a way that he recognized as a worry over one of her schemes.

"Just what?" he asked in a firmer voice.

She inhaled then it all came rushing out. "Mamm doesn't know about the quilting I'm doing for the shop. I didn't want to have to tell your mother I couldn't do it. After all, I plan to make many more quilts for the shop after we're married. This set was a special order, and I did it not for the money but to be a help to your mamm. So mostly it's not working . . . But . . . Mamm doesn't know. What if your mamm tells her about it, or if she sees the quilt?"

Joshua absorbed all this in silence, giving himself a moment to sort through all the words and what they actually meant.

"Oh, Joy." He groaned.

But that only pulled her to a frowning stop, hands flying to her hips. "Don't you start with me, too, Joshua Kanagy."

"You should have been honest with both my mater and yours," he pointed out.

"Do you think I don't already know that? I've already been working on these quilts at night in my room, or when she's not around, so she doesn't ask what they're for." She tugged at one of her kapp strings. "I only have one last quilt to do, and we're almost married. It'll be fine."

"As long as she doesn't find out before then."

"I can't let your mamm down," she pointed out.

"You should have thought of that before you agreed."

Disappointment darkened her eyes, dulling the color to the muted brown of fallen leaves already turned crunchy. "I'm not telling you so you can berate me for something I already know," she said, quietly again, the same way she'd spoken to her mamm.

"Then why are you telling me? So I can fix it?"

"Nae."

"I could talk to Mamm and see if the customer will extend the deadline."

"That's not why—"

"Or help you confess to your mater and see what she suggests."

"Joshua." The snap in Joy's voice was a sound he rarely heard from her. Usually, even a small annoyance was tempered by a shake of laughter.

"What?"

"All I wanted from you was a hug or a pat on the arm."

"Oh." That disappointment was still there, but he realized now it was with him, not herself, and that clenched inside him.

"You don't have to fix *everything*," she said. "I'm not . . . broken."

"I never said you were," he insisted.

She huffed a laugh, but humorless. "You didn't have to," she murmured quietly. Then started them on down the sidewalk.

"What is that supposed to mean?" he asked as he hurried to catch up.

"It means . . ." She paused and took a breath. "It . . ." Another breath and a shake of her head this time. "Ach vell . . . I think it means I'm tired and grumpy," she finally said.

That clenching inside him didn't ease. Hadn't he noticed how tired she was? "Then you should go home and rest. I can help Mary."

"Nae." She shot him a smile. A real one finally, though her eyes were still heavy. "It won't be for long, and I promised."

More promises. Once they were married, he'd have to keep an eye on all her promises to others, or he'd have a wife too tired to raise their kinder.

Still caught up in his thoughts, he kept going while Joy's steps slowed. As soon as he noticed, he did a double take and stopped to discover her standing still, gaze fixed on a spot down the street. He turned his head in that direction to find Katie Jones standing next to a lopsided buggy.

"That's too bad," Joy murmured. "Let's see if she needs help."

Katie had her back to them as they approached, watching in the other direction.

"Do you need help, Katie?" Joy asked, and the other girl swung around on a gasp.

Katie's gaze slid from Joy to Joshua, and her cheeks

turned red. She hemmed and hawed for a second. "I . . . That's so kind, of course, but . . ." She tossed a glance over her shoulder. "I'm sure . . . errr . . . help will be along in a second."

Joshua crossed his arms, certain now of what was actually going on—she was waiting for a particular man to come by so she could get him to help her. She'd done the same thing to him after singeon a few months back. He'd been flattered at the time. Somebody needed to tell Katie's mater that she pulled tricks like these to snare unsuspecting men.

JOY KEPT A surreptitious eye on Joshua and his reaction. He'd assured her he'd had no other girl in mind, but he was being unusually quiet, not acting like himself.

I should give them a chance to talk.

If they worked things out, then that was Gotte's will. Her heart wobbled at the thought, giving a protesting thump. One Joy ignored. After all, she wanted Joshua to be heart whole when he married her. It would pain her to know that she'd hurt him in any way, and it often took men a knock in the head to figure out what was going on with their hearts.

Her own heart aching something fierce, she pushed through the pain and the sudden pile of rocks in her stomach and did the most selfless thing she'd ever done. "Joshua . . . why don't you drive Katie home so that her family can figure out the buggy."

His head swung sharply her way.

"That's really not needed," Katie insisted before he could open his mouth.

Disappointment and relief turned into a confusing tangle of thorns inside her. Because she really didn't want to send them off alone together. Except how selfish could she be? This was for Joshua's happiness. That meant more to her than her own needs.

"So you have someone coming?" Joy asked slowly.

"Oh . . . errr . . ." Katie shrugged.

What was that supposed to mean? "Ach vell, we'll wait with you until they get here." she offered instead. Then, deliberately, she wrinkled her nose. "Although I promised Mary I'd help with her booth." She turned to Joshua. "Can you wait with Katie?"

The small lines that formed between his brows could have been anything, but the intent way he searched her face had Joy pinning what she hoped was a carefree, helpful expression to her face. He studied her a moment longer, then almost seemed to sigh, though he made no sound, and lifted his gaze over her head to Katie. "I'm happy to either wait here with you," he said, "or take you home. What would you prefer?"

Joy turned to find Katie staring back at Joshua, her expression almost embarrassed, but of course she'd be emotional over this chance to set things right before it was too late.

Katie nodded, though the movement was reluctant. Maybe she was playing hard to get, making him work for it? That sounded like a silly thing to do to Joy. If she was Katie, she'd probably throw herself into Joshua's arms and beg for a second chance.

"Denki, Joshua," Katie said softly. "That would be . . . helpful."

"Wunderbaar," Joy sang out, internally wincing at how extra chipper she sounded. "I'll leave you to it. Mary must be wondering where I am."

Before either Katie or Joshua could comment, she hurried off down the walkway and into the maze of booths at the market, her heart cracking more with every single step.

She'd done it.

She'd given Joshua a final chance to choose his heart over his head. This afternoon when she got home, would she be learning her own wedding was now off? Joy refused to think about that, mostly because she suspected she'd break down crying right here in the middle of town if she did.

She rounded a corner and slowed at the sight of Leroy Miller standing in front of the quilting booth talking to a glowing Mary. Deliberately, Joy stepped into the nearest booth to hide—one operated by an Englischer selling premade sheds. Only she didn't see anyone else in the booth, so she stuck her head back out to watch right in time to see Leroy laugh at something Mary had said. Not a polite chuckle either, but a satisfying belly laugh, and Mary's cheeks turned pink with pleasure.

Joy sighed, her own happiness for them a salve to the sting of leaving Joshua and Katie alone together. At least one thing had come of this entire marriage business . . . Leroy and Mary seemed to be connecting. If Joshua broke off the wedding, Mamm would simply have to pick someone other than the bishop's son for Joy.

With a wave, Leroy left, heading the opposite way from where Joy was hiding.

"Can I interest you in a shed to store all your gardening tools?" a gravelly voice said behind her.

She jumped and turned to find the booth owner standing there. An older gentleman with gray hair and a thick beard. Not like Amish married men, who wore their beards around the outside lines of their jaws, shaving clean the area where a mustache would go. His filled up his entire face, putting her in mind of the Englischers' Santa Claus at Christmas. Right down to the jolly twinkle in his blue eyes.

"Um . . . No, denki. I was just waiting for . . ."

Oh, help.

No way could she explain why she was standing here. She shook her head with a laugh and decided to be truthful. "I was giving my friend a second alone with the man she likes," she explained.

"I see." He chuckled, thankfully finding that amusing rather than annoying. "That makes you a very nice friend."

Joy lowered her gaze automatically, not wanting to be prideful. "Ach vell, he's gone now. Gute dag to you."

"You too," he called after her.

As soon as Mary sighted Joy hurrying over, a smile lit up her entire face. "Joy. Ach du lieva, you'll never guess what happened."

Trying to hide her own smile, Joy joined her in the booth. "What?"

"Leroy Miller stopped by. Just to speak with me." Mary gave a contented hum, bliss written all over her face.

"I am so happy for you!" Joy said, and spontaneously hugged her friend. Usually Amish didn't show affection in public, reserving such things for the privacy of their own homes, but Joy couldn't help herself. At least one of them was happy. "Maybe he'll ask to drive you home Sunday night."

Mary's eyes sparkled. "You think so?"

At the pace Leroy moved, maybe not. Maybe she shouldn't get Mary's hopes up like that. "I hope so. You are welcome to get a ride there with Joshua and me, just in case."

It would be their last singeon. After that they'd be married and starting a life together. That was, if Joshua was still marrying her and not Katie by then. Hope shoved down the growing ball of worry that was threatening to drag her into a lonely pit. She was doing the right thing.

Mary scrunched up her face. "I don't know. Leroy is wonderful shy; it might take longer for him to work up the courage."

Then she chuckled, seemingly unworried about this fact. The change in Joy's friend was visible. In a few short weeks, Mary had truly come out of her shell, her confidence growing. Normally that would make Joy's world so happy, the birds practically bursting into song around her, but her worries were silencing the birds.

"Besides," Mary continued, "I wouldn't want to play gooseberry."

To Joy's and Joshua's supposed romance, Mary meant. Only they didn't have a romance. That ball was dragging Joy lower by the second, that pit yawning beneath her feet.

"We'll have plenty of time to be alone after the wedding," she said with a wave of her hand. "Think about it and let me know, jah?"

"Jah. And denki, Joy," Mary said, laying a hand on her arm. "You've been a true friend."

She placed her hand over Mary's and squeezed. "It's easy to be a friend to someone with such a sweet heart. I hope everything works out for you. For sure and certain."

For her, too, although she still wasn't sure what that looked like. Because she didn't want it to work out for her if that meant Joshua's heart was broken. But if his heart went elsewhere, she was scared hers might shatter.

I should ask him if it's Katie. Because last time she'd been a coward and only asked about "someone." He'd held something back that night. Joy could tell he had.

Why was she acting like such a child? After all, if they married, they needed to be open and honest with each other. She straightened at the thought. If nothing happened with Katie today, she'd still ask him, to be certain. Only this time, she'd get the full truth, even if it hurt.

Not that the decision made her feel better, but at least, in the end, she'd know.

Chapter Sixteen

JOSHUA PULLED THE buggy into the open yard in front of the Hershbergers' house. Mary was already waiting outside for them, and he got out to help her in. He'd been looking forward to time alone with Joy but understood why she'd offered the other girl a ride. Hopefully they'd be alone on the way home.

"I should have driven myself," Mary said after greeting Joy and settling in her seat.

The tone in Mary's voice wasn't quite right. That was not a polite platitude. Joy turned in her seat, and he would have, too, if he hadn't been driving, though Frank was old and trained enough for Joshua not to have to focus as hard with him.

"What do you mean?" Joy asked.

In the pause that followed, Joshua could practically feel the glance that landed on the back of his head. "Leroy isn't interested in me," Mary said quietly, with a decided wobble to her voice.

Oh, sis yucht. Joshua suddenly had a sickening feeling he knew what was coming next.

Beside him Joy stiffened. "What makes you say that?"

"Because he was seen driving Katie Jones through town." Mary's voice had turned into a wail by now.

"Driving Katie—" Joy cut herself off and turned slowly in her seat to face Joshua. "What happened?"

Before he could answer, she turned back to Mary. "Katie's buggy had broken down in town and *Joshua* was supposed to take her home," she explained in a rush.

"Oh?" Mary's voice was still watery and now warily confused.

Joy turned back to him in an abrupt swing. Joshua flicked her a glance from the corner of his eye and tried not to shift in his seat at the accusation scrunching up her face. He'd done nothing wrong.

"Leroy happened along in his buggy shortly after you left," he offered. "Since he was already headed that way, and it would have taken me longer to get Frank hitched up, it made more sense for him to take her."

The hole of silence beside him didn't bode well. Joy only didn't talk when she was too upset to get out the words. He turned his head to find her glaring at him—a glower as dark as a spring thunderstorm, which was maybe the first time in his life that Joy had ever looked at him in such a way.

He didn't like it. "He offered. She was happy to have his help."

But even he winced at the last part. Katie had been almost too quick to accept Leroy's offer. If anything, she'd fished for it and Joshua had been blind to it. Deliberately so, he realized, since he hadn't wanted to drive her in the first place.

But . . . had Leroy been who Katie was waiting on? Come to think on it, Katie could bake just fine. Had Leroy been the reason she'd wanted to join Joy and Mary's little weekly get-togethers?

Oh, sis yucht, he thought again.

The trouble was, he already knew what Katie was like. If it had been only him and Joy in the buggy, he'd have even told her, though he'd been reluctant last time the girl's name had come up with Joy. However, speaking ill of a person who wasn't there to defend herself in front of more than Joy was something he wouldn't do. He'd been raised better than that.

"Of course Leroy would be happy to help Katie," Mary said, so quietly he barely caught the words. "He is wonderful considerate, and she's one of the prettiest and kindest girls in the area and does everything so well."

Joshua had to hold in a derisive snort. He'd thought so, too, once. But then he'd spent a little time with her and discovered Katie knew she was considered perfect. More than that, she had trouble believing him when he said he wasn't interested. He'd learned that the hard way.

"She can bake wonderful gute, too," Mary continued, sounding so forlorn, Joshua winced.

"So can you now," Joy insisted.

Mary was quiet a moment. Then, "Leroy might like her for her."

At an elbow from Joy, Joshua cleared his throat. "I'm sure Leroy was only being helpful. He didn't act all that excited about having to drop her off. Something about his mamm and being back in time for lunch."

"Beatrice Miller does like to do things right on time," Mary murmured.

She did? Joshua couldn't say he'd noticed one way or another.

"Katie can also . . ." How did he put this without sounding judgmental or speaking out of turn? "Katie is a little boy crazy," he settled on.

Beside him Joy coughed, or it might have been a disguised laugh. Except a glance showed her frowning still, so probably not.

Did she not believe him? He hadn't said anything about Katie specifically when Joy had asked if he'd had his eye on another girl. Maybe it had gotten back to Joy that he'd driven Katie home that one night? Or that she'd been around him a lot lately. Only that hadn't been *all* his doing.

After one moment of showing his initial interest in her, she'd become the one who pursued him. It had started innocently enough. Playing on his team for a game of volleyball. Greeting him with a smile at church on Sunday. Saying hello when she popped into the store. She'd moved on to doing small things, like making his "favorite dessert" just for him at a frolic. Though the seeming kindness had set an odd pit of concern in the center of his gut, he'd thanked her reluctantly.

But then she'd turned into a . . . pest, for lack of a kinder word.

Katie had started coming around the store more. When she couldn't come inside because she'd already been there, she'd linger outside, hiding and giggling as though he couldn't see her. She showed up at his home on the excuse that her mamm had sent her for a jar of Daniel's honey, which could have been true. Except the next time, she'd come to talk to Aaron about commissioning a piece of furniture, then laughed at her own silliness that she'd forgotten he'd moved into his own home with Hope, or that he now worked at the Troyers' store and she could have gone into town to talk to him there during working hours.

She'd even pulled the same "my buggy broke" stunt at singeon one night, getting Joshua to drive her home in his buggy instead. When he had refused to come into her house, she'd gotten angry, accusing him of leading her on. To his astonishment, she'd also proceed to "break up" with him, which was interesting since they'd never dated.

The difference between Katie and Joy suddenly struck him. On the surface, before all this, he would have picked Katie, who presented herself as quiet, humble, and sweet. But Joy would never have done any of the things Katie had. Never pushed herself on someone clearly not interested. If anything, she would hate to think she was a bother or wasn't wanted.

So after all that with Katie . . . maybe he'd been more than happy to foist her off on Leroy when he'd happened by. Except apparently, that had been the wrong thing to do. Apparently, she'd set her sights on Leroy. Hopefully he would be smart enough not to encourage her either.

"The boys all seem to like Katie," Joy commented slowly. Then glanced back at Mary and hurried to add, "Only I'm positive Leroy is *not* interested."

Joshua would have agreed, if only to set Mary's heart at rest, but he wasn't certain that was the truth. Leroy was extremely private. He didn't show his emotions much. He was also hopeless when it came to women.

He'd messed up big, letting Leroy take Katie home.

"Besides," Joy added slowly. "I thought Katie had her heart set on . . . someone else."

Why did those words, which were directed to Mary over the back of the seat, sound as though they were more significant than just that? Joy better not think that meant him.

"Why not wait until we get to singeon and see how they are together?" Joy suggested next.

Joshua grimaced. Given the way Katie had single-mindedly pursued him, if she'd decided Leroy was the man for her, to the outside looking in, it might appear as though Leroy was interested back. After all, he wasn't likely to make a scene or reject her publicly, and Katie could be . . . tenacious.

"I guess so," Mary murmured.

"You made his favorite dessert," Joy said. "He'll appreciate that, for sure and certain."

Joshua tried not to grin. Leroy didn't strike him as the observant type, and given how his mamm pushed him to do whatever she felt was best, he might be susceptible to someone like Katie, versus Mary, who wouldn't say boo to a ghost. Though a girl like Mary would probably blend better with Leroy's mamm and family life.

Sending a little prayer to Gotte that tonight didn't end in disaster, Joshua turned Frank's head down the Millers' drive—no relation to Leroy, lots of Millers lived in northern Indiana Amish communities—and hoped hard that Mary got her wish. She was a nice girl; she deserved to be happy.

What's more, Joy was invested in their growing friendship, and she would be equally as unhappy as Mary if this didn't work out. Joshua wanted his future wife's happiness with a growing intensity that almost surprised him. Love was a funny thing.

Which was why he'd wanted to be alone with her tonight. Yet another reason to hope Leroy had the sense to ask Mary to ride home with him.

Maybe someone else needed to play interference with

Katie. He grimaced as he realized that someone might have to be him.

PRACTICALLY DRAGGING MARY along beside her, Joy followed in Joshua's wake. He'd kindly taken Joy's plates of goodies and was leading them over to the table where refreshments were being set up.

"Is Leroy here?" Mary asked. "I can't look."

Joy cast a furtive glance around the yard. The evening was so lovely, the Millers had apparently decided to host the event in the front yard, which was already crowded with die Youngie. Suddenly, she spotted Leroy at the best place possible.

"He's at the table with the food."

Mary's grip on her tightened almost painfully, but she didn't say anything. In fact, she kept moving when Joy almost expected her to stop in her tracks. Not only that, but Mary walked right up to the table, across from Leroy. Her smile might have been stiffly determined, but she *did* smile. "Wie gehts, Leroy," she greeted him.

A soft color tinted Mary's cheeks, probably at her own boldness, and Joy quietly tried to scoot away to give them a little privacy.

"Where do you want this?" Joshua asked, holding up her own dish. He spoke overloudly, probably thinking the same thing about giving them room.

"Oh, over here, I think?" she said, taking the opportunity to move closer to him and get them both farther down the table.

Leroy meanwhile lifted his gaze from the goodies and blinked at Mary through his glasses, but Joy thought a pleased light lingered about his eyes. "Gute, denki."

Mary held up the pie she'd made from scratch that day. "I made a schnitzboi pie . . . with Joy's help, of course."

"That's my favorite." Surprise tinted Leroy's words.

"I know," Mary said. "I—"

Katie's distinctive laugh cut her off. "What a coincidence," the other girl said as she sidled up next to Leroy, across the table from Mary. "I made the *same* kind of pie."

Joy had never once in her life before now contemplated so much as a mean word. Not just because that was the Amish way, but it went against her nature. But right then, she could have happily done something like trip Katie Jones. The other girl had *known* that's what Mary was going to make. She'd been part of the discussion, and now she'd set herself up as the superior baker.

Mary's small bout of confidence visibly dissolved like stomach tonic tabs in water.

"I'm sure both pies are wunderbaar," Leroy assured the girls, his expression an almost comical mix of panic and wonder. After all . . . when had he ever been the center of attention for two women? At the same time yet. Joy would've laughed if she still wasn't hopping mad.

"Katie." Joshua suddenly rounded the table. "I was about to go play volleyball. Do you want to be on my team?"

What was this now?

Even Katie couldn't hide her surprise, staring at Joshua with her mouth open for a long second before sliding a sidelong glance in Joy's direction. A smug glance that did nothing to calm Joy's ire.

Joy forced her stiff face into a semblance of being carefree because her only options were either a forced smile or an extremely mean stream of words. Not for Joshua, but for Katie. Despite all her doubts and questions surrounding him and the other girl, she had a feeling she knew why he was offering this now. He'd decided to keep Katie away from Leroy.

For that alone, despite the ugly swell of jealousy—she gave the slimy feeling a name—she could have cheerfully thrown her arms around his neck and hugged him.

"You know I love to play volleyball," Katie cooed at Joshua. Then turned to Leroy. "Do you want to join us?"

"Uh—" Leroy glanced around, pale blue eyes panicked, as though wishing he were anywhere else but right there. Everyone knew Leroy wasn't . . . coordinated. Yet another reason Mamm's plan to have him help with horses wasn't exactly the most well thought out. She must have been that desperate to get Dat out of the barn to save his hands.

And Joy hadn't known of his affliction at all. What kind of dochder did that make her?

"I promised Micah I'd help him with . . . errr . . . something," Leroy finally mumbled, and suited action to words, walking quickly away.

At least he wasn't with Katie. Still, the slump to Mary's shoulders was difficult to witness.

Even harder was watching Joshua lead Katie away to the game. He didn't bother to ask if Joy wanted to join in, not that she would have wanted to. Suddenly, her last singeon before they were married on Thursday and started a new life together wasn't nearly as fun as she'd imagined it might be.

Glancing around, she searched for a distraction. "I haven't talked to Sarah and Rachel Price in forever," she chirped to Mary, trying her best to appear upbeat. "Do you want to come with me?"

Mary glanced after Leroy, then drew back her shoulders, as though determined to push forward. "Jah. I like them."

Sarah and Rachel were sisters, and close friends of Hope Kanagy's in particular. As soon as Joy stepped near, Sarah lit up. "There's the new bride," she called. "Thursday yet, isn't it?" With a smile, she reached out a hand and tugged both Joy and Mary into their circle. "Tell me all about it. Are you all ready for the big day? I know Hope was honored to be asked to stand up with you."

"Mary is as well," Joy said, her cheeks already starting to hurt from the forced smiling.

"That's right," Sarah said, then gave a dreamy hum. "I wish I was marrying a man as handsome as Joshua Kanagy."

As handsome. As thoughtful. As strong. As kind. That pit in her stomach, the one whispering how she wasn't good enough for him, that he deserved more, gnawed a bigger hole.

"Sarah!" Rachel admonished in a shocked voice only to have her sister laugh at her.

"You said the same thing to Hope right before she and Aaron started courting."

Rachel shook her head, but a chuckle still escaped. "Maybe I've matured," she ventured.

Matured.

Which was what Joy was supposed to be now. Married, and with a job yet, one day soon with a family of her own to tend to. Only had she truly put aside all things childish? She was still as impulsive as ever, even if kindly meant. She still got herself in trouble, she'd thought less lately, but in the last few weeks she'd torn her dress and had to sneak into her house, worked all hours of the night on those quilts, had to rescue her bruders from that tree haus, and now Joshua was spending time with Katie because of the Leroy and Mary plan.

Maybe she wasn't as grown up as she'd wanted to believe. Maybe Joshua was right, and he'd always be having to save her.

Her gaze slid unerringly to where he was playing volleyball. Only he was laughing at whatever Katie was saying. Katie laughed back, the sound echoing across the yard, making Joy want to scowl.

With a jerk, she dragged her gaze away.

"What color did you pick for the dresses?" Rachel asked, forcing her to focus.

She explained about the yellow, pink, and green. While a few of the girls around them lifted their eyebrows—after all, the choice was slightly unconventional in their community—she was able to ignore them as Sarah and Rachel gushed over how lovely they would look together.

"Oll recht, everyone," Ezra Miller called out in his booming voice. "Time to gather. Kumme, get yourselves a blanket if you didn't bring one."

A general air of organized chaos took over as all die Youngie found blankets and loaded up plates of food, before they searched out friends and a place to sit in the yard.

A warm hand grasped Joy's elbow. "I have a blanket for us," Joshua lowered his head to murmur in her ear.

She did her best to push away the bite of self-doubt still bothering her, but apparently it didn't come out in her smile because he frowned.

"Something wrong?" Joshua asked.

She shook her head, only his narrow-eyed gaze told her he wasn't convinced. Luckily this wasn't the place for him to pester her for more. A plate in hand for the both of them, she followed him to where everyone else was laying out their blankets on the ground. This could have been such a romantic night—the two of them sitting together cozily, singing in harmony with their friends and peers, maybe sharing a whispered conversation.

Instead, she waved at Mary. "Over here," she called.

She ignored the sharp look Joshua cast her direction.

Unfortunately, in the same instant, Leroy approached Mary, a blanket over his arm, and Katie popped up out of nowhere. Together, all three made their way to where Joy and Joshua were spreading out and Leroy fluffed out his blanket to overlap slightly with theirs.

Somehow, Joy found herself on the outside edge of the little group, with Katie right next to Joshua, Leroy on her other side, and Mary the farthest away on the other edge.

Oh, sis yucht.

Katie said something Joy couldn't catch to Leroy, but before he answered, Joshua turned to her—away from Joy. "I forgot how gute you were at volleyball, Katie," he said.

Sparking that laugh. "I practice with my bruders when the weather is nice," Katie said.

Joy shoved a deviled egg in her mouth and chewed it hard as she glared at Luke Raber's back. Not that he or his back had done anything to deserve it. But even if she was mostly sure of Joshua's motivations, Katie Jones was taking all the fun out of the night.

She crunched on one of Sarah's cookies next, trying to let it go.

Somebody started singing, and everyone joined in. They never had a leader or a moderator of what they sang or for how long. Naturally, they started with the familiar German hymns from church.

Except Joshua and Katie, who continued a murmured conversation, leaving Joy and the others out. She had to sit there and sing softly—not wanting to inflict her off-key ear on the prettier voices—all by herself.

Gotte encouraged his people to be slow to anger, and this was definitely a slow build, the confusing burn over so many different things that had flown out of her control. Irritation, an emotion she generally didn't bother with in her life, grew hotter and bigger inside her with each passing moment. The guilt of including Joshua in the irritation when he wasn't doing anything wrong—beyond being slightly rude to her just now—only made it worse. So did the jealousy.

Even when one of die Youngie started a round of her favorite Englisch gospel song—one so full of the joys of loving Gotte, she always had to sing it out loudly—she only grew quieter. Because through the irritation, sadness was creeping up on her.

She and Joshua needed to talk—about a lot of things. Tonight. Before she was too late.

Finally, they concluded the singing portion of the evening with a "Thank You" song for the host family, and she'd never been so happy to see the end of a Sunday evening get-together. Since they'd all eaten during it—getting up as needed to refill plates—the Millers didn't serve additional treats for afterward. No one left yet, though, gathering in groups to chat longer.

"Redd up," Joshua said to her, clearly expecting that she was ready to go.

Except Joy tried to subtly turn his attention in Mary's direction. Her friend was at the table gathering her pie tin and taking her time about it, casting furtive glances in Leroy's direction.

Only Leroy didn't go over and ask to drive her home. Instead, he walked off toward his buggy. Katie, who'd been lingering as well, scurried after him. Joy couldn't overhear what was said, but Leroy shook his head and Katie's expression turned mulish as he left her standing there without a ride as well.

"We'll give you a lift, Katie," Sarah Price called out.

Thank heavens. Because if Joshua had offered, Joy might have started wailing right here in the middle of the Millers' front yard. With a sigh, she waved Mary over and they piled into Joshua's buggy. The second he snapped the reins and Frank rolled them away, Mary burst into tears.

Joy bit her lip and turned around. "There's nothing to—"

Mary shook her head so hard, her kapp came unpinned, sticking up on her head all askew. "Don't," she said in a fierce little voice. "Please don't, Joy."

So, heart even heavier because she'd been focused on her own problems and not her friend's, Joy nodded and turned back around, hating the pit in her stomach. This was her fault. She'd helped lead to this. All she could do now was give Mary as much privacy as could be had in a shared buggy all the way back to her house, cringing with each snuffle and hiccup.

"I'll let her out," she said to Joshua when he pulled up outside Mary's house.

Jumping down, she opened the door on her side and walked Mary up to the steps. At the top Mary turned watery, swollen eyes her way. "I know you meant well," she said. "But I wish you had never got my hopes up where Leroy Miller is concerned. Let's . . . Can we not talk about him again?"

Joy opened her mouth to protest, to assure Mary that it would all work out, but she didn't know that. Not for sure. Slowly, she closed her mouth again. "I hope . . . you can forgive me."

Mary swallowed hard. "You wanted only my happiness. Nothing to forgive."

But she was wrong. Joy's impetuous need to jump in and fix things had ended up in hurt rather than the help she intended. Probably because the reason she'd helped in the first place was for her own selfish needs—to find Leroy a different job.

Mary went inside and Joy made her way slowly back to the buggy, where Joshua was waiting. His frown made the darkness even gloomier.

Now, for the tougher conversation.

Chapter Seventeen

JOSHUA TURNED FRANK'S head toward the Yoders' house and set the horse at a slow clip, not only to reflect the drag on his own mood, but because he needed to say something to Joy and was still trying to figure out how to word it. He inhaled, readying himself to speak, then paused, and repeated the action.

Only Joy beat him to it. "Were you in love with Katie before she broke it off?"

The words building stuttered to a halt in his throat. All except one. "Nae."

Joy's head went forward, dipping as though she was hiding her face from him. "But she's exactly what a gute Amish man would want, isn't she?"

She was what Joshua thought he wanted . . . until he learned better. Until Joy.

"I told you . . . no other girl is in my life. Definitely *not* Katie. Why would you ask that? Tonight was me helping you and Mary, you realize that?"

Except she didn't answer his question. "Leroy is not interested in Katie either. I just know it," she said in a tone that sounded as though she was trying to convince herself as much as him.

Either? But I never was. He let that go, seeing as she appeared to believe him about his own relationship with Katie, which he still had to tell her about. But he couldn't let her keep making Mary miserable.

"It's time to stay out of it, Joy." There was more of a snap in his voice than he'd intended, and she twitched her head around to stare at him.

Joshua cleared his throat, reaching for calm. But after an entire evening spoiled by having to distract Katie Jones and pretend any kind of interest in her when he was engaged to the woman beside him, whom he'd only recently figured out he was knee-deep in love with . . . he was not in the mood to make this easy. "You got poor Mary's hopes up and now look at her. If Leroy is supposed to be the man Gotte intended for her, it's up to him to make that move."

Joy made a derisive snort in her throat. "But Leroy moves like the tortoise—"

"And the tortoise gets to the finish line eventually, just as the hare does," he pointed out.

"You were perfectly happy for me to try to make this match when I started," she shot back. "What about your job with the horses?"

"Would you have gone ahead and done as you wished without me?"

He didn't need to look away from Frank's slowly bobbing head as the horse plodded along to know Joy was frowning at him.

"You are like Amos sometimes," Joshua pointed out. "Determined to build a fort in a tree because in your mind the benefit is so important, it blinds you to how dangerous it could be."

"I am *not* dangerous," she said on an outraged gasp.

Joshua clenched his teeth together. This was not going anywhere productive. Joy's back was up now, and she would only argue with everything he had to say. "Do you think Mary feels the same way? That poor girl is *heartbroken*."

"I already feel horrible about that," Joy said, suddenly quiet. "Berating me is not going to fix anything."

"Except maybe make you think twice about a scheme like this next time."

Silence greeted that. Not a contemplative silence, but a heavy one full of emotions on both sides. A silence that sat between them the rest of the ride home.

He directed Frank to pull the buggy down the Yoders' long drive, and still she didn't speak. Not until he'd brought them to a stop outside her front door. Setting the brake, he went to get out, only she swung sharply around to face him on the seat, her expression a mess of emotions.

"You realize that one of my 'schemes,' as you put it, is the reason you and I are getting married in the first place, don't you?"

"That's different."

"But it's not," she insisted. "If my plans and promises are always getting me into trouble, and dragging you into it, then why is our plan to marry going to end any differently?"

He stared at her. Trying to untie that logic was like picking out a badly knotted rope. "Because it's not just your plan," he said slowly. "It may have started out that way, but now we're doing it *together*."

Her intent expression descended into a scowl. What did he say to make her look that way?

"What?" she demanded. "So your involvement makes it okay? Fixes everything that would have gone wrong if this was just me?"

Everything inside Joshua, every single part of him, froze stone still. *There it was.*

The thing that had been prodding at the back of his mind since he'd agreed to her proposal. Why her wording it that way made the realization suddenly clear to him, he didn't know, but as though sunshine suddenly broke through night to illuminate the problem, he could see it.

Their marriage *was* another scheme.

Yes, one based on solid, well-intended reasons, but Joy always had reasons for doing the things she did. Her heart was always in the right place. On the surface, her idea to wed was like that. They both got so many things that they wanted, he hadn't been able to see the pitfalls, or maybe, because he loved her, he hadn't wanted to. But a big problem was right there, staring him in the face, if he'd only seen past his own selfish wants to recognize it.

Joy.

In the middle of helping them both, she'd lost sight of what could go wrong . . . what *she* was giving up. He had, too, convincing himself that they were making mature choices together.

Joshua clenched his jaw against the pain swelling around his heart, squeezing tight, because he knew what he needed to do now. Only, the fact that he'd fallen in love with her was going to make it a thousand times harder.

This was going to hurt.

Swallowing hard, he opened his mouth, only Joy dropped her gaze to her lap, where her hands were twisting together, a sure sign she was building up to something. "I wanted to marry you because I thought we'd work well together. That you wouldn't try to change me," she said. "That's what my mammi used to tell me. Find a man who would accept all my parts and that would be a solid basis for a happy marriage."

Joshua's world tilted a bit. She thought he didn't accept her?

"I *do* accept all your parts, Joy," he insisted.

Even with what he was about to do, especially because of that, he'd never want her to change. Even if he had to rescue her every day of his life, married or not, her schemes to help others were part of her, and he loved all of her.

"But you want me to . . . stop."

He shook his head, then shook it again. He was in an impossible position. Nothing he could say or do was going to end up well.

"I think . . ." Joy paused and took a long, shuddering breath, then lifted a gaze gone remote—almost coldly distant—to look him directly in the eyes. "I think we shouldn't get married."

He'd already decided to confess that he loved her and insist they marry only if she felt the same way—so that she didn't have to give up that dream. Despite the fact that he'd known her answer wouldn't be what he wanted, hearing those words from her about tore his heart out of his chest and threw it on the ground to be rolled over by the buggy wheels and trampled by Frank's hooves.

"Joy—" Only he shouldn't try to convince her otherwise.

He loved her, and love meant doing what was right for that person. Joy deserved that beautiful love like her grandparents had that she'd talked about her entire life. He could give her that, but she didn't feel the same, so it wasn't right. To her, he was a friend and a partner, but she didn't love him. Not in the way that mattered most . . . to them both.

"Don't say anything," she begged. "You are still the best friend I've ever had, always . . . watching out for me. I hope—" She had to stop to swallow, her voice choked as she started again. "I hope I haven't ruined our friendship with another . . . scheme."

An ache so deep it hurt everywhere wrapped itself around his heart, choking off his air and his thoughts and his voice.

Gotte help me let her go. Help me do the right thing.

Because with everything he was, Joshua wanted to reach out for her, kiss her lips again, and find that sense of peace they'd started all of this with. But it would be wrong, like keeping a butterfly in a jar so he could enjoy its beauty while at the same time depriving it of the delight of fluttering on the wind from flower to flower.

"Are you sure?" The words were out of his mouth before he could stop them.

Joy's eyes went wide, and an emotion flashed in those dark pools that he couldn't quite pin down. Disappointment didn't make sense, except maybe disappointment that they'd have to give up all the benefits that had come with marrying. "Jah," she said after a long pause. "I'm sure."

Breath punched from him. He ran a hand through his hair but nodded. "Oll recht," he said in a voice threatening to break. "I'll . . ." Oh, help. What did they do now? "I guess . . . I'll . . ."

Say something, he shouted at himself. He cleared his throat. "I'll speak with my parents tonight and the bishop tomorrow."

After a long moment where he couldn't bring himself to look at her, she finally said. "I'll tell my parents tonight, too."

Before he could say another word, or even get out to

walk her to the door, she was out of the buggy and inside her house. Joshua flinched at the soft snick of the door closing.

Shutting him right out of her life.

Heart trying to cut off his breathing, Joshua removed the brake and flicked the reins, sending Frank plodding their way home. To a life without Joy in it.

JOY WATCHED THROUGH the window as Joshua turned the buggy around and left, heading home. It was done. She'd done the right thing. Not because of Katie—she believed Joshua that he wasn't interested in the other girl specifically. Not because of Leroy and Mary, or even herself either. But for Joshua. They both deserved love in their marriage. He'd wanted a gute, quiet, traditional Amish girl, and that wasn't Joy.

Maybe I am finally making better choices.

Mary's tears had told her, more than anything else, that she needed to change her approach to helping others. Starting with Joshua.

Katie hadn't really been the problem tonight, not as far as worrying that Joshua had feelings for her. It was more that Joy had put him in that position of having to be the buffer. A position she'd put him in the rest of his life if they married. One he would clearly end up resenting.

That wasn't fair to him.

Swiping a hand over tears she hadn't even realized were falling, she spun away from the window and the sight of his taillights disappearing around the bend. Only to pull up short at the sight of her mamm sitting on the couch. She wasn't doing anything. Not knitting, sewing patches onto the boys' pants, reading . . . nothing.

Just staring at Joy with pinched lips, the skin around her eyes tight, a sure sign she was angry.

"Mamm?"

Ach nae . . . Her dat's hands. Joy's already broken heart shattered into a thousand pieces too small to ever put back together again. Joshua wouldn't take over now that she wouldn't be working in the shop. This would be terrible news for her family. How could she be so selfish? No matter what she did, she was hurting someone.

"We need to have a talk," Mamm said.

That pulled her up short. Uh-oh. The two other times her mother had started with that had been the time Joy had accidentally burned down a neighbor's shed and the time they learned the boys would be coming to live with them. One had turned out to be a blessing, but still . . . after what she'd just gone through, having to tell Mamm about calling off the wedding when she was about to "have a talk" was terrible timing.

"Sit down," Mamm said.

Trying to rein her emotions under control, Joy sat beside her mater on the couch. Mamm opened her mouth then paused and took a closer look at Joy's face. "You've been crying."

Oh, sis yucht. No use trying to deny it. "Jah, but I'll tell you after whatever you have to say."

Anna Yoder studied her face, frowning a bit as though coming to a realization. "As you wish . . . When were you going to tell me about the tree haus the boys built?"

Joy's mouth dropped open. Of all the things she might have guessed, that wasn't it. The quilts, the wedding, or something to do with Joshua maybe, or even Leroy and Mary, but the boys?

A shaft of fear split through her. “Are they hurt? They didn’t go back and try to rebuild it? Because they promised—”

“No.” Mamm shook her head. “But your dat needed the wood, and in confessing that they took it, they told us about the tree haus . . .” She side-eyed Joy, ire pressing her lips tight. “And what happened.”

“I’m sorry,” Joy said, too relieved her bruders were unharmed to worry about her own punishment. “Joshua and I talked to them about how dangerous it was and made them promise never to do anything like that again. I thought that was enough.”

Mamm was silent a long moment, as though turning that over in her head. “I saw the wreckage,” she said. “You saved them, Joy, even though you could have been hurt.”

Then she yanked Joy into her arms, settling her chin on the top of her head, and held her for the longest time.

“They’re my bruders,” Joy said into her mother’s shoulder.

Mamm pulled back to search Joy’s face. “But . . . If they are doing dangerous things, I need to know.” Her strong, steady mater, with her boundless energy and sharp gaze, suddenly appeared all of her almost sixty years, tired lines deepening around her eyes and shoulders sagging.

Spontaneously Joy reached out to squeeze her hand. “I won’t keep anything from you again. I promise.”

Still, Anna Yoder nodded her acceptance of that. “Though it probably won’t happen again. You will be gone in a few short days.”

Joy winced, her stomach turning over. *Dear Gotte. Help me to tell her this part.*

A thousand different ways to approach the topic flew through her mind, but what came out was a blurted . . . “We’ve called the wedding off.”

Saying the words out loud was so jarringly painful, Joy stared at her mother's shocked face for all of two seconds before her own face crumbled and the tears came in earnest. Only she couldn't stop them, like water surging past the banks of a river in a flood. Covering her face with her hands, she turned her back and sobbed. Her entire body clenched with the tumult of emotions.

But Anna Yoder was having none of that. Gentle hands on Joy's shoulders turned her back into her mater's arms, which wrapped around her tight, one hand flowing over Joy's back in comforting sweeps. "Get it all out," Mamm murmured soothingly.

And she did, crying into her mother's shoulder until she spent the emotions, her sobs turning into hiccupping, shuddering breaths. Finally, when she quieted, her mother set her upright and handed her a handkerchief.

Mopping up her face, she offered a waterlogged grimace. "Sorry," she said. "I don't know what came over me."

"Don't you?" Mamm searched her gaze.

Maybe she did, but she wasn't ready to face it. Not yet.

"Why don't you tell me what happened from the beginning," Mamm prompted when Joy said nothing.

Joy grimaced again, dropping her gaze, because to truly explain, she was going to have to confess to all of it. "You're going to be so mad at me," she whispered. "And . . . Dat's hands . . ."

After a beat of silence, her mother reached out and tucked an escaped strand of hair back under Joy's kapp, then she took one of Joy's hands between hers. "Let's not worry about either of those things for now. Jah?"

Joy lifted her head, taking in her mother's steady gaze. Then, haltingly at first, she confessed the lot. All of it—not wanting to marry Leroy, wanting to run a quilt shop, Joshua and the horses, marrying to solve all those problems, Katie Jones, quilting for Ruth at A Thankful Heart, the mess with Mary and Leroy, and finally tonight and calling it all off.

Through it all, Mamm held her hand and never once frowned or scolded or interrupted.

"So . . . that's why I can't marry Joshua," Joy said, winding down. "But Dat needs him, Mamm. He *needs* him. What should I do?"

Her Mamm was quiet so long, Joy worried at her lower lip with her teeth, waiting for what on earth Mamm might say, semi-expecting a punishment fit for the crimes. Finally, she spoke. "I think you've been punished enough," Anna Yoder said slowly. "I won't add to it, but I hope you've learned a lesson about that impetuous heart of yours?"

"For sure and certain."

Mamm tipped her head. "You said that the marriage was only because you are friends?"

"Jah." To start with at least.

"You don't feel more for him?"

"I—" Joy cut herself off, falling silent.

"Because it seems to me that a woman who cries as hard as you just have over ending it feels more than friendship."

Joy gulped as the one thing she knew, deep down, but hadn't been ready to admit even to herself until this second struck with all the subtlety of her bruders' tree haus coming down on top of her head. She loved Joshua. She always had. . . . always would.

Merciful heavens. What did I do?

"I love him, Mamm," she whispered. Her chin wobbled, face trying to crumple again under the onslaught of emotions, but she sucked in and got it under control. "Like Mammi and Dawdi. I always have and that makes it all worse."

"Worse?"

"Don't you see? I wasn't trying to follow Gotte's will, or be helpful, I was being selfish."

Mamm patted her hand. "And Joshua? Have you asked him how he feels?"

Joy shook her head. "No. I'm only his friend."

"And you are certain of that? He told you so?"

"Nae, he didn't say so. He didn't have to. If he loved me, he wouldn't have let me break off the wedding."

"Hmmm . . ." Mamm's expression remained unsure, but Joy was positive. "Maybe tomorrow you should ask him?"

Joy hopped to her feet, agitation driving her up. "If he found out I'm in love with him, it would ruin our friendship even more than I already have," she insisted, her hand slashing through the air. "He'd be horrified. I . . . I can't risk that."

"Okay," Mamm said. Then patted the seat beside her. "What do you want to do?"

"Do?" What else was there to do other than face the entire gmayna after the wedding was canceled, then try her best to return to normal?

Mamm patted the seat again, and Joy dropped down beside her. "It seems to me," her mater said slowly, "a lot of your troubles could be solved if I weren't being so stubborn."

Joy's mouth dropped open as she stared. Shock holding her immobile, all she could do was squeak.

Mamm actually chuckled at her reaction. "I didn't realize I was hurting you, Joy. I thought . . ." She stopped talking, glancing away as though sifting through all her thoughts. "I was a lot like you at this age. Growing up and marrying your fater was the best thing for me. It grounded me. I saw so much of me in you, I was certain that's what you needed."

She shook her head, running her gaze over Joy as though seeing her for the first time. "But I was wrong."

Joy's lips twisted as she tried to hold in more tears. "You always want what is best for me, Mamm."

"True." She cleared her throat. "Now . . . if I let you pursue this quilt business without marrying"—she stopped to give Joy a stern stare—"and there would be rules, of course. But if I let you do that, then you have two options."

The air rushed out of her in a long burst. "What two options?" she asked tentatively. Was this really happening?

"You could start your quilt shop out of our home to start with. If the business was gute enough, Dat and I would help you set up a permanent location."

Joy's eyes went wide, and she suspected that if her heart weren't so laden with sadness over losing Joshua, she might have tackled her mother to the ground with a hug. "And the other option?"

"Ach vell . . . we could talk to the Kanagys and see if they'd be willing for you to work in the shop while Joshua comes here. No marriage needed. You could set your quilting idea up out of their shop, like you'd planned."

Which would save Dat's hands, too, though Mamm didn't say so. Was it really that easy? Joy's heart gave a heavy, hopeful thump. Joshua could have his dream, as well. Without being tied permanently to her, and that hurt her so much, she could hardly face the ache. But he'd be happy, and that was all she wanted for him.

Everyone would be happy. Well . . . except her broken heart, they all would be.

"I—"

Mamm squeezed her hand. "Don't decide yet," she said. "Such a big decision shouldn't be made when you are so emotional. A little time and distance are what you need first."

"I do?"

Mamm nodded. "Your onkle Andrew—your fater's oldest bruder—his wife runs a small bakery in Louella. I'm sure they would welcome a visit and helping hands. It's not quilting, but you could ask her questions about starting and running a business and give your heart time to . . . settle . . . before you decide what to do. A week or two should be enough."

"Oh, Mamm," Joy whispered. Then threw her arms around her mother's neck, squeezing tight and trying to hold back another wave of tears. "Denki, Mama," she whispered.

Because the last thing she would ever have thought to expect from her mater was this. She'd envisioned returning to a life stuck in the house, helping clean and cook, only doing quilts as gifts, and having every proper Amish boy in the district thrown at her head.

Finally, they pulled apart.

Mamm grabbed the handkerchief and dabbed under Joy's eyes. "In between, you could finish that last quilt for Ruth," she said.

"Actually . . ." Joy paused. "I think I'll give her the one I made for Joshua's wedding gift. We . . . won't be needing it now."

And she was fairly certain looking at it would only break her heart over and over and over again. Best to get it out of the house.

If Mamm was surprised by that, she didn't show it. She merely nodded brusquely and got to her feet, pulling Joy up with her. "Tomorrow morning, you pack to leave. I'll take the quilt to Ruth and use their store phone to call Andrew. Dat can take you—he's been wanting to try that new horse in a longer buggy journey anyway."

"Even with his hands—"

"He might need you to do some of the driving, but don't you worry about Dat's hands. Okay?"

Not possible, but she nodded anyway. This was all happening so fast, Joy felt as though the world was spinning underneath her feet, making her dizzy.

Mamm patted her cheek. "Go try to sleep. Everything will work out the way it should."

She gave her mater one last hug, closing her eyes tight and hanging on like she had as a little girl.

"I love you, liebling," her mater whispered in her hair.

Pulling away, Joy swiped a hand over fresh tears running down her face. "I love you, too."

Chapter Eighteen

TELLING HIS FAMILY the next morning that he and Joy had called off the wedding was the second-worst moment of Joshua's entire life. Second only to actually calling off the wedding.

Piling on was the moment he'd remembered Mervin Yoder's hands. He may as well have used a trowel to smother guilt all over the rest of the terrible emotions inside him. Leroy was never going to be able to take over that business, especially not in time to give Mervin the rest he sorely needed. Something had to be done, but Anna wouldn't let Joy work in the shop unmarried, so Joshua had no idea what. There were no easy answers.

He'd passed that night sleeplessly, for once grateful he had a job that got him up and moving early the next morning. His parents he'd informed over breakfast, the shock and disappointment and worry reflected back at him only adding to his own pain over the breakup. Now he knew how a fish being gutted felt.

His parents only cared, he knew that, but he'd rather everyone just . . . forget.

If the people around him forgot and went back to normal, then maybe he'd have a small chance of forgetting, too. What happened with Joy . . . he'd have to see what that relationship turned into from here. He missed his friend already.

He made it all the way to the shop, got through the routine tasks of opening up and getting ready for customers, then proceeded to man the register as Mamm turned the sign to OPEN and unlocked the door.

Only a few minutes later the small bell over the door jangled and he glanced up to find Anna Yoder standing there, holding something wrapped in brown paper.

Oh, sis yucht.

"Anna," he greeted her slowly. Then floundered, having no idea what he was supposed to say to the woman who would have become his mother-in-law if he'd married her dochder in a few days. Did she even know?

"Joshua," she greeted, face set in stern lines, eyes narrowed as she studied him closely. "I am sorry it didn't work out between you and Joy," she said finally.

He blew out a silent breath. "Jah," he agreed. "Me too." More than she realized.

She gave a single, sharp nod. "Is your mater in the back?" she asked next.

Probably she wanted to talk with Mamm about the best way to deal with calling everything off. "Jah."

Briskly, she strode into the back, calling out, "Ruth?" as she passed through the curtain.

Beyond the murmuring of female voices, he didn't catch specifically what was said. All he knew was that Anna was back there sixteen minutes. He'd counted every single one. Then she left, giving him a polite nod on the way out.

That was it.

Nothing about Joy. Nothing about the wedding, to him at least, beyond that one expression of regret. Nothing about his job with Mervin and the horses. Would she also push Leroy at Joy all over again? After all, he hadn't officially started dating Mary yet. Or Katie. He was a man free to make a different choice, and his parents had wanted Joy for him as well.

Joshua gritted his teeth and glared at the register. Anyone but Leroy. He wasn't right for Joy. She'd be bored to tears with him and probably chafe under his mater's apparently tight lunch schedule. Not Eli Bontrager either. He laughed too loud. Or . . .

You've got to stop this, he told himself.

And meant it. He needed to let Joy figure out her own life. But heavens how that hurt. He rubbed at his sternum, but it didn't help any.

Joy stood by the buggy as her dat loaded up her belongings for the ride to Louella and her onkle Andrew and aendi Dinah, whom Mamm had called from the Kanagys' shop as soon as they'd opened.

Her parents exchanged yet another speaking glance as Dat went back into the house, though Joy couldn't think of anything else they needed.

She forced herself to face her mater. "I guess this is it."

This was the right thing to do, wasn't it? Give herself a small break through the worst of the speculation about the breakup of her wedding plans and figure out how to hide her broken heart from Joshua. Cowardly maybe, but Mamm had arranged everything. They had turned some kind of corner in their relationship, so Joy would go and make the most of it.

"Did he see the quilt?" she asked. Then bit her lip. She had convinced herself not to even ask about what happened at the shop. "Don't answer that."

"He was there," Mamm said slowly, "but nae, he didn't see it."

Joy's emotions were so all over the place, she had no idea how she felt about that. Even if he did see it, he probably wouldn't catch the significance anyway, which had been her biggest worry about sending that particular one to Ruth instead.

Dat came out of the house carrying nothing but also taking away the need for her to respond. "Redd up," he said.

Joy turned into her mater's arms. Then, her feet as heavy as her heart, which was a useless lump of clay in her chest, she climbed in beside her father and they rolled away, the new buggy horse taking most of Dat's attention as it danced in the harness, showing its eagerness. He winced but, catching Joy's gaze on him, offered her a smile. Sensing he wouldn't want an offer of help until later, she buttoned her lips around the instinctive offer.

"Mamm told me everything," Dat said after a second.

Joy cringed, waiting for whatever he'd say next. Not that she expected recriminations, but Joshua's job working with the horses impacted her dat's business. "I'm sorry about the horses. Dat, your hands—"

"Nae. What's important is your happiness. Don't make a decision that will affect your entirely life because of me. I have options of my own. Jah?"

Joy stared at her hands in her lap, guilt nipping at her heels all the same. "Jah," she whispered.

"Gotte will guide your feet," Dat murmured. Reaching over, he patted her hands, his own fingers sort of cupped oddly. "If you turn your eyes to Him."

She hoped so. Gotte had been there for her all her life. He didn't turn his back on his people. "Denki, Dat."

"And if that doesn't work, I'll go beat a little sense into Joshua Kanagy."

Joy made a sound between a choke, a gasp, and a laugh. "Dat!" she cried in a scandalized voice. "What about your vow of nonviolence?"

"Gotte will understand," he grumbled, his expression perfectly serious.

The ache around her own heart eased slightly, and she gently covered his hand with her own. "That won't be necessary. I made this mess. It's not Joshua's fault."

"He broke my baby's heart."

Joy shook her head. "I did that all on my own. He has no idea how I feel."

Dat sighed and sort of grunted at the same time, an entirely male sound of doubt. "If he doesn't love everything about you, then he's a fool."

That her soft-spoken, soft-hearted father would threaten violence and call someone a mean word had Joy shaking her head. "I love you, Dat."

"Ach jah." He snapped the reins and turned the horse down the road to Louella.

Rather than go to the house, they drove into the heart of the small town and directly to the bakery. The second they opened the door, her aendi gave a soft screech. "You're here!"

Or at least, she thought this was her aendi. She hadn't

seen Dinah in quite a while. Before she knew it, Joy was wrapped up in an embrace from a woman tinier than a pixie, but soft and round with it. Dinah took her by the shoulders and held her out where she could see her properly. "Your mamm didn't give a reason for this sudden visit, but since your wedding was supposed to be Thursday, I'm guessing that has something to do with it."

Joy nodded dumbly, trying to hold her emotions together. "We . . ."

"They called it off," Dat said briskly, leaving no room for questions.

After flicking him a glance, Dinah squeezed Joy's shoulders. "Ach vell, there's nothing for a broken heart but a change of scene and lots of work. Can you cook?"

Dat visibly bristled. "My dochder is the best baker in the district," he declared, as though Dinah should already have known that.

The subtext seemed to fly right past Dinah, who gave Joy a delighted grin. "Wunderbaar. You will be a huge help to me."

"Denki for having me," Joy murmured.

"Kumme, kumme." She hustled Joy away.

Looking over her shoulder, Joy mouthed a goodbye to her dat, who waved, and didn't entirely succeed in hiding the worry in his eyes. Something that would make this harder if she had to see it every day.

Maybe a quick, clean break *was* better, even with her family.

Joshua would find the right girl for him. One who didn't laugh in church or get in trouble when she tried to help. Or who didn't love him so much, her heart ached with it. They could have had a gute life together, but not the kind they both deserved. She wanted cuddles and laughter and understanding from a man whose heart was as full of her as hers was of him.

Looking around the kitchen where Dinah had led her, she did her best to shove Joshua Kanagy to the back of her mind. "What do you need me to do?" she asked.

LONGEST DAY OF Joshua's life. An unendingness to it where the seconds crawled to a stop. As though the world were turning to the rhythm of the slow, painful beats of his heart. He worked in the barn now, doing his evening chores for the animals, an aching hole in his chest, and tried to convince himself that tomorrow would be better.

After all . . . today was the hardest of it. Except he still needed to talk to the bishop.

"Joshua?" Aaron's voice floated up to where he stood in the hayloft pitchforking fresh hay down. He'd need it tomorrow, and this would save time before going to the shop.

"One second," he called back. Then climbed down the ladder to the ground floor, turning to find both Daniel and Aaron there waiting, their expressions serious . . . concerned.

"Ach du lieva," he groused. "If these sad expressions are how you intend to be around me, then go be somewhere else."

Immediately both his bruders rearranged their faces. Daniel's went completely blank, which might have been the worse of the two. Aaron was more successful, with a raised eyebrow.

"So you're going to go back to being friends?" he asked.

Joshua was in no doubt whom he was referring to. "I don't want to talk about it."

"Too bad," Daniel said.

They both blinked at him, and Daniel shrugged, visibly uncomfortable.

Joshua blew out a harsh breath, seeing he was going to have to talk about it. "Jah. Joy and I are friends."

But were they? Could their friendship survive this?

Could he be "just friends" with the woman he loved to distraction while he watched her eventually fall in love, marry a different man, and move on with her life . . . all while he stood by as she continued to let that generous heart of hers get her into trouble? He wanted to be part of her life, but not the way she wanted. He wanted to kiss her every day, and laugh with her, and tease her, and save her from her soft heart and determination to help others in misguided ways. He wanted Joy.

"You don't think you can work things out?" Aaron prompted. "The two of you together . . . you both were so happy with the arrangement. Anyone could see that."

"I'm sure."

"Maybe if you talked to her—"

"I'm in love with her," Joshua stated baldly.

Daniel rocked back on his heels, then suddenly, he shot a triumphant grin at Aaron. "Told you."

Aaron grunted, his eyes narrowed as though trying to discern the truth for himself.

Joshua stared at Daniel. "You told him I was in love with Joy?"

His brother shrugged. "I think I've known you were in love with Joy since her first year of Rumspringa. The first time she came to singeon, you scowled at every single buwe who dared to speak to her."

Joshua crossed his arms. "I did not."

Aaron snorted a laugh. "Even I noticed that."

That made Joshua pause. Daniel was the observant one

of the three, but Aaron . . . obliviousness was part of who he was. If he saw that, too, then . . .

"Why do you think no one was surprised when you announced you were getting married?" Aaron asked.

"I didn't think about it, I guess," Joshua muttered, glancing away.

But then realization struck, and he turned back with a frown. "But . . . if you know I loved her, why were you okay with me marrying a girl who doesn't love me back?"

Guilt sat uneasily on both their faces, and the two exchanged a look as though debating who was going to address that first.

"To be honest . . . at first, I assumed that you'd only proposed because Joy loved you, too," Aaron said.

Daniel nodded.

True, they hadn't told anyone other than the bishop that theirs was a marriage based on mutual liking but not love. Amish didn't publicly show affection, so no one would have expected them to act any differently around each other.

"Are you certain Joy doesn't love you?" Daniel prompted gently.

Joshua's mouth twisted, though he was doing his best not to be bitter. After all, he couldn't blame Joy for the way she felt, or didn't feel, about him. "To her I'm a friend only." He swallowed the lump in his throat back down. "She was the one who broke it off, actually."

"Oh," Aaron and Daniel said in unison, both grimacing.

Exactly.

Only Daniel paused thoughtfully, then tipped his head, studying Joshua closely. "But you told her, right? That you love her?"

Joshua shook his head. "She was so worried she'd hurt our friendship, I couldn't. I would have made it all worse, ruined the relationship we're trying to keep." A patched-up, tattered relationship he still wasn't sure would survive this.

Daniel rubbed a hand over his jaw. "I still think you should tell her."

"Be honest with her," Aaron encouraged. "Trust in Gotte to set the relationship to rights between you—whether that's as friends, as more, or as less."

Would any good come from telling her that? Joshua shook his head. "Nae. I will only make her uncomfortable, and she'll feel guilty that her plan broke my heart. I can't do that to her."

He'd work through his own feelings. They'd diminish over time surely. Maybe he'd find another girl to love, and Joy would move on—

He cut that thought off.

"It's up to you," Aaron said, clapping a hand on his shoulder. "Whatever you decide, we're here for you."

Daniel nodded.

They left him alone after that, and vaguely Joshua was aware of the sounds of Aaron and Hope leaving to return to their own home. Frank put his head over the barn door and whickered softly. Moving to the old, faithful horse, Joshua patted his nose. "Pathetic, aren't I?"

Frank blew out a long breath that sounded like a harsh agreement.

Joshua sighed, too. "That's what I thought."

THAT NIGHT, AS Joy lay in the bed in what used to be her cousin Martha's room staring at the ceiling, she acknowledged that Joshua hadn't stayed in the back of her mind like he was supposed to.

Keeping busy helped. Mamm had been right about that

much. Plus her onkle and aendi were lovely people. Andrew was older than dat, and all her cousins were already married and living nearby with lives of their own. Their bakery was clearly successful. Joy's still aching feet told her so. She'd worked without a break. After baking and serving all day, they'd gone home, where she'd helped put dinner on the table and worked on a new quilt—one for Dinah and Andrew as a thank-you for putting her up on such short notice.

Even so, every single second—the seconds when she was in the kitchen, the seconds when she was serving customers, the seconds sewing, the seconds doing dishes, even the seconds when she was whisking or stirring or measuring—her mind was on Joshua.

What had the bishop said when he told him? What had the Kanagys said? What about when Mamm had dropped the quilt by the shop? Who else knew yet? After all, the wedding needed to be called off.

Because of the speed with which they'd organized the festivities, most out-of-town family and friends weren't coming. Only those close enough for easy travel, which meant they wouldn't arrive until Wednesday, which meant they'd need to be told immediately. Without phones in many households and mail moving too slowly to get to them in time, that meant working by word of mouth, and having friends or neighbors in their communities taking the news to them. Andrew and Dinah didn't mention anything, but surely they'd made sure her cousins knew.

One day.

Not even one day away from Charity Creek, away from Joshua, away from the promise of their life together. Though it had been one whole day since the breakup, and if anything, the ache inside her was growing worse.

How selfish was she to want to run home? Beg him to take her back. She could live without his loving her more than a friend, couldn't she? And yet, she'd be taking away his chance at real love, and she couldn't do that to him.

Heavens, she didn't know hurt could go this deep. To the bottom of her soul.

She should try to sleep. Try to forget and escape the long hours of trying to heal and move on without him in unconscious bliss. After all, they had an early wake-up to get to the bakery. Gute thing she wanted a quilting shop. Apparently, bakery customers expected fresh goods daily, which meant extremely early mornings, even by Amish standards.

But despite her eyes feeling as if sandbags were attached, and her body drained from being on her feet all day, and her soul exhausted from everything else, sleep wasn't coming.

Joy squeezed her eyes shut tight and wondered how long it would take before she'd go more than an hour without thinking about Joshua.

Chapter Nineteen

JOSHUA PULLED FRANK up outside the back of the shop and his family filed out—his parents, Daniel, and Hope. Technically, today was Daniel's day to do chores, but Dat had given some excuse about needing his help with a mumbled something or other. Not that they'd fooled Joshua. He hadn't thought he'd been too bad yesterday, or not too distracted at least, but if they needed all hands in the shop, he must've been pretty useless.

He hadn't argued, though. They were watching out for him as well as the business, and he'd never fault them for that. Maybe today he could pull himself together better. Clicking, he flicked the reins and didn't need to direct Frank into the fenced-in field beyond; the horse knew the way after so many years. After parking the buggy, unhitching, and seeing to Frank, he headed inside the shop.

Only his mater wasn't in the back room. She was usually the one who doled out needs and tasks. Trying not to heave a sigh like a pathetic lovelorn puppy, he pushed through the curtain to find her over by the quilts, hanging a new one up. She seemed to be moving things around to give this one pride of place at the front of the display.

"Mamm, what do you need me to—"

Joshua skidded to a halt at the sight of the quilt she was hanging, his heart shooting up to get lodged in his throat as he stared at the lovely design.

One of Joy's. He knew it. No doubt in his mind.

A traditional Amish wedding ring quilt hung on the rung. He remembered that much about designs because of how many girls gushed over them when they had them in stock. A white field with rings of blue, his favorite color, and yellow, Joy's favorite. In the center, though, she'd left an open space, which had two intertwined hearts instead of rings—one blue and one yellow. The yellow one had a design in the center—an embroidered spool of thread and two needles crossed together with what appeared to be a trailing piece of thread winding around into another small heart. At the center of the blue heart were two embroidered horses running together, and the reins flying into the air also formed a heart.

"Joy," he whispered.

He hardly noticed his mater standing there watching as he moved closer to pick up the corner of the quilt. The material she'd used was both soft and the perfect weight, and her stitches were neat and even. Overlaying the design in white thread were more hearts and rings.

His heart dropped out of his throat and back into his chest, where it tried to pound through his ribs in painful jolts.

"Did Joy make this, Mamm?" he asked without turning his gaze away from the beautiful work.

"Jah. She sent it with Anna yesterday."

The package Anna Yoder had been carrying when she'd come in to speak with his mother? *Ach du lieva.* He'd wasted an entire day hurting when, if he'd seen this sooner, he could have—

He jerked his gaze around to his mater. "I have to go find Joy."

Ruth Kanagy frowned. "She's left town."

What? No. "Where?"

"I don't know. To stay with family. Anna called them from our phone yesterday. But you shouldn't—"

He shook his head, already backing toward the exit. "She loves me, Mamm." A grin burst from him, even as uncertainty threatened to topple his surety. "She made that for us."

In fact . . . He stopped backing away and hurried to the quilt, which he plucked right off the rack.

"Joshua—" Mamm tried to protest.

"If I'm wrong, I'll bring it back." Joy wouldn't have designed such a thing without love in her heart, would she?

Please don't let me be wrong. Gotte, please let her love me.

He had to know either way. Joshua shot away from his mother. "I'll send Mervin to bring you home after work," he called over his shoulder. "I need the buggy."

Dat and Daniel shot him shocked glances as he burst past them and outside. Mamm must've explained quickly enough, though, because he'd only got a hold of Frank to hitch him back up when both of them appeared at his side, helping him get going faster.

"Are you sure this is what you want to do?" Dat asked.

Joshua fit the bit in Frank's mouth. "Don't start canceling the wedding until I get back," was all he said.

Thank goodness they'd decided to wait until today to

start that process. Yesterday had been hard enough. Now . . . maybe . . .

Hopping in the buggy, he took up the reins then paused and leaned forward to catch his father's attention. No more leaving questions unasked because he was worried about the answer.

"Dat . . . does it break your heart that I want to work with horses instead of in the shop?"

Joseph Kanagy's eyebrows shot straight up practically under his hat. "I thought I told you—"

"You did, but I need to know for sure."

That seemed to give his parent pause. "Has that been worrying you?"

"Jah."

His fater shook his head. "Nae. I'm not heartbroken. It surprised me, that's all."

Daniel's head swung sharply to stare at their father, but Dat didn't notice, still going.

"I want all my buwes to do what Gotte wishes them to do, and Gotte wants us all to use the gifts he gave us."

The rightness that had been off in a way he hadn't been able to pin down all these weeks he'd been engaged to Joy finally took shape, settling inside him. "Denki, Dat."

"We'll be praying for you."

Dat and Daniel both raised a hand in farewell as he flicked the reins and got Frank moving. He forced himself to set an easy pace for the horse. After all, once he found out where Joy was, he'd need Frank to take him there.

Knee jiggling from nerves and anticipation, he finally pulled up to the Yoders' property. Making sure the buggy was properly braked and Frank taken care of, he ran for the house and knocked, probably harder than was polite.

No one came and he couldn't hear anyone moving around, so he knocked again.

"In the back," a feminine voice floated to him on the breeze.

Trying not to run, Joshua hurried down the porch and around the side to find Anna getting up from her knees in the garden at the back, gloved hands holding a trowel and a fierce frown descending over her face.

"Joshua?" she asked.

"I love your dochder," he burst out.

Her lips compressed as she stared at him. "You've always loved her," she finally said. "You are gute friends."

"Nae." He shook his head, but her frown only deepened. "That's not what I mean."

"Joshua?" Mervin's voice interrupted as he made his way to the house from the direction of the barn. He glanced at his wife, who shrugged. "I hadn't planned on you working with the horses . . . errr . . . today. The medicine is working fine, and I don't need the help—"

Joshua shook his head again. He didn't believe a word of that, though he appreciated Mervin wanting to give him a way out of the guilt. Still, around the frustration building and the impatience to go to Joy, he realized he should take the time to settle things with her parents first. This was not how reuniting with Joy was supposed to be going at all.

"I love your dochder with all of my heart," he said to them both. "The way a husband loves a wife. The way she wants to be loved. I want to marry her and start a family and take over the horse farm. But especially marry her."

Mervin rocked back on his heels, a slow smile forming, but Anna . . . she crossed her arms. "Why didn't you tell Joy this?" she demanded.

"Because I didn't want her to feel bad that she didn't love me back the same. We—" Oh, help. What exactly did Joy tell her parents about the reason they broke off the wedding? Too late now. "We were marrying as friends, as partners, but not for love."

"We know," Anna said. "She told us."

She did?

"I think a small part of me had hoped after we married that she'd come to love me the same way, but then, when I admitted to myself that hope, I realized it wasn't fair to her. She's always wanted a relationship like her grandparents', and I couldn't take the possibility of that—even if that love was for another man—away from her."

Anna's expression remained intractable, a hard stare that was highly unimpressed. "Why now?"

"The quilt." He smiled, practically bursting at the seams with it. He couldn't help himself, because the elation flowing through him had no other place to go but out.

Please, please, please, Gotte, let me be right about it. "What if she *does* love me like that?" he asked.

Anna's expression didn't change, but her arms dropped to her sides as she studied him closely.

When she didn't speak, though, suddenly Mervin clicked his tongue, like he would to a horse. "Tell the poor boy where she is, Anna," he said softly.

"But—"

"This is for Joy and Joshua to work out, with Gotte's help," Mervin insisted gently. "Our job now is to pray for our dochder."

Anna bit her lip, dropping her head to stare at the trowel in her hand unseeingly, clearly struggling.

"She's at our onkle and aendi's," a small voice piped up,

and Joshua spun around to find Joy's bruders with their heads stuck out the back door listening shamelessly.

"Amos Yoder," Anna scolded on a gasp.

Amos's chin jutted out, and for once Joshua thanked Gotte for stubborn buwes. "He loves her, Mamm," Amos insisted, pointing at Joshua. Beside him, Samuel's head bobbed in decided agreement.

Anna shook her head at them, but finally her expression cracked, a tiny smile tugging at the corners of her mouth. With a sigh, she turned to Joshua. "She's at the Faith Made bakery in Louella. Mervin's brother Andrew and his wife, Dinah, own and run it."

"Denki," Joshua said, already starting to turn away. "Denki from the bottom of my heart."

"Joshua," Anna called.

He stopped, glancing over his shoulder.

"Go put the happiness back in my baby's eyes," she said. A request rather than a command and one that came from her heart.

He swallowed. Anna wouldn't have said that if Joy wasn't upset, too, would she? The excitement rising inside him pushed out more. "I hope and pray that I can," he said, then ran for the buggy.

He sprinted around the side of the house and almost took out Leroy, who was apparently headed over to work. "Joshua. What—"

Turning to run backward, Joshua grinned at him. "If you have any interest in Mary Hershberger, Leroy Miller, you need to do something about that soon or she'll give up all hope of you. And that's all I'm going to say about that."

Turning his back on a stunned, gabbling Leroy, Joshua vaulted into his buggy. Louella would take a little time to get to. This might be the longest journey of his life. At least he'd have plenty of time to decide what to say to Joy.

JOY BENT OVER the industrial-sized oven, testing with a toothpick the cupcakes Dinah had set her to baking to be sure they were done. Satisfied, she slipped potholders on her hands and pulled the large rack out. Except she hadn't quite got one of the potholders all the way on and managed to accidentally brush her arm on the searing hot oven rack.

Pain was instant and sheer instinct had her jerking back with a hiss, but still holding on to the pan.

"Are you hurt?" an achingly familiar voice sounded behind her.

On another yelp Joy whirled, but she moved so fast, cupcakes flew into the air, one smacking the man she loved right between the eyes.

"Joshua!" she gasped. "What—"

Except he was across the room, gently forcing her to put down the pan before he slipped off the potholder to check her arm.

"You burned yourself," he murmured, concern deepening his voice to a gruff rumble that sent shivers tiptoeing up her back.

His sudden appearance had knocked the burn clean out of her mind, but as she dropped her gaze to the long red welt rising on the delicate skin of her forearm, the sting and throb made themselves felt.

"Ouch," she muttered.

"Let's get cool water over it," he said, and led her to the sink, turning on the faucet and testing the temperature before shoving her arm beneath the running water.

From under her lashes, she stared at the top of his bent

head. Joy didn't know if she was coming or going. Her arm hurt, her heart hurt, and Joshua was here. And . . .

"Oh, the cupcakes," she wailed. "I'll have to start all over."

Joshua shot her a look that was part exasperation and part amused tenderness. Tenderness that she wanted so badly to reach for, but her arm was under water. Plus he moved away to start scooping the fallen cupcakes off the floor, throwing them into the trash bin as he went.

Joy drank in the sight of him—broad shoulders, capable hands, familiar and oh-so-handsome face. Her heart cracked wider even as hope was trying to weld those cracks shut.

"Why are you here, Joshua?" she asked, softly voicing the question. *Please don't say because of Dat's hands.*

If he was only here to fix more of her problems, she would definitely cry. Buckets and buckets.

Bent over and mid-scoop, he stilled, then slowly rose and turned to face her. She tried not to bite her lip or appear as desperate as she felt as he studied her face for a long, silent moment. As much as she wanted to prompt him—so many what ifs chased around her head like dogs after their own tails—Joy waited.

Joshua opened his mouth, then closed it. Then opened it again. "Joy . . . When two people—"

He cut himself off then shook his head.

Still she waited. Maybe the hardest thing she'd ever done, she was so desperate to know why he was here, optimism trying to rise up inside her. She couldn't let it yet. She had to know first. No more assumptions or thinking she knew how he was thinking or feeling.

"Marriage is—" Another shake of his head and he ran his hands through his hair in a distracted move so unlike her Joshua, sticking it up on end.

Even with her heart taking off at the word "marriage," Joy refused to jump to conclusions. "Joshua," she said, half reluctant and half hopeful. "You came all this way. Talk to me."

He stared at her, an emotion akin to panic in his eyes, unspeaking. Long enough that he dropped his gaze, then chuckled and strode back to where she stood to turn off the water. With a sound low in his throat, he took her hands in his.

Then he sucked in a deep breath. "Joy . . ." Another breath. "Will you marry me?"

Good thing she wasn't still holding the cupcakes, because she would have dropped the pan for sure and certain.

"Ach du lieva." Only that was all she could think of to say at first, too many questions crowding into her head to be able to pick just one to start with.

Panic flared in his eyes, unmistakable now.

"This isn't about friendship or partnership," he hurried to tell her, and suddenly Joy found herself unsure of what was up and what was down all over again.

"What's it about yet?" she asked slowly. Hoping beyond all hope that he would say . . .

"Love."

Relief and disbelief and sheer happiness hit her all at once in a confusing jumble of emotion, clogging her throat with tears. Happy ones this time. "Love?" she choked.

He squeezed her hands, searching her face.

"But—"

"Don't say no," he rushed. "Not yet. Let me say this first."

She closed her mouth but nodded.

"I think I've always been in love with you, Joy, but we were so comfortable as we were that I was blind to it. I should have known, though. Any boy that so much as looked at you wasn't gute enough. Leroy Miller," he scoffed. "What was your mamm thinking? He's all wrong for you. They *all* are because . . ." He took a deep breath that she could feel in her own body. "Because I'm the only one for you."

She couldn't hold back the tears any longer, though she didn't crumble, just silently let them slip from her eyes.

At the sight Joshua's gaze dulled, his brows dropping. With a swallow he reached out and dried the tracks of tears with the pad of his thumb. "You don't have to say anything," he mumbled. "I understand. You don't feel the same. I saw the quilt you made for us and I thought—" He stopped and seemed to realize the way he was touching her. With a jerk he stepped back. "Don't feel bad, though. I'm sure—"

Finally Joy's frozen body thawed enough that she stepped forward, putting her finger over his lips. "Shhhh," she said softly. "You sound like me all of a sudden."

He chuckled, the sound vibrating against her finger, even as he searched her face.

Joy smiled as everything in that jumbled mess of words righted itself inside her head . . . and her heart. "Yes," she said.

Joshua's breath audibly caught. "Yes what?"

"Yes, I love you, too. Yes, I made the quilt for us." Her smile broadened, joy radiating from her heart, which was bursting with it. "And yes . . . I will marry you."

With a whoop, Joshua caught her up in his arms, spinning her around the room, their laughter intertwining. Only as fast as he'd grabbed her, he stopped, putting her down to take her face in his hands. "You mean it. Right? You're not just saying you love me to spare my feelings, to—"

"I ended the wedding because I love you. Because you deserved more than just a partnership, even if we are such gute friends."

Air whooshed from him—relief, she hoped. Then he leaned forward, touching his lips to hers in a sweet kiss that was more like a promise, sealing their own vow to each other. No need to weld the cracks in her heart shut anymore. That one simple touch made everything whole, like a miracle.

"Now, now, none of that." Onkle Andrew was suddenly rushing into the kitchen.

With a huff of a laugh, Joy buried her face in Joshua's shoulder, hiding her pink cheeks.

"I take it that we will be coming to your wedding on Thursday after all?" Andrew asked, grinning and patting his round belly.

Joshua pulled back, raising his eyebrows at her in question, and Joy chuckled. "Jah," she said softly. "I'm marrying the man I love on Thursday."

"Well, thank Gotte for that," Dinah said, bustling into the space behind her husband. She looked at Joshua. "Welcome to the family, but I have a business to run. Why don't you take your bride back to our house? You can stay the night and give your horse a rest. Return to Charity Creek in the morning. Jah?"

Joshua grinned. "Denki. That would be perfect." He paused. "May I borrow your phone?"

Eyebrows raised, Dinah waved a hand in the direction of the small office in the back. Not letting Joy out of his sight, Joshua rushed to make a phone call . . . to the shop to tell his parents the wedding was back on and asking them to let her parents know.

Then, hanging up on Ruth's ecstatic voice, which Joy could hear from where she stood beside him, he grabbed

Joy by the hand, tugging her right out of the shop to where Frank was hitched outside. As she climbed into the buggy, he reached into the back, then joined her and spread the quilt over their laps.

He traced the horses and the needles and, finally, the smaller hearts. "I knew when I got a close look at this that I had to tell you I loved you," he said.

She gazed up into dark eyes that reflected all the hope and love she knew were in her own gaze. "I figured you wouldn't even notice it," she murmured.

"Why didn't you tell me sooner?" he asked.

She canted her head, lips tipping up. "I imagine for the same reason you didn't tell me."

He shot her a lopsided grin. "We should really work on our communication."

Joy tossed her head back on a laugh. "It's a gute thing you used the word 'we,' Joshua Kanagy," she teased.

"Jah, but only so that we're on the same side. Always. I wouldn't want to change your heart for others, Joy, but be your helpmate and your biggest supporter. Your need to help and spread happiness to those around you is what I fell in love with first."

She gave a happy little hum, her last worry laid to rest, her happiness complete. "And I promise to listen to your advice. Most of the time."

"That's all I ask." He wrapped an arm around her, pulling her up against his side, then took the reins and set Frank to moving. "Let's go home and get married, Joy," he murmured into her hair. "I can't wait to start this new adventure with you."

"Me too," she sighed, and snuggled closer to Joshua, finally right where she knew Gotte had always meant her to be.

Epilogue

"GESCHENK IS COMING along nicely," Mervin said, clapping a hand on Joshua's shoulder.

He clucked at the colt, who'd luckily inherited his sire's height. He and Joy had named him Geschenk, which was German for "gift," which was perfect for them. Full of spontaneity, much like Joshua's wife, but settled in the buggy, Geschenk was a fine horse. The colt tossed his head, as though agreeing with both his thoughts and his father-in-law's comment.

They both chuckled.

"I'd better get inside," Mervin said. "Anna will be expecting me."

Joshua nodded and continued putting away the equipment he'd been cleaning and oiling before Mervin came in. Joy would be here any minute. In fact . . . she should have been here by now.

A loud hissing sounded from the other end of the barn,

and he glanced over to find the massive tabby barn cat batting his paw in the air in the direction of outside.

"Hello?" he called.

"Shoo," a female voice laden with irritation said. Then Joy's head poked around the side of the door. "Is Dat gone?" she whispered.

Joshua grinned at the sight of his wife, though he tipped his head, eyeing her odd choice of entrance. "Ach jah," he said. "Why are you hiding?" Then he crossed his eyes, giving her a mock-stern look, and put his fists on his hips. "Did you rip your dress again, Joy Kanagy?"

As she came out of hiding and moved down the long aisle toward him, she chuckled at the reminder of the last time she'd snuck into the barn. "Nae. I have a surprise for Dat and Mamm and I wanted your help."

"What is it?"

"Kumme see."

She beckoned him out to the buggy that she'd left standing in front of the house. Inside, he found a quilt similar in pattern to theirs, but instead of blue and yellow, she'd made it in pink and green, which Joshua had to guess were her parents' favorite colors. In the center of the green heart were horses, like theirs, and in the center of the pink were flowers and a garden trowel.

"They'll love it," he said, smiling.

Joy's quilts and the classes she'd started holding at the shop, using what used to be Aaron's carpentry space, which she'd converted into a quilting room, were so popular that she'd gone into business with Mary, who provided the materials and helped run the classes. Leroy still hadn't proposed to the poor girl, but at least he'd finally started courting her, which might have thrilled Joy even more than

Mary. Katie Jones, meanwhile, had moved her sights to a man in another town.

"The boys are going to distract Mamm and Dat," Joy said now. "Can you help me get this laid out on their bed? Then we can sneak out and it will be a surprise when they go to sleep tonight."

"Oll recht."

Somehow, they managed to accomplish the task, despite Anna trying to come upstairs and the buwes loudly stopping her with a made-up excuse about a toad outside they wanted her to see. Also despite Joy giggling too loudly as they ran down the stairs and out the front door to their buggy and drove away.

Another adventure . . . a small fun one. His days were full of them with Joy in his life, and he loved her more every day because of them. Even the ones that caused him heartburn. She was his sunshine. The light of his life. He'd made it his mission to make her happy the way she did for him.

Gotte had truly blessed them both.

"I have another quilt I wanted to show you," Joy said through her chuckles.

He flicked her a glance, eyebrows raised in question, smile tugging at his lips. "Vell . . . let's see it."

She fished around in the back and pulled out a pale yellow quilt. One small enough that she was able to spread it out across her lap and show him most of it.

Joshua didn't look too closely, his attention on the road. "Beautiful as always."

"Uh-huh."

Something in her tone caught his attention, and he peered at her more closely to find the danger dimple in full view. He loved that dimple. "What?"

"It's a baby blanket," she pointed out.

"Jah," he said. He knew that, but not why she felt the need to point it out.

She waited patiently, a look of expectation on her face, eyes glittering with happiness, and suddenly he knew.

"Ach du lieva." Joshua barely managed to pull the horse to a stop without crashing, then turned to face her, elation thrumming in his heart. "Are you telling me . . ."

He could hardly ask the question around the excitement welling up inside him.

Joy broke out in a smile as beautiful as the one she gave him the day of their wedding. "We're going to have a baby."

Joshua whooped and pulled her—gently, of course—into his arms, burying his face in her neck and inhaling the scents of sunshine and sugar cookies.

Married to the love of his life, both their businesses going well, and now a baby on the way. "Blessed indeed," he whispered. "What a gift life is."

Acknowledgments

NO MATTER WHAT is going on in my life, I get to live out my dream surrounded and supported by the people I love—a blessing I thank God for every single day. Writing and publishing a book doesn't happen without the support and help from a host of incredible people.

To my readers (especially my Awesome Nerds Facebook fan group!) . . . thanks for going on this ride with me. Sharing my characters with you is a huge part of the fun. Joy and Joshua were two of my favorite characters to write. Something about them just clicked, and I hope you love their story as much as I loved writing it. If you have a free sec, please think about leaving a review. Also, I love to connect with my readers, so I hope you will drop a line and say "Howdy" on any of my social media!

To God . . . thank you for the journey and the blessings of imagination and words.

To my editor, Kristine Swartz . . . thank you for the support and loving this sweet series!

To my Berkley team . . . thank you for the amazing and appreciated support and all the hard work to make these books the best they can be.

To my agent, Evan Marshall . . . thank you for everything you do for me!

To my author friends . . . you are the people I feel most *me* with, and you inspire me every single day.

To my support team of beta readers, critique partners, writing buddies, reviewers, RWA chapters, friends, and family (you know who you are) . . . thank you, thank you, thank you.

Finally, to my wonderful husband and our awesome kids . . . I don't know how it's possible, but I love you more every day.

Amish Words & Phrases

THE AMISH SPEAK a variation of German called Pennsylvania Dutch (some speak a variation of Swiss) as well as English. As happens with any language spread out over various locations, the Amish use of language includes different dialects and common phrases by region.

As an author, I want to make the worlds I portray authentic. However, I have to balance that with how readers read. For example, if I'm writing a romance based in Texas or in England, I don't write the full dialect because it can be jarring and pull a reader out of the story. Consequently, for my Amish romances, which hold a special place in my heart, I wanted to get a good balance of readability and yet incorporate Pennsylvania Dutch words and phrases so that readers get a good sense of being within that world. I sprinkled them throughout and tried to use what seem to be the most common words and phrases across regions, as well as the easiest to understand within the context of the story.

If you read books within this genre, you'll note that different authors spell the same words in several different ways. Each author has her or his own favorite references, and not all references use the same spellings. I preferred to go with a more phonetic spelling approach.

The following are the words and phrases most consistently used in my books:

WORDS

ach jah—oh yes
ach vell—oh well
aendi—aunt
appenditlich—delicious
Ausbund—the Amish hymnal used in worship services
boppli—babies (alternate spelling: bobbli)
bruder—brother
dat—dad (alternate spellings: daed, daadi)
dawdi and/or grossdawdi—grandfather (alternate spelling: daddi)
deerich—silly, idiotic, foolish
denki—thank you (alternate spelling: danki)
dochder—daughter
dumm—dumb
fater—father
fraa—wife
Gelassenheit—yielding or submission to the will of God. For the Amish, this is a central tenet to living their beliefs. Translations in English include serenity, calm, composure, and equanimity—essentially the result of that yielding.
Gmay—capital *G* when referring to worship/church services held biweekly

gmay—lowercase *g* when referring to the Amish community who worship together (alternate spelling: gmayna)
Gotte—God (alternate spellings: Gott, Got)
gute—good (alternate spelling: gut)
jah—yes (alternate spellings: ja, ya)
kinder—younger children
kumme—come (alternate spellings: kum, cum)
liebling/liebchen—darling (term of endearment)
mamm—mom (alternate spellings: maem, maam)
mammi and/or grossmammi—grandmother
mann—husband
mater—mother (alternate spelling: mudder)
nae—no (alternate spelling: nay)
narrish—crazy
Rumspringa—"running around," the term used to describe the period of adolescence starting at around age sixteen with increased social interaction and independence (alternate spelling: Rumschpringe)
scholar—student
schtinke—stink
schwester—sister
singeon—a Sunday evening social event for the older youth / teenagers / unmarried young adults. They bring tasty food, play games, sing hymns and other favorite songs of faith, and enjoy other social activities. Often part of courtship (especially offering to drive a girl home in a buggy).
sohn—son
vell—well
wunderbaar—wonderful (alternate spellings: wunderbar, wunderlich)
yet—used at the end of a sentence in place of words such as "too" or "still"

youngie/die Youngie—young folks, usually referring to teenagers or unmarried young adults

PHRASES

for sure and certain
it wonders me
oh, help
wonderful gute ("wonderful," as a way of saying "very," can be placed in front of many words)

PHRASES IN PENNSYLVANIA DUTCH

ach du lieva—oh my goodness
Er is en faehicher schreiner—He is an able carpenter
Gotte segen eich—God bless you
oh, sis yucht—oh no, oh darn

SAYINGS & IDIOMS

"Blowing at the smoke doesn't help if the chimney is plugged."
"Difficulty is a miracle in its first stage."
"If you aim at nothing, you're bound to hit it."
"If you want a place in the sun, you will have to expect some blisters."

Keep reading for an excerpt from

The Gift of Hope

by Kristen McKanagh
Available now

THE KNOCK AT the door was expected, but a bit early.

"I'll get it," Hope Beiler tried to quietly shout down the stairs from her doorway. Her sister was always saying she was too loud, but she was trying. She needn't have bothered this time. The front door squealed a protest at the use. Over the indistinguishable murmur of voices, Hope mentally added the task of oiling the hinges to her unending to-do list.

She would just have to hurry to finish getting ready. Hopping around her room, she put on her shoes as quickly as she could. Voices drifted up to her, but she couldn't make out the words. Hopefully Mammi wasn't in one of her moods and was keeping her comments to the weather—or something equally neutral . . . or normal.

Her grandmother had moved in this year. While Hope loved Mammi with all her heart and was grateful for her cheerful if somewhat scattered presence every day, she was also never entirely sure what might come out of Mammi's mouth, particularly when guests arrived.

Snatching her hard-saved money off the dresser, Hope hurried down the stairs to find Mammi standing there with her hands on her hips, talking to Sarah and Rachel Price. Tucking back an errant strand of her wayward strawberry-colored curls, which never wanted to stay pinned under her white kapp, Hope made her way to Mammi's side in time to catch the words "Find my Hope a husband."

She had to hide her snort of laughter.

A husband wasn't exactly high on Hope's list of worries, not these days at least. That topic was better than last week, when Mammi had asked Elam Hershberger if he thought he saw a turkey every time he looked in the mirror. To be fair, the poor man had a hunk of skin that sort of hung under his neck, but still . . .

"We'll try," Sarah said, glancing at Hope over Mammi's shoulder, eyes twinkling with amusement. "But she is wonderful picky. She seems almost . . ." She paused and wrinkled her nose in thought.

"Hopeless," Mammi filled in. Then nodded solemnly as though her granddaughter weren't standing right there listening. "There must be *some* young man."

As if men grew on trees like apples, and you simply had to pluck one from its branch, rotten or not.

Hope lifted her gaze heavenward, sending up a quick prayer for patience. She was always praying for patience but found that to be more and more the case lately.

"Dat needs me at home too much," she said firmly. "A husband can wait."

Her mamm's sudden passing last year had been hard on them all, but hardest on her dat. Levi Beiler had shrunken in on himself without his fraa at his side, turning into a ghost of the strong, dependable provider and father he'd always been. With only the two girls—she and her sister,

Hannah—he had to work the family farm alone. Hannah was getting married, focused on preparing for the wedding. Mammi was a dear but getting older and less able. Which left Hope, who tried to help in her own way.

Speaking of which . . . "Where is Dat?" she asked Mammi.

"He's already in the north field," she was informed.

She exchanged a quick glance with her grossmammi that said everything. Every day her father went to "work the fields," but as far as she could tell, not much was getting done.

She hadn't voiced her concerns out loud, though. No need to burden others with worry when little could be done. The signs hadn't become obvious until recently because, after Mamm's passing, the community had gathered around them in so many ways. The blessing of a close-knit community. Their Amish neighbors and friends had helped get the farm through summer and fall harvest, after which winter had been relatively slow with no need for extra hands. But now that spring had come . . .

Unfortunately, Hope was fairly certain Mammi had noticed as well.

Mammi might be prone to saying odd things and having an outlook that bordered on overly optimistic, but beneath that, she was surprisingly sharp. Not much got by Rebecca Beiler. While neither Hope nor her grandmother had voiced any of their concerns outright, they'd both done their best to fill the gap left by both of Hope's parents.

The general air of neglect in the fields was equally true around the house. Not the cleanliness or tidiness, which the women were on top of. But the place was quickly falling into a state of disrepair—the roof needed patching, a gutter was hanging on by a thread, and there were various other fixes that they were waiting on Dat to get to.

Hope tried her best. In addition to her usual chores, she'd been trying her hand at repairs, but she could only do so much in a day. Also, several larger repairs needed a man's muscles, like digging up the massive dead rosebush in the front yard. She'd reminded Dat about it until he'd asked her not to repeat herself, but still the rosebush sat outside, untended.

Nothing she could do about that either.

In addition, the wedding preparations were a lot. Getting ready to host and feed over three hundred people took planning, coordinating with their close community of friends and neighbors, and money they didn't have, which meant getting creative.

Things would get better, though. Dat was in mourning and would find his way home again eventually, with Gotte's help, the wedding would pass, and everything would get back to normal.

As her mamm used to say, "Difficulty is only a miracle in its first stage."

"Can I get anything from town for you, Mammi?"

"Nae, denki." Her grandmother patted her shoulder. "Enjoy your outing with your friends."

"I will," Hope promised.

Other than Gmay every other Sunday, and the daily walks to her spot in the woods where she went to think, this was the first she'd been away from the house in some time. She'd stopped attending singeon with the other youngie Sunday evenings. Enjoying the social time felt selfish when so much needed doing at home.

She leaned in and placed a kiss on her grandmother's cheek, the skin soft and paper thin under her lips, a reminder her mammi wasn't as young as she liked to act. "Keep an eye on Dat?"

"I always keep an eye on that boy. It's what gute maters do, even when their sons are grown." Mammi winked.

Hope chuckled at the image of her strong, silent father as a boy.

With a deep breath, trying to rid herself of the anxious feeling that the house might collapse without her there to hold it together, Hope followed Sarah and Rachel down the stairs. As she hit the third step, she wobbled slightly. Peering closer, she discovered the wooden tread was starting to split right along the overhang. Yet another thing to add to her list of concerns and fixes.

Maybe while she was in town, she could ask about how to fix a breaking stairstep and even get the supplies she'd need.

Except there was no money for it. So perhaps not.

"Your grossmammi is precious, Hope," Sarah said, pulling her from her thoughts.

Giving herself a mental shake, she smiled. "Yes, she is."

Sarah and Rachel lived just down the lane and had been her closest friends, along with Hannah, since childhood. They knew about many of the troubles in the Beiler house. Dawdi had passed away a few years ago, leaving her grandmother alone, and after Mamm . . . Regardless of the sad circumstances leading to it, having Mammi here now was a blessing in the midst of sorrow.

"Denki for the ride," she said to Sarah and Rachel's father as she climbed into the waiting buggy.

"My pleasure, Hope." He pulled the wide brim of his hat lower over his eyes to shield against the bright sun and snapped the reins to set the horses to an easy pace.

Intending to enjoy the day shopping for wedding gifts for Hannah, the girls planned to walk the three-mile trip home afterward.

Hope turned her face to the warmth of the sun and let the pleasant chirping of the birds sing her worries away. While the air remained brisk in mid-spring, which meant she'd brought a sweater with her, the sun would keep them warm well enough. This was always Hope's favorite time of the year, when small green shoots sprouted in the fields and the last of winter snow, clinging to the shadowy bases of trees, melted away. Soon enough, flowers would bring color to their community of Charity Creek.

Many blessings to thank Gotte for today. Hope laid her worries aside, determined to enjoy her outing.

"How did you keep Hannah from coming with us?" Sarah asked. "It wonders me she could not join us today?"

Wedding shopping meant keeping her schwester away. "She and Noah are looking at a house he wishes to buy for them."

"How wunderbaar!" Rachel clapped her hands. "Hannah is lucky to have caught Noah Fisher."

"I think he's lucky to have caught Hannah," Hope said, though in her sweet way. Hannah was perfect. Exactly what Hope tried to be, though she often fell short. Especially in the kitchen.

"True," Rachel agreed easily. "Too bad he is an only child."

All three of them nodded. Poor Noah's mamm had died in childbirth when he was born. Hope had wondered if Noah and Hannah had bonded over that small sadness they had in common. The loss of a parent.

"I wish I was picking a house with my handsome husband," Sarah sighed.

She earned a sharp glance from her dat for the trouble. "I hope I've raised dochders who wish for helpmates, men who can walk beside them in life and faith, rather than wishing for houses or material things."

Sarah lowered her eyes. "Yes, Dat."

Rachel wasn't as meek as her younger sister, and merely chuckled. "Handsome wouldn't be so bad."

"Ach." Zachariah Price shook his head, though Hope caught a small twitch of his beard that she thought might be hidden amusement.

"What do you think you'll get for Hannah?" Rachel asked Hope.

"Something she could use in the new house maybe. Or in her garden."

Thankfully, talk turned to the wedding and gift ideas and plans for the future. Hope let Sarah and Rachel's cheerful chatter pour over her as she debated her own purchase in town today. The Amish lived a plain and simple life with not a lot of fluff, but a new house would require many useful things. They planned to visit A Thankful Heart—the only Amish-owned and Amish-run gift store for several towns around, popular with the Amish and Englischer locals and tourists alike. Granted, the Kanagys owned it, and Dat wouldn't care for her giving them any business. She could hear his gruff voice now saying, "No dochder of mine should have anything to do with the Kanagys, even if I *have* forgiven them."

He said he had, but anyone in their family could tell he still harbored bitterness. Not that her parents had ever explained why. As far as Hope could tell, the Kanagys, whom she knew because they were part of the same church, were honest people of faith. Well . . . all except Aaron Kanagy maybe. Granted, she didn't know the Kanagys well, mostly because of the tension between the two families making them acquaintances more than friends. Still, their shop had to have some small item appropriate for Hannah on her wedding day.

The way Hope saw it, she had no other choice. Given the pittance in her purse, saved over time for rainy days, finding anything would be difficult. She'd thought she might paint something, but Hope's paints had dried up these last months, thanks to lack of use, and she hadn't wanted to waste money on new ones.

She straightened in her seat, determined to find at least a little something.

Despite it being a Wednesday in the middle of spring, Charity Creek was as busy as she'd ever seen, bustling with cars and people on foot, as well as several buggies. The town itself was small enough to recognize most anyone—both Amish and, to a certain extent, Englischers—who lived in the area. Everyone in everybody else's business, especially within her Amish community. However, they were in the heart of Indiana Amish country of the Elkhart-LaGrange counties and drew tourists and outsiders for various reasons. Especially their lovely little downtown with its shops and places to eat. But this was more than usual. Perhaps the weather had drawn people out—a hint of coming warmth and skies as blue as she remembered her mother's eyes.

Zachariah pulled his buggy up right outside A Thankful Heart, and Hope jumped out, giving a quick wave to Luke Raber, who stood across the street and thankfully nodded in return but didn't come over. As she waited for Sarah and Rachel, Hope peered in the shop window, already mentally discarding items as inappropriate wedding gifts.

Then a small, simply carved chair, obviously intended for a child, caught her eye and sparked an idea. Perhaps the new couple could use a simple piece of furniture for the new home. Noah's family were selling their farmland, as most of his sisters had married and moved away and his dat had started working in the nearby factory, as many Amish men in this area had out of necessity. A farmer born and raised, Noah intended to move to the Beiler farm and help her dat, who'd only had two girls. Luckily, a small home on three acres that backed up to their southern border had been put on the market. If that didn't work out, Noah intended to build eventually.

"Did you hear me, Hope?" Sarah's voice pulled her from her thoughts.

She turned away from the window with what she hoped was an interested smile plastered to her lips. "I'm sorry. I was caught up with this little chair."

"Which one?" Sarah and Rachel pressed closer to peer through the glass and Hope pointed it out to them.

"Oh," Rachel said. "That is sweet. Aaron must've made it, for sure and certain. He does all the woodworking for the store."

Hope tried not to let her smile slip at the sound of Aaron's name, and a picture immediately formed in her mind. Dark hair, laughing dark eyes, a too-easily-given grin, and strong hands made for hard work. Why couldn't it have been one of Aaron's brothers, Joshua or Daniel, who'd carved the chair? She could've dealt with one of them much better.

"Why do you need a child's chair, though?" Rachel turned to her with a frown.

Hope quickly shook her head. "I don't, but I was thinking I could have whoever made that build a small table or a rocking chair perhaps. For Hannah."

"She would love that," Sarah enthused. "I'm sure Aaron could build you something right quick."

Hope shook her head.

She had no intention of asking Aaron Kanagy any such

thing. Just the thought of him still made her wince, the sting of her hurt pride not dimmed by time. No doubt he hadn't meant for her to overhear him telling his friends that he had no interest in her after singeon one night about a year ago. He hadn't known that Hope had been standing outside to escape Barnabas Miller's attentions. She'd been taking a needed break around the corner from where the group of boys Aaron was with had gathered, mid-conversation, talking about girls they were interested in. One of the boys brought up her name.

"Hope Beiler is okay, I guess," Aaron had said, his voice unenthusiastic.

Hope's heart had shriveled in the same way she'd shrunk herself into the shadows, the burn of mortification heating her skin.

True, her curls were a tad unruly and brightly colored, and she was on the short side and skinny with it. Next to Hannah, with her golden hair and flawless ways, Hope had often felt inadequate. Regardless, Aaron shouldn't have said such a thing to all those other boys. No one would want to show interest in her after that.

The memory still had the power to turn her ears hot and no doubt bright red, and she was suddenly grateful for her kapp, which covered them.

"I'll ask at the Troyers' store where they make larger furniture," she said firmly, glad for the excuse. "They might have something already finished."

"I guess so." Sarah puckered her brows, but then a sly glint came out to play. "But wouldn't you want to spend time with Aaron? I would."

Hope was well aware how all the Kanagy boys—men in their early twenties now, actually—were considered quite the catches. They never wanted for girls to talk to at the various community events and frolics. Even Daniel, who tended to keep to himself.

Rachel widened her eyes dramatically. "Hmmm . . . But think if it led to more, and he fell hopelessly in love with you, and you married him."

When they turned to Hope with such expectant expressions, words of denial popped out of her mouth. "Aaron Kanagy is the last man I could ever think to marry."

The instant she'd said it, Hope clapped a hand over her mouth and wished she could pull the words back in and swallow them whole.

Unfortunately, Sarah and Rachel, instead of appearing shocked, exchanged glances filled with a knowing that set Hope's teeth on edge. "What's wrong with Aaron?" Rachel asked.

Hope lowered her hand. "Nothing. That was an unkind thing to say. Please don't repeat it. I would feel terrible."

The words spoken in haste made her no better than Aaron telling those boys she was just okay. Worse even. Hope glanced around, relieved to find no one else close enough to overhear.

"But you don't like him?" Sarah prodded, confusion evident in her tone.

"Nae. He's . . . fine . . ." Hope stumbled over herself to get words out. "He's not who I would . . . choose, is all."

She barely kept from closing her eyes in despair. What could she say to fix this?

"You're so picky, you don't choose anyone," Sarah pointed out. "I, for one, wouldn't mind his interest."

"Me neither." Rachel waggled her eyebrows.

Hope managed a laugh that sounded just the right type of light and airy. "Then *you* commission him. Let's save the gift shop for last and see if anything in Troyers' will do?"

At least her friends allowed her to lead them away. Hope couldn't possibly go in there right now. Not with them watching her extra closely, especially if Aaron was working today. Given her behavior, they no doubt assumed she either disliked him or harbored a secret crush.

Too bad, since she'd so wanted a closer look at the little chair. Affording anything in Troyers' was not an option. She'd have to be extra persnickety and reject everything in there, which no doubt would earn her more teasing.

Or maybe she'd manage to find a small item. Probably tiny. Because asking Aaron Kanagy for anything was not an option.